Lost and Found in Paris

SASHA WAGSTAFF

Lost and found in Paris

CANELO

First published in the United Kingdom in 2019 by Canelo

This edition published in the United Kingdom in 2020 by

Canelo Digital Publishing Limited
Third Floor, 20 Mortimer Street
London W1T 3JW
United Kingdom

A CIP catalogue record for this book is available from the British Library.

Print ISBN 978 1 78863 798 5
Ebook ISBN 978 1 78863 319 2

Look for more great books at www.canelo.co

Printed and bound in Great Britain by Clays Ltd, Elcograf S.p.A.

For my Dad… my hero. Thank you for everything X

Chapter One

'Now *that* is the perfect dress to wear for a proposal.'

Sophie Marchant turned away from the mirror. 'We don't actually know that's what's going to happen, Jo!'

Jo pulled a face and flopped down on the bed. 'We actually do.'

Sophie gazed at her reflection again. 'On a serious note... the right outfit?'

Jo considered Sophie. 'Yes. The perfect blend of naughty girl and... girl next door.'

Sophie rolled her eyes. Jo was a straight-talking girl with a blond quiff, a no-nonsense attitude and three glorious tattoos Sophie wasn't brave enough to have herself. Sophie's best friend and all-round superstar, Jo could always be relied upon to tell the truth and shoot from the hip.

Sophie gazed at her reflection. What on earth did a girl wear for an evening like this anyway? She had plumped for a ruby-red, lace skater-style dress with spaghetti straps and a fitted bodice, teamed with strappy, golden heels and a brand, new matching golden box clutch for the occasion.

The occasion? Sophie smiled and bit her lip. She had been asked out to dinner at a beautiful, London restaurant with her boyfriend of three years, Ryan. Handsome, ambitious and caring, Ryan had impeccable manners, a great job and he was pretty much the model boyfriend. And tonight felt special. Different. As though something momentous might happen. It wasn't something Sophie had necessarily ever *wanted* to happen because it wasn't really her thing, but she was fairly sure it was going to happen. And despite her views on such things, Sophie did feel excited.

Slipping on a gold cuff bracelet her mother had given her for her birthday, Sophie decided she was as ready as she could be for what might be ahead. Her heart thumped forcibly. Was she ready for this? Could a girl ever be ready for this? Sophie gave her long, dark hair a final brush and stepped away from the mirror.

Jo got off the bed and put her hands on Sophie's shoulders. 'So, my friend,' she began gravely, 'this is most likely our last moment as single girls.'

'Jo, neither of us is single,' Sophie stated.

'You know what I mean,' Jo laughed. 'Single girls as in… not… betrothed.'

'Betrothed?' Sophie shook her head. 'Who even says such things?'

'I do,' Jo said solemnly. 'In situations like this. And even though I'm an uber-independent estate agent and you're a boho-chic photographer, we are just girls, standing in front of guys, waiting to be…'

'Oh stop it.'

Jo removed her hands from Sophie's shoulders and picked up her golden clutch bag. 'Godspeed. Go get him. Go get engaged.'

Sophie held onto her clutch bag tightly. Engaged. Gulp. She was so… bohemian. Was getting engaged something she had ever envisaged for herself?

'Come on. Your sister has been trying to marry you off for years.'

Sophie pulled a face. It was true. Her twin, Eloise, seemed to be under the impression that Sophie's life was incomplete because she didn't have a ring on her finger and an actual husband on her arm. Eloise had married the first man who had asked her, a Parisian businessman called Georges, who was a good but rather lazy man, and really not Sophie's idea of fun. Eloise still lived in Paris, near their mother and they were literally worlds apart, despite being deeply connected as twins.

'Yes, well, Eloise is the marrying kind,' Sophie explained. 'I was and then I wasn't and now I'm...' She faltered, not sure what she was now.

'We could be completely wrong about this...' she said nervously.

'Oh stop it,' Jo scoffed. 'Perfect boyfriend... tick. Everything going brilliantly... tick. Been acting strangely for a few weeks... tick. Clearly has something on his mind... tick, tick, tick. What else is it going to be?'

'Well...'

'You're about to be proposed to,' Jo insisted. 'Come on, Soph. You've even seen the ring.'

Sophie checked her hair. That part was true at least. Ryan had come home one night looking secretive and while he was in the shower, she had moved his rucksack and a small, black box had fallen out. Gasping, Sophie knew she should put it back without opening it but she was a normal person and a bit of a control freak with a need to know things. She couldn't help herself: before she knew it, she had opened the box and was staring at an impressive solitaire diamond in a white-gold setting, nestling in lush, red velvet. Snapping the box shut, she had put it back in Ryan's rucksack just in time as he emerged from the bathroom with a towel round his waist. Sophie hadn't been sure whether to feel flattered, excited, sick, scared or all of the above.

Ryan. Thirty three… two years older than her. Handsome in a rugby player kind of a way: tall, stocky and well-built. He had dark hair and blue eyes and was considered handsome and rugged by most people's standards, Sophie's included. Ryan worked for a forward-thinking corporate insurance company and he was rapidly working his way through the ranks towards having his own team. It meant that he spent a fair amount of time entertaining clients, but he was also a real homebody and he and Sophie spent plenty of quality time together.

Was their relationship all candles and romance and passion? Sophie wasn't sure. But it was stability and security and a kind of serene happiness. It was rightness. It was everything she needed. Sophie had experienced passion and excitement, a thumping heart and a spinning head before; it had left her reeling and it simply hadn't been worth the pain. She had been left broken and battered, unsure she would ever find happiness again. Sophie threw the thought away, shrugging it off expertly, something she had learnt to do over time. And out of necessity.

Jo was right about Ryan acting strangely of late, however, Sophie thought to herself, switching her thoughts back to her boyfriend. For the past few months, Ryan had seemed deeply preoccupied and distracted.

'Jo. Could there be… any other reason for Ryan acting so strangely lately?' Sophie was suddenly gripped by anxiety. 'Maybe we've got this totally wrong. Maybe he's…'

'What? Leaving the country or something?' Jo said, making her scorn of such an idea patently obvious with a dramatic eye roll. 'No, Soph. No way. He's besotted with you. He's been acting weird because that's what guys do when they're about to propose. Trust me,' she added confidently.

Sophie smiled to herself. If anyone would know, it was Jo. She had been proposed to a record number of eight times. *Eight times*. Seriously. Sophie knew Jo was special; it was one of the reasons they were best friends. But still, eight times? It was impressive and oddly fascinating, because who knew what prompted a man to propose to a woman? It took some men a few weeks, some several years. It was one of those inexplicable things. Either way, it meant that Jo had incredible – and proven – credentials when it came to proposals… and men's associated behaviour.

'Besides, you asked him recently, didn't you?' Jo probed, clearly believing that Sophie needed further validation.

'I did, yes,' Sophie admitted. 'And he said he's never been happier in his life and that I have nothing to worry about.'

Jo nodded resolutely. 'Well, there you are then. He's nervous, he feels weird, he's a man and he's resisting settling down, because that's what he's programmed to do.'

Sophie checked her reflection in the mirror again. Jo had all these theories about men being 'genetically predisposed' to resist settling down and getting married. Which didn't seem to… marry up, ha ha, with all the proposals she'd received over the years, thinking about it.

'And he works long hours,' Jo stated reasonably and finally. 'He's tired, he's stressed, he's losing his shit because he wants to propose, but he doesn't want to and he's a man and therefore he's…'

'Genetically predisposed, yes, yes.' Sophie cut her off and pulled herself together. 'Ok, I'll trust you. I'm sure it's all going to be fine. I really should go.'

'You should definitely go,' Jo said, pushing her towards the door. 'You have a fancy restaurant to go to and a gorgeous diamond to wear.'

Sophie kissed her best friend on the cheek.

'Enjoy it,' Jo said with a grin. 'I've enjoyed all of mine. All eight of them,' she finished without a trace of ego. That was one of the best things about Jo: she was the epitome of modesty and self-effacement. She wasn't sure what made men propose to her all the time either.

Sophie left the house and jumped into a taxi. She hated tubes because she suffered from slight claustrophobia but she tonight felt as though it warranted a taxi.

If Jo was right, Sophie thought to herself, breathing out jerkily.

Arriving at the restaurant Ryan had chosen and booked, Galvin at Windows, Sophie looked up at the Park Lane hotel in awe. The London Hilton. How very Ryan: classy, elegant, refined. After a short lift ride, Sophie arrived at the twenty eighth floor and stepped out. Wow. What a restaurant! What a view!

Ryan was seated at one of the tables by one of the vast windows and Sophie knew he must have asked for it specially. It was typical of him to go the extra mile and she loved him for it. He put down his beer and stood as soon as he saw her. He was wearing a sharp, navy suit with a crisp white shirt and a navy, silk tie. Classic, stylish… perfect. Sophie actually felt giddy. Maybe an engagement was what she did want after all. Maybe her cynicism was simply down to her parents not making it. Ryan was everything she needed and wanted.

'Soph.' Ryan kissed her cheek and squeezed her hand. She smiled back at him, feeling a rush of happiness.

'You look amazing,' Ryan said, staring at her dress. 'You always do, but that… that dress is absolutely stunning.'

'Thanks.' Sophie took her seat, glad she had gone with the strappy red number. 'I can't believe this place… check out the view!'

'I know, right?' Ryan gestured to a waiter who immediately came over and took Sophie's drinks order. 'I didn't know what you wanted so I thought you could choose when you got here because they have such lovely cocktails.'

Of course. How very Ryan. If he wasn't sure he was going to get something exactly right, he'd act the gentleman and get her input. Sophie decided to go for a cocktail called the 'Portugal'. It was made with pink pepper Gin, white Port, lime, mint and homemade strawberry tonic syrup. Sophie wasn't entirely sure about the whole gin craze that was sweeping the country, but she felt like being daring.

Glancing at Ryan, Sophie realised he was nervous. Like, really nervous. He was fiddling with his tie and rearranging the cutlery, something he always did when he was on edge. He had done the exact same thing when he had met Sophie's mother for the first time in Paris a year ago and when Sophie had first taken him to meet Jo and her boyfriend Paddy.

'Are you ok?' Sophie asked, starting to feel apprehensive again.

'Me?' Ryan nodded rapidly. 'Absolutely. I'm ok. Thanks. You?'

'I'm fine.'

Sophie smiled and picked up her menu. The food looked and smelt incredible as it went past in waiters' hands as they moved discreetly around the dining area. She wasn't sure what she wanted to eat. She looked over the top of the menu at Ryan and noticed the front of his suit bulging at one side. She said nothing, hiding a grin behind her menu. Jo had specifically asked her to look for the bulge in Ryan's suit jacket and it was there. Tick.

'I need to talk to you about something,' Ryan blurted out suddenly.

'Oh?'

Sophie lowered her menu. Her stomach was fluttering in a strange fashion and her heart was beating extra fast. God, this was it. Ryan was about to propose. This was the big moment.

As Ryan appeared to be composing himself, Sophie randomly wondered what her mum would think. All of her friends loved Ryan to bits and thought he was the best, but Mariele had been typically reticent. She had liked Ryan when she had met him, but Sophie knew her mother was still absurdly hopeful Sophie might get back together with an old French boyfriend one day. Lord only knew why; he had hardly turned out to be suitable.

Ryan cleared his throat. 'Yes. The thing is… God, I really don't know how to say this.'

Sophie's brow furrowed slightly. She had imagined that Ryan being Ryan, he would have the most beautiful little speech prepared and that he would have learnt it off by heart and rehearsed it to within an inch of its life.

'Are you ready to order?' A waiter smoothly appeared at their table.

'Er… no.' Ryan shook his head. 'Could we have a minute please?'

'Of course.' The waiter withdrew.

Ryan raked a hand through his hair. 'God. Shit. I thought we would have dinner first and then… but…'

'So let's do that,' Sophie said, picking up her menu again. 'No hurry.' She didn't want Ryan to be stressed out. This should be one of the best moments of their life after all!

'I can't.' Ryan reached into his pocket and pulled out the ring box. He placed it on the table between them.

Sophie lowered her menu. This wasn't quite what she had expected, but she was more than happy to go along with it. And unconventional was more her vibe to be fair. Jo always said she was quirky and bohemian like her mum.

'I bought this a while ago,' Ryan said jerkily. 'With a view to… you know…'

Sophie swallowed. The vibe had changed. Oh crap. What was happening?

'But then something happened and I can't do it.'

Ryan looked up but seemed unable to look Sophie in the eye. Whatever was over her left shoulder was receiving his full attention. Sophie stomach was now doing horrible cartwheels. Bloody hell. What was Ryan saying? Was he saying… God, the thought was too terrible for words. Had he… met someone else? Sophie felt rather sick.

'I've been offered a job in Dubai.' Ryan finally met Sophie's eye.

'Ok…' she said slowly. 'That's a good thing, I'm thinking?'

'It is.' Ryan nodded, but he wasn't smiling. 'They want me to head up an area and run this huge team of staff.'

'Awesome!' Sophie was still baffled. This was exactly what Ryan had always wanted! Why on earth did he look as though he'd been hit by a bus? And why had he placed the little black box containing the engagement ring on the table between them like that, as though it was now sad and redundant, rather than about to be the star player?

'Yes, it's awesome,' Ryan agreed, straightening his tie again. 'Really awesome. Except that it's only me who can go, not both of us. And it's for a year.'

'A year?' Sophie's buoyant mood plummeted. A year? And only Ryan could go? 'I could still come, surely? I could… get photography work in Dubai. I'm certain I could and I could pay my way. I still have that huge pay off from that posh wedding I shot in Windsor so I'm…'

'Sophie.' Ryan interrupted her. 'I want to go on my own. I mean, I'd love you to come, but there is so much riding on this job. My company have stipulated that I need to knuckle down and focus on the job because if the team they're putting together doesn't succeed, the company could fold.'

Sophie blinked. Was Ryan saying he was choosing his work over her – over them? That he was leaving for a whole year and she had to stay away? She felt more upset about this than about the engagement ring or possible wedding, or lack of.

'Have they… asked you to go alone?' Sophie said, feeling confused. 'Have they said I can't come with you?'

'No.' Ryan bit his lip. 'And I know you're probably going to think I'm being an absolute arse. But I've been thinking it over for the past few months and I know that this is for the best.'

'Right.' Sophie wasn't sure how to react. But she was fairly sure tears might feature shortly.

'I'm so sorry, Soph,' Ryan said, reaching across the table to grab her hand. His arm thumped down on the ring box and he winced.

'I don't get it,' Sophie said slowly, allowing Ryan to take her hand, even though she wasn't sure she wanted him to. 'You were going to propose and now you're not because your work have promoted you. And you're going to Dubai. On your own. For a year.'

Ryan looked back at her guiltily. 'I'm sure you can still visit and all that. I just don't feel it's fair to propose and for us to be engaged and thinking about a wedding when I have all this work stuff going on. I want to come back to you in a year's time with this huge experience under my belt, ready for us. And… with an awful lot of money if it's not crass to mention that,' Ryan added awkwardly. 'I'll be able to afford the wedding of your dreams by then. And we can buy a proper family house together.'

Sophie nodded, feeling tearful. Oh man, this was awful. It wasn't the wedding thing; she hadn't even been sure about that herself. She knew she would want any wedding of hers to be quirky and different and that she wouldn't have an alphabetised file or a subscription to

Bride Monthly magazine. But… going away for so long and cooling off their relationship like this? Sophie took her hand out of Ryan's.

'Sorry, I'm just trying to get my head around this. Are we still together, but just not getting married? Or just… not getting married yet? Or are we actually splitting up here? Is that what's happening? Did we just break up?' She gazed out of the window. 'You brought me here, to this gorgeous place, to… to break up with me?'

'No, of course not.' Ryan looked affronted. 'I don't want to break up, Soph. Not at all. Well, what I mean is, perhaps we should just… put us on hold for a while.'

'Put us on hold,' Sophie repeated in a dull voice. 'For a year.'

Ryan screwed his face up. 'You make it sound awful. But it's not, it's just… sensible.'

'Sensible.' Sophie looked down at her place setting. She had to stop repeating what Ryan was saying. She sounded like an idiot.

'Yes, I honestly think it's for the best. You could come to Dubai – of course you could. But I think I'd neglect you,' Ryan said. 'And I'm just being honest, Soph. I don't think I'd have time for us and for you. Not with everything I've just committed to at work.'

'Right. So… you just don't want to get married anymore?' Sophie felt dazed.

'Not… right now,' Ryan confirmed, moving his knife and fork around the table again.

Sophie wasn't sure what to do or what to say. 'But… we live together, Ryan. We share the same house – until you move to Dubai, obviously – but I don't even know what we are now.' She stood up. 'I just know you bought a ring and you're not giving it to me, and you're going away for an entire year and it feels like we're over.'

'We're not over,' Ryan said, looking upset. 'We're... on hold. Sophie, I just don't know what else to do. This job will set me up for life and if we can get through this, we can revisit all our plans for the future then and see where we're at.'

Sophie put her hand on the ring box and pushed it across the table. He hadn't once said he loved her. That everything would all be alright. All he had given her was doubts and uncertainty. Sophie felt overwhelmingly sad.

'So you want me to... wait for you?'

'Yes. Yes, if you can.' Ryan gave her a small smile.

'And you'll wait for me,' Sophie said, raising her eyebrows. 'No other girls in Dubai?'

'Of course not! If I'll be too busy for you, I'll be too busy for anyone else.' Ryan stopped. 'God, that sounded awful. What I mean is, I don't want anyone else. I promise you, Sophie.'

Sophie stood up. 'Ok, Ryan. I'm a bit... this is all a bit...'

'I know, it must be. I'm so very sorry.'

Sophie nodded. 'Yes, of course. I... I have to leave if that's ok. Maybe... stay at a Darren's house tonight? Give me some space to think?' She closed her eyes for a moment. 'Which is silly, as I'll have all the time in the world to think soon. But I need it. Tonight, I need it.'

'Sophie...' Ryan stood up, but Sophie turned away and headed out of the restaurant, gratefully stepped into a waiting lift. Calling Jo, Sophie halted all of her best friend's excited gabbling and asked Jo to meet her at the nearest bar. Jo, being the incredible best friend she had been since Sophie had abruptly moved back to England from Paris five years ago, didn't question or stutter out confused sentences; she simply said she'd be there as quick as she could and put the phone down.

Sophie walked unsteadily but quickly to the nearest bar and sent a text to Jo with the address. She then ordered two Porn Star Martinis. And immediately downed both of them. Catching her breath, Sophie then ordered two more and waited for her best friend to turn up and tell her what to do.

Chapter Two

A Month Later

'It's really cool here,' Ryan was saying, shouting a bit.

'I can't really talk, Ryan,' Sophie said in a low voice. Juggling her camera and her phone, she gestured to the happy couple who were busy picking confetti out of their heavily lacquered hair and ducked around the corner of the church to take the call properly. 'I'm working. I only have a minute or two…'

Ryan carried on talking. 'As soon as they let you come out here, I'll get you a plane ticket, Soph!'

Sophie said nothing. A ticket to Dubai? She really wasn't sure Ryan would ever produce one, nor was she remotely sure she wanted one. Not now. In fact, Sophie wasn't even sure why Ryan periodically phoned her. He was still talking to her and she could hardly hear him over all the background noise of music and chatter.

'Where are you?'

'A buffet lunch,' Ryan shouted. 'It's the thing over here; buffet lunches. Loads of drinks and food and

Sophie leant against the wall. 'Doesn't sou
work.' She wasn't sure she cared, but
nonetheless.

'My clients are here,' Ry
babe, I have to go. Mi

Sophie felt glum. She missed Ryan like crazy because she couldn't simply switch her feelings off, but she was inwardly fuming at what he had done. Jo was of the opinion that Sophie should turn her back on Ryan and kick him to the curb after the non-proposal, but Sophie wasn't sure she needed to take any particular action. She could either remain in no-man's land until such time when Ryan would change his mind, or she could take the view that the relationship was effectively over and somehow try to move on. Ryan had literally left a few days after the awful non-engagement dinner and Sophie had spent the first two weeks paralysed over what Ryan might be up to over in Dubai. But she had since come to the conclusion that it was a pointless way to live. Ryan didn't want to be with her so it didn't really matter what he was up to.

Sophie's phone rang again. She glared at it irritably, then answered because it was Jo.

'Yo! What are you up to?'

'I just spent three hours photographing a nauseatingly loved-up couple who just got engaged,' Sophie replied gloomily. 'And now I'm at a wedding.'

'An engagement and a wedding?' Jo tutted. 'Nightmare. Last thing you need.'

Sophie nodded. She was hearing that. 'Yep. And Ryan just phoned.'

Jo tutted again. 'Hmmm. What did he have to say for himself?'

'He was at a buffet. There was loads of music and it didn't sound like work; it just sounded as though he was partying.'

⸺ out a derisive snort.

Sophie silently agreed with the sentiment. Ryan's career might be important, but he had totally sidelined their relationship and that hurt like mad. Sophie was bouncing back and make no mistake about it. But she hadn't decided to write Ryan off completely. Yet. For now, she was just going with it.

Sophie heard her name being called. 'I have to go, Jo. The happy couple needs me.' She rang off, took a deep breath and headed back round the church.

'Right. Can I have all the bride's family in front of the weeping willow please…' Sophie put all the confusion and disappointment that came with thinking about Ryan out of her head, and focused on taking the most breathtaking photographs she could.

—

Later that day, Sophie popped in to see her boss at the photographic studio she worked for three days a week. Paul Pinter (rhymed with 'splinter') was a ruggedly handsome man in his fifties, who had the silver fox thing down to a fine art. No one ever called him Paul because he just didn't suit it.

'How was the wedding?' Pinter asked. He rearranged some photographs he was viewing, shuffling them into a different order on his desk.

'Beautiful,' Sophie admitted, perching on the edge of his desk. 'Rose-gold, pink and baby blue colour tones, pseudo-rustic table settings, and adorable bridesmaids tugging puppies with bows on their collars around. Attractive couple, very much in love.'

'Standard. Ish. Must have been tough for you.' Pinter raised his eyebrows sympathetically and held up a photograph.

Sophie took the photograph from him. 'It all feels rather tough right now, Pinter. Weddings, engagements, babies. Everything reminds me of Ryan… or rather, what's now not happening with Ryan.' She handed the photograph back. 'This is gorgeous. *She* is gorgeous.' The photograph was of Pinter's wife, Esther. A former model, ten years younger than Pinter, Esther was impossibly glamorous and pouty, and in black and white especially she had sculpted-out-of-marble lips and cheekbones.

'Thanks.' Pinter lounged back in his chair. Typically, he sat in a very non-conventional chair that belonged on a garden deck not in an office. 'I can't really take a bad photograph of Esther, to be fair because she's off the charts beautiful and I'm punching a tad. But this is all stuff we know. What's new?'

'Not much.' Sophie shrugged. 'Feeling a bit blue. Missing Ryan even though I hate him. I feel as though I need to get away, but I don't know what from exactly.'

'I see.' Pinter eyed her shrewdly and laced his fingers together. 'Well, feeling blue is to be expected.'

Sophie nodded.

'And I think you probably just need a fresh start of some kind, rather than getting away from it all.'

Sophie pulled a face. 'God. Are you firing me?'

'Never.' Pinter grinned then looked serious again. 'The hatred for young Ryan is absolutely to be expected. I'm not feeling the love for him much myself right now, either to be honest.'

Feeling flat, Sophie got off his desk. Wandering round the brightly lit studio with its vast windows, skylights and discreet lamps, she let out a breath. Being at the studio was always soothing; it was peaceful and elegant with cream, fern-green and silver tones, courtesy of Esther. And Pinter had that kind of charismatic, pent-up energy that worked fantastically well on a photo shoot where it was required, but he was equally capable of stillness and calm when in the office. Which was just what Sophie needed.

Pinter was also talking rubbish; he'd never really warmed to Ryan, so why he was making out he'd gone off him because of recent events was anyone's guess. She said as much out loud.

'I cannot tell a lie,' Pinter confessed, getting up to make coffee. 'I always thought Ryan was rather clean cut and prissy. And not very... you.'

'Prissy?' Sophie couldn't help laughing. She hadn't heard Ryan described that way before. Clean cut, yes, because Ryan was fastidious about his hair and his appearance, but prissy...?

Pinter spooned coffee into cream mugs with silver handles. 'Yep. I see you with someone more rugged. A bit older. Stylish.'

Sophie frowned. 'What... like you?'

Pinter looked at her sternly. 'Don't be ridiculous. I'm old enough to be your... bleurgh, what a horrible thought. Whatever. No, I do not mean like me... God forbid. I'm a nightmare, and you and I are platonic and always will be.' He handed her a mug. 'But Ryan... I don't know. I know it's hard on you at the moment, but I can't help feeling that this is a blessing in disguise.'

Sophie sighed into her coffee. That was easy for Pinter to say. Regardless of his rather chequered past, which involved a heavy alcohol habit and a penchant for partying and sleeping around, Pinter had it all together now. He had the studio, he had a lovely home, he had Esther (so he no longer slept around) and neither of them wanted kids, so they loved to travel and see the world together. By comparison, Sophie just felt lost. She definitely didn't have anything together right now.

Her phone rang and Pinter picked it up. 'It's your twin,' he said, sliding her phone across the table.

'Eloise?' Sophie felt a flash of concern. She and Eloise chatted every few days even though Eloise still lived in Paris near their mother. But she knew something must be wrong.

'Sophie!' Eloise sounded relieved.

'Something's wrong.' It was a statement, not a question.

'It's mum.'

'What about mum?' Sophie rolled her eyes, feeling herself relax. Their mother could be erratic at times.

Pinter held his hands up, clearly affronted at not being able to hear what was going on.

'She's disappeared,' Eloise said.

Sophie put Eloise on speakerphone so she didn't have to fill a very nosy Pinter in later. 'Ok, but she's done that before.'

'Yes, but this is different. And she's only disappeared for a few days before. This time it's been a week.'

Sophie looked at Pinter. Pinter pulled a face.

'A week?' Sophie shook her head. 'Why didn't you say something before?'

'I didn't want to worry you,' Eloise said, sounding stressed. 'Not with the whole Ryan thing going on.'

Pinter nodded gravely as though he agreed. Sophie rolled her eyes at him. 'Don't worry about me. I've put Ryan on the back burner for now; I can cope.'

Eloise continued. 'Ok, so mum left this cryptic note… something about finding her heart or some such nonsense.' She let out an audible sigh. 'I need your help, Sophie. There's the shop to think about, but I'm mostly worried about mum. She's never gone for this long before. And I don't even know where to start when it comes to looking for her.'

Sophie frowned. 'And you think I do? You're closer to her than I am, Ellie. You live in the same country, at least.'

'But you're more like her,' Eloise insisted. 'You know you are, Soph.'

'Quirky… weird…' Pinter mouthed to Sophie.

Sophie silenced him with a pointed stare.

Eloise continued. 'Please help. Come over, help me track her down. The shop… Hang on, Albert needs me. I'll call you back in a bit.'

'Well,' said Pinter, after Eloise had rang off. 'Saved by the nephew. Is that the nephew? Or is Albert the lazy husband?'

'Albert is the nephew,' Sophie replied. 'Or rather, one of them. Georges is the lazy husband.' She felt exasperated. Where on earth had her mum gone? And what was she playing at? Disappearing like this, leaving behind a cryptic little note. Honestly.

'Right.' Pinter rubbed his chin ruminatively. 'Well, well, well.'

21

Sophie looked at Pinter. 'What, Pinter? Why are you looking at me like that?'

Pinter flung himself into his chair. 'Looking at you like what?'

'Like you're having a lightbulb moment.'

Pinter grinned. 'Because I am. You wanted a change of scene, yes? A fresh start of some kind?'

'Yes, but…'

'Well, if Paris isn't a fresh start, I don't know what is.' He sat back as if he'd made an oracle-worthy announcement.

Sophie let out an impatient sound. 'You're making it sound as though I would be jetting off to Paris to start a new life, Pinter! That's not what this is. This is my sister wanting me to go over to Paris… a place I left years ago for… for my own reasons… and track down our errant mother, who could be literally anywhere.' She threw herself into the chair opposite Pinter. 'And by the sound of it, I'd get roped into running the bloody macaron shop and I can't think of anything I'd rather do less.'

Pinter fixed Sophie with a pointed gaze. 'And what exactly were your reasons for leaving Paris, Sophie? You've always been very mysterious about that.'

'Hardly,' Sophie threw back quickly. 'I left Paris five years ago. And my reasons aren't half as exciting as you think they are. It's not mysterious at all.'

She swallowed and looked away. She wasn't about to open up about leaving Paris to an already over-excited Pinter who was clearly in the process of making up a back story in his own head about Sophie's arrival back in England years ago, filling in the gaps she had never provided answers for.

Sophie faltered for a second. No, she wasn't going to think about any of that. She'd left all that behind her a long time ago. She had left Paris and she had had very good reasons for leaving – reasons that had nothing to do with her family, whom she adored and was still exceptionally close to. Eloise and her family visited a few times a year – their mother even more often than that if she could get time off work. Sophie spoke to Eloise constantly, and to their mum every week or so. Not about why she left, because Sophie didn't talk to anyone about that mostly because people tried to make her feel as though she might have made a mistake and that she should go back and see. Jo had only mentioned this to her once because it was her genuine take on the situation, but she respected Sophie's right to believe what she believed.

It was also the very reason why Sophie had never confided in Pinter about her reasons for leaving Paris. It wasn't that he was disrespectful, but he was a romantic at heart and Sophie knew he would have been fascinated and intrigued by the story and that he would have pushed her to find out if she had done the right thing. And Sophie had to believe she had done the right thing, even now.

She turned her attention back to Pinter.

'Ok, listen.' Pinter leant forward, resting the rolled back sleeves of his shirt on his desk. 'I'm not grilling you; it's your stuff. Even though I desperately want to know, obviously, because I'm horribly nosy. And I bet it's about a man and I bet I'd like him more than I like Ryan. Sorry!' He held his hands up at the expression on Sophie's face. 'But anyway, on a serious note, you did say you wanted a change of scene. This could be the perfect thing for you.'

Sophie hadn't seen Pinter looking so earnest before, but she still wasn't convinced. Heading back to Paris on a wild goose chase didn't exactly feel like any kind of fresh start. But then again…

'Time away from England and everything that reminds you of Ryan,' Pinter was saying. 'And your mother is missing… you'd feel far too guilty if you didn't help your sister find her. And what about the fresh challenge with the macaron shop? I doubt you'd have to do much, to be fair, but who doesn't love a macaron? Not to be confused with a "macaroon", of course – that sickly thing with coconut in it, but anyway.'

Pinter paused and took a swig of coffee. 'You could continue with the photography over there… weddings, babies, engagements and suchlike, and maybe some lovely shots of Paris. I have loads of contacts, so I could arrange work for you over there. As long as your mum is ok, of course.'

Sophie hesitated. It wasn't so much that she was being swayed by Pinter's long list of reasons for her to dash over to Paris, but at the end of the day, she *was* desperately worried about her mum.

Pinter snapped his fingers. 'A-ha! Esther's sister is getting married in Paris in a few months' time. You could be the photographer. I was going to ask you anyway and see if I could get you back to Paris somehow.'

Sophie frowned. She couldn't prove that either way, but it all sounded rather convenient. Plus, she certainly hoped – *if* she decided to go over to Paris – to find her mum within a few days, not a few months! So Esther's sister – Savannah, if memory served her correctly – would most likely have to hire a different photographer.

'You're half French, aren't you?' Pinter asked, probably to distract her.

'A quarter, if we're being technical about it,' Sophie corrected. 'I had English grandparents but they're dead now and I have a French grandmother who is still alive. Fifi. She's a proper character… very flamboyant.'

'How fabulous.'

Sophie shrugged. She loved her family dearly.

'But anyway… just think. We could host an exhibition on your return,' Pinter finished grandly. 'And…' – he paused for dramatic effect – 'a change is as good as a rest, as they say.'

He sat back, clearly feeling that he had put forward a rather splendid case for Sophie to drop everything and decamp to Paris at a moment's notice.

Sophie thought for a second. Not much of what Pinter had just outlined made much sense to her mostly because it was an idealised version of events, and Sophie wasn't remotely convinced that any of the points he had made would actually help her own situation. But one part made sense and was the crux of the matter.

'You're right,' she allowed finally.

Pinter looked exultant.

'About one thing.'

Pinter's face fell.

'I'd feel far too guilty about not helping Eloise search for my mum. I only have one parent – and it's been that way since Eloise and I were tiny – and she's a bit flaky, but I love her to bits and I need to know she's alright.'

Sophie's phone rang again and she answered it quickly. It was Eloise again, having dealt with whatever her son had needed her for. In that moment, Sophie made a decision.

'Yes, ok. I'll get a flight and be with you tomorrow or the day after,' she said. She hadn't used the Eurostar before so flights were easier in her head. 'Ok. Try not to worry. I'll let you know when I've booked a flight.' She ended the call, feeling a shiver of excitement. And something else. Apprehension maybe?

'Happy now?' she asked Pinter.

Pinter shook his head. 'Not in the least. I'll miss you loads.' He gave her a sage smile. 'But I think you're doing the right thing.'

'I'm glad one of us does,' Sophie said doubtfully. Was she doing the right thing? She had no idea. But with everything that had happened with Ryan, maybe she did just need to get away? And see if she could figure out what had happened to her mum. She couldn't have got far, surely? As for everything else from her past…

Sophie strengthened her resolve. The past was the past. There was no point in dwelling on it and it was all so long ago now. As Pinter said, it was time for a fresh start. Even if it was going to come about by tracking down her errant mum in Paris of all places.

'*Bon voyage*,' Pinter said, chinking his coffee mug to hers. 'And looking on the bright side, because I'm sure your mother is probably just having one of her funny moments, you're just about to go to Paris in the spring. Wait until Esther hears; she'll want us to join you.'

'Please do,' Sophie said, raising her mug. 'I'll probably need all the help I can get.' She bit her lip and felt another ripple of excitement. Or apprehension. Or both. Paris. She was going back to Paris. For the first time in five years. Sophie had no idea if she was doing the right thing, but she was doing it. With her mum missing, she simply had to.

Chapter Three

Two days later, Sophie had said goodbye to Jo and to Pinter and all her other friends and she had messaged Ryan to let him know she was heading to Paris. Walking out of Charles de Gaulles airport with a loaded suitcase she hoped would be sufficient for her stay, Sophie got into a taxi. It was late in the afternoon, but Sophie told the driver to go the long way round Paris so they could take in all the sights before heading towards the 10th arrondissement. She was surprised that her command of the French language came back to her so easily.

Sophie gazed out of the window. She'd forgotten how beautiful Paris was, how elegant: the Sacre Coeur, stunning in its simplicity, majestically placed upon a hill and surrounded by the artistic, bohemian flavours of Montmartre; the Arc de Triomphe, immense, solid and a central feature for the constant flow of frantically weaving traffic that coursed through and around it; the Eiffel Tower, tall, magnificent, breathtaking, Sophie remembered being taken there as a child. She had thought she might be terrified at the top because of how high it was, but instead, she had loved it. She had stood there with her sister Eloise and her mum, and she had looked across the whole city, amazed at how tiny everything seemed. Houses that looked as though dolls should live in them, miniature cars like little toys driving around narrow streets and mini people going about their business. As a child, Sophie remembered always being excited when the Eiffel Tower was lit up by different coloured lights at various times of the year, because it looked magical.

'You're too early for the lights,' the driver commented in French.

Sophie nodded. It was a shame she wouldn't see the sparkling golden lights that flashed and twinkled for five minutes at a time today, but she guessed she might get to see them at some point. Although she had no idea how long she would even be here…

'How long are you here for?' the driver asked her chattily.

Sophie smiled and craned her neck to get a last look of the Eiffel Tower. 'I was just thinking… I honestly have no idea,' she said.

The driver shrugged, clearly not sure what to say in response.

Tearing her eyes away, Sophie allowed the memories to wash over her as the taxi approached the Île de la Cité in the 4th arrondissement. She took in the awe-inspiring sight of the cathedral of Notre-Dame, impressed as ever by the stark, Gothic architecture. They sailed past the Père Lachaise, the cemetery that was resting place to, amongst others, Edith Piaf, Oscar Wilde and Jim Morrison, whose tombstone was covered in graffiti, and Sophie suddenly found herself entering the 10th arrondissement, where her mum's cottage was.

Giving the driver more precise directions, Sophie sat back, feeling a flash of apprehension. Seeing Paris again was easier than she had imagined it to be, but coming back to the cottage she had once shared with her mum and sister was something else. Sophie felt the sudden need to slow things down.

'Could you stop here, please?' she asked the driver. There were a few streets away from her mum's macaron shop and house, but there was somewhere Sophie wanted to stop off at first.

'Here?' The driver pulled over. 'Aaah, the bistro. The food is good here.' He jumped out to help Sophie with her suitcase and having settled her on the pavement by the bistro, he drove off.

Sophie stood outside the bistro. *Chez Josephine* was a typical, art-nouveau French bistro on the corner of the street – old-fashioned and traditional. It served 'old school' dishes such as boned pigeon with foie gras, and chicken with morel mushrooms and cream. But more than that, to Sophie, it was the restaurant her mum used to take her and Eloise to as children as a treat.

Sophie stepped inside, lugging her suitcase in with her. It was promptly taken somewhere safe and she was greeted like an old friend, much to her surprise.

'Sophie!' Bernard the rotund, affable owner kissed both her cheeks exuberantly. 'We 'ave not seen you for... three... no, five years.' He had always loved speaking English with her.

'Aaah, Sophie.' Adele, Bernard's wife, a still-beautiful woman with grey hair in a chignon and fantastic cheekbones, pulled her into a hug. 'You have returned.' She didn't favour speaking English.

'It's good to see you both,' Sophie said, feeling overwhelmed. She hadn't expected anyone to remember her after so long.

'Your usual table?' Bernard turned and swept an arm out with a flourish. 'It's free, but if it wasn't, I'd make sure it was.'

Sophie smiled. 'You're too kind. Thank you.' She took a seat, and while Adele and Bernard busied themselves with getting her a carafe of water and a basket of fresh bread, Sophie took in her surroundings. The walls were painted a pale yellow and decorated with pictures and huge mirrors. The tables were sat close to one another and were covered with pristine, white cloths. Small lights studded the ceiling, like upside down ice cream cones, throwing circles of light across the restaurant. The rest of the light came from the elegant, but somehow rustic candles on the tables, the white wax oozing and dribbling into the sparkling glass cups they were held in.

Sophie's mum, Mariele, loved this restaurant because of its personal service and family-run vibe, but also because of the chic, art-nouveau décor. As for the food… Mariele would sometimes treat herself to the excellent white chocolate *panna cotta* with raspberries or the delicate citrus *millefeuille* they served, which she always declared a '*triomphe de patisserie*'.

'You will have the *joue de boeuf en daubes*?' Bernard asked. 'The beef cheeks in red wine and thyme? With extra orange, as you like it. The *terrine*? Or maybe the *escargots* in *provençale* butter?'

'The *joue de boeuf* please,' Sophie smiled, touched by Bernard's excellent memory and always impressive attention to detail. Eloise, always rather squeamish as a child, had been put off by the idea of eating the 'cheeks of a cow', as she put it, but Sophie had always found them to be tender and moreish. And far easier to stomach than snails, which Sophie found tough and gristly, much to the horror and disbelief of her French friends.

Bernard smiled. 'And the Bordeaux, naturally.'

'Naturally.'

Sophie watched Bernard bustle off to attend to her order and Adele arrived at the table with a glass of the very good Bordeaux wine they favoured. 'On the house,' she smiled, the apples of her lovely cheekbones broadening. 'You are home to see your mother?' she asked.

'Sort of,' Sophie said cautiously, slipping easily into speaking French with Adele.

'I haven't seen her for a while, actually,' Adele mused, her brows knitting into a frown.

Sophie hesitated. She wasn't sure what to say to people about her mum; Mariele might not want people to know she was missing.

'I'm looking forward to seeing my sister,' Sophie said by way of a distraction. 'And my nephews.'

'Aaah, *les garçons*,' Adele said, looking sentimental. 'They are handsome, yes?'

'Umm… yes,' Sophie replied vaguely. Her nephews were very handsome, if rather boisterous and also loud.

Bernard brought up a small slice of the delicious *terrine de campagne* the bistro was famous for, to start. 'Just for you,' he said expansively.

Sophie felt overwhelmed by the attention, but at the same time, she couldn't deny it was lovely. What a great start to her return to Paris! She tucked into the mouth-watering *terrine* and sipped the rich, mellow Bordeaux. There was jaunty, accordion-style music playing in the background, which was rather clichéd, but it reminded Sophie of times spent here with her mum.

'*Superbe,*' she told Bernard as he removed her *terrine* plate. 'Even better than I remembered.'

'You are too kind,' he grinned, loving the compliments. 'And your beef cheeks.' He placed the dish in front of her with a grand sweep. He stood over her expectantly, clearly wanting to see how she found it. Luckily, Sophie found the dish as exquisite as she remembered it. The sauce was thick, and the orange, thyme and strong seasoning burst in the mouth.

Sophie kissed her fingers and dipped the last of her bread in the sauce. '*Formidable!*' she exclaimed. 'I am very happy to be in Paris.'

'And we are happy to have you back,' Adele gushed, giving her an unexpected hug. 'And I hope your mother is alright,' she said close to Sophie's ear.

Sophie nodded and said nothing. After settling what seemed to be an extraordinarily small bill for the lovely meal she had just enjoyed, she left, dragging her suitcase behind her. A few streets down, she swallowed as she caught sight of the family home: it was an unusual, but beautiful property. Pastel-pink coloured and rather huge, it was set back from the street, but had an annexe attached to it, which was the macaron shop. MARIELE'S MACARONS was written in pretty cursive above the front of the shop, which was in darkness because it stayed closed on Sundays, but memories still swam in front of Sophie's eyes. Five years. Five years since she had last been here. She took in the sight of it. Five years was such a long time to be away from somewhere she had always seen as home, but when she had left, she had felt that she had no other choice. Her heart had been shattered into tiny pieces; what else could she have done?

Taking a deep breath, Sophie unlocked the door and went into the house. All of a sudden, standing there in the hallway, she felt overawed by all the childhood memories that were assailing her. Sophie could hear echoes of herself and Eloise, running around as young girls, screaming with laughter. In her mind, she could see them playing in the surprisingly large garden, hiding behind trees... or mostly up them, in Eloise's case.

Sophie could see and feel her mum in every room as she started to walk through them. She felt oddly reassured that nothing much had changed inside the house. The lounge area was light and airy with mismatched colours and furniture. Cream and brown sofas with non-matching armchairs, strewn with plump, fluffy cushions in neutral tones and the odd, velvet jewel-coloured cushion scattered here and there – amethyst, ruby red and emerald green. There was an unusually shaped raw oak coffee table in the centre, and on top the copies of Vogue magazine Mariele had collected over the years and coasters from different places they had visited in France. The same photographs that had always adorned the walls were still there... photographs of Eloise and Sophie at various ages. The walls were full of them and Sophie smiled inwardly because she and Eloise used to hate the embarrassing pictures of them with gappy smiles and bizarre, bohemian clothes.

Sophie sniffed. There was a faint scent of Anais Anais in the air, the Cacherel perfume Mariele always wore, and whenever Sophie smelt it, it reminded her of her mum. She used to spray it on her pillow when she was a kid, and after moving back to London, Sophie would go into department stores and spray it on herself whenever she missed her mum. Eventually, she bought her own bottle and started to wear it because she loved it so much and because it held such wonderful memories. Anais Anais was probably considered to be a bit of a throwback now, but Sophie still adored it.

She wandered into the kitchen. It was homely and cosy even though it was of a decent size, and Sophie felt a rush of memories wash over her again. How much time had the three of them spent in here together? Cooking, experimenting, eating, talking, laughing. Like many houses, it had been the heart of the home especially since Mariele had trained to become a pastry chef after realising that art didn't pay the bills. She would often try out recipes and get the girls to help; they had been chief tasters to Mariele's weird and wonderful creations. Eventually their mum got into making macarons, and by the time Mariele had opened her shop, Sophie and Eloise had tasted hundreds and hundreds of the delicious, crunchy little biscuits.

Sophie ran her hand over the edge of the wooden worktop. She felt a renewed anxiety. Where was her mum? Why had she disappeared like this? What happened to make her run away, leaving a cryptic note? Sophie found the note on the work top where Eloise had left it. She read it, nonplussed.

> *I have to go away for a while and I am truly sorry.*
> *My heart isn't happy and I have to work on that.*
> *Please don't worry about me! I'll be in touch soon*
> *X*

What on earth did it mean? *My heart isn't happy.* Sophie had no idea what her mum meant by that. Did she miss someone from her past? Was she unhappy alone? Was she sick?

Sophie tucked the note in her back pocket and headed into the macaron shop. It looked strange in the dark, so she turned all the lights on and instantly, the shop came to life. Spotlights in the ceiling and small, non-matching lamps threw light into every corner. It was a beautiful, eclectic little shop and apart from some new cream wooden chairs and tables scattered throughout, it looked the same as it had five years ago to Sophie. A sweet, familiar smell hung in the air and Sophie was instantly transported back to her childhood.

She wandered around the shop, smiling to herself. There was a glass case at the front to display plates of pretty macarons – empty at the moment – and neat piles of pink boxes sat at the side, ready to be filled. They were lined with puffs of tissue paper in jewel tones: ruby, emerald, aqua. Mariele loved bright colours and she was everywhere in the shop. Her taste flooded the space and imbued every aspect.

Sophie ran her hand along a pretty dresser; there were many in all shapes and sizes that Mariele had painted in different pastel shades. There were shelves with random ornaments on them, that were… unusual: boxes shaped like books and treasure chests, shells and driftwood and glass figures that danced and twirled. Everything should clash, but somehow it didn't. The shop still looked slick and professional in places, but it was also inviting, warm and cosy.

The thing Sophie had always loved about the macaron shop was that it wasn't trying to be something it wasn't. It wasn't in competition with the big players in Paris such as Ladurée or Pierre Hermé, companies Sophie knew her mum admired greatly. It was a family-run macaron shop with bags of charm and some pretty delicious macarons that had a solid, constantly growing following.

Sophie let out a breath. Why would her mum leave this little shop that she loved so much? Why would she walk away from something she had spent her life creating? Sophie had no idea who was helping out in the shop in the meantime – Eloise hadn't elaborated on that – but Sophie sincerely hoped it was someone who understood how Mariele liked things done. How she ran the business with an unrivalled passion and unique energy.

Switching off the lights, Sophie sent Eloise a text to say she'd arrived and immediately received one back saying that Eloise would come over to see her first thing in the morning. Eloise had two young children; it was under-standable that she couldn't rush over tonight.

Sophie decided to have a coffee and she got the coffee machine up and running. Mariele refused to buy instant coffee so they would always, always make the real thing, and Sophie did the same thing in England. In fact, it had annoyed Ryan as he was a fan of instant and didn't like waiting for a proper cup.

Ryan. Sophie listened to the familiar, comforting chugging of the coffee machine and took out her phone. It still hurt to think about him and Sophie had no idea what the future held for them. He was keeping in touch but the contact was erratic so she was never sure when she might hear from him. She was about to dial his number, but at that moment an incoming call from Pinter lit up the screen.

'Pinter. Did you have a sixth sense that I was about to call Ryan?'

Pinter gave a throaty chuckle. 'I'd love to say yes, but… no. Haven't given him a second's thought. I only worry about you. Anyway, how does it feel to be back in Paris?'

Sophie poured herself a coffee. 'Weird. Paris is beautiful, of course. And the house is the same. Gorgeous. Evocative. Like, exactly the same. It smells of her, you know?'

'Is that good?'

Sophie laughed. 'Yes, you idiot. It smells of her perfume. But I feel all anxious about her now, which I know is silly.'

'It's not,' Pinter said reasonably. 'It makes perfect sense. You're at your old home so you feel closer to your mum. And now you're feeling more worried because you're wondering where she is and what's happened.'

'That's exactly it.' Sophie wandered back into the lounge. 'I just went into the shop… it feels strange when it's closed but it still brought back so many memories.'

'Who runs it with your mum?' Pinter asked. 'Someone must be manning the fort.'

Sophie shrugged. 'Not a clue. It's a guy, I think, but I don't know much more than that.'

Pinter whistled. 'A *guy*. How exciting. Maybe he's handsome and sexy and he'll take your mind off Ryan, the big plonker.'

Sophie rolled her eyes. 'I doubt it. He's probably ninety and smells bad.'

'Well, beggars can't be choosers,' Pinter reasoned kindly. 'He might still have that *je ne sais quoi*. Now, what about food? You need to eat tonight.'

'I've just eaten at the local bistro. And you're not my dad, Pinter.'

He tutted disapprovingly. 'You keep saying that and it's just weird. I worry about you, alright? Eat something.'

'There will be something in the fridge if I get peckish later,' Sophie reassured him. 'Eloise will have stocked up. She's very efficient like that.'

'Good. Right, I'm off. Esther's here. She sends her love, but she wants my attention now.'

'Tell her I love her too. Bye, Pinter.'

Sophie tucked her phone into her pocket. She supposed she should sleep in her old room tonight. Turning the TV on for some background noise, Sophie headed upstairs with her luggage. Feeling a stab of trepidation, she was relieved to find that her old room looked nothing like it had when she left five years ago. It now resembled a smart spare room with mint-green walls, a large bed with a brass bedstead and a shabby chic dresser topped with pretty pink candles and cerise silk flowers.

Feeling exhausted all of a sudden, forgetting about her coffee and the TV she'd left on downstairs, Sophie tiredly lay on the bed. Within seconds, she was fast asleep.

Chapter Four

Sophie lifted her head from the pillow. It took a few seconds to remember where she was and she struggled to sit up. She hadn't slept well and she knew she had tossed and turned, worrying about her mum most of the night. Frowning, Sophie realised she could hear noises downstairs. Getting up and shaking her head when she saw that she was still in yesterday's clothes, Sophie made her way downstairs.

'Eloise?' she called.

'Sophie!' Eloise appeared in the lounge, holding out a plate loaded with croissants. 'I got us breakfast...' She plonked the plate on a nearby table and rushed over for a hug.

'It's so good to see you,' Sophie said, returning the hug. She and Eloise had always been close; they were twins after all. They were as different as chalk and cheese because Eloise was uptight and orderly and Sophie was creative and impulsive, but they were close. They even shared odd moments of 'twin bond' where they felt each other's pain – when Sophie had left Paris all those years ago, Eloise had reportedly felt sad for weeks and not just because she had missed her twin. And when Eloise had had her two sons, Sophie had known before she was even told of their births as she had oddly 'felt' it from afar. Sophie suddenly realised how excited she was to see her nephews again; Eloise and Georges had brought them to England several times and they were full of fun and as loud as anything.

Eloise held onto Sophie tightly. 'You too. Thank you so much for coming. I'm so glad you're here. So glad.'

Eloise drew back and Sophie couldn't help noticing that her twin looked apprehensive. Anxious about their mum Sophie could understand, but apprehensive?

'What's wrong, Ellie?'

Eloise smiled briefly at the nickname only Sophie used but the smile slowly faded.

'I know you're worried about mum, but why are you looking like that?'

Sophie searched her sister's face for clues, but couldn't work out what she was feeling. All she could pick up on was trepidation. It was odd coming face to face with Eloise again; they weren't identical twins, but they looked very similar. They both had dark hair, delicate features and green eyes; it was only their body shape that was different. Sophie was slender and Eloise had curves. Which Sophie had envied her for all their lives and of course, Eloise wished she was slimmer like Sophie. Standard.

Sophie searched her sister's eyes for a clue, but couldn't properly read her. She turned as she heard noises beyond the kitchen. 'Is that someone in the macaron shop?'

'Yes. Listen, it's…' Eloise tailed off and looked down at her hands. 'Oh, Sophie…'

Sophie started to feel panicked. Why on earth was Eloise looking so petrified? 'Is it mum? Have you heard something? Oh God, is it bad news? You just need to tell me if it is…'

'This isn't about mum.' Eloise met Sophie's eye and awkwardly bit her lip. 'It's about…'

'Sophie?'

Sophie gasped and closed her eyes. That voice. She knew that voice. She opened her eyes and turned her head in the direction of the voice. It felt as though she was moving in slow motion… as though she was drowning in shock.

Raphael. Raff was standing in front of her. Sophie caught her breath. Raff couldn't be here… he simply couldn't be here.

Six Years Ago

'I just want to meet someone and fall head over heels in love,' Sophie said, flicking her hair.

'You're so idealistic, Soph.' Eloise pulled a face and fiddled with the waistband of her trousers. 'God, these are tight. Are they yours?'

Sophie peered at them. 'Don't think so. What's wrong with being idealistic?'

'It's just… pointless,' Eloise muttered, clearly wishing she'd worn something more comfortable.

Sophie rolled her eyes. Eloise was only saying that because she'd met Georges a year ago and he was Mr Stable. He had a good job working at one of the big banks in central Paris and he was nice-enough-looking and he was probably going to propose soon. But he wasn't exciting and that was a fact. Eloise and Georges had met in a bar like this one near the Eiffel Tower. A desperately self-conscious champagne bar full of… Georges types.

With a stunning view of the Eiffel Tower, admittedly, Sophie thought to herself. It looked magnificent in the autumn… well, all year round, of course, but there was something special about the swirl of gold, orange and russet leaves around the base of the monument and the stark sight of a misty moon as a backdrop.

Sophie sipped the drink she had been nursing for the past few hours and gazed out of the window despondently. What on earth was she doing here? This wasn't her kind of place at all. She didn't like the look of any of the guys hanging out in this bar. They looked as though they were more interested in business propositions than falling in love. And Sophie was fed up with meeting guys who just wanted to have fun and mess around and who didn't do stimulate her intellectually.

'Let's leave,' she said decisively.

'Leave?' Eloise looked shocked. 'But you haven't even chatted to...'

'I really don't want to,' Sophie replied, not wanting to hurt her twin's feelings and tell her she wasn't after a Georges lookalike. 'Come on, Ellie.' Grabbing her twin's hand, they made their way out of the bar, accosted several times by various sharp-suited types begging them not to leave.

'Actually, that was pretty bad,' Eloise giggled as they spilt out onto the pavement. 'Shall we get something to eat?'

Sophie tucked her arm through Eloise's. 'Why not?' They walked along the pavement arm in arm, laughing at the evening they were having until Eloise stopped outside a pastry shop. It was a cosy, little shop that doubled up as a bakery in the mornings, but for now, it was all about the cakes. The smell wafting from the shop was delicious and enticing.

'Wow. Look at these!' Eloise went into a predictably excitable place in the face of such beautifully crafted sugar.

They went in and surveyed the vast array of cakes and pastries on offer. Eclairs, choux buns, madeleines, palmiers and of course, pretty, pastel-coloured macarons. A dark-haired guy emerged from the back of the shop, shouldering a tray of macarons.

43

'I can't decide what to have,' Eloise was saying. 'Maybe one of these eclairs or a bun…'

Sophie wasn't listening. She was staring at the guy. And he was staring back at her. He put down his tray and continued to stare, a grin spreading across his face. Sophie felt herself grinning back like an idiot. It was as though they were silently saying to one another 'Oh. It's you. That person I've been waiting for.'

Sophie ran her eyes over him. Dark hair shaved short, and kind, sexy, chocolate-brown eyes framed by those ridiculously long lashes girls went crazy for. Broad shoulders and big thighs. That was the snapshot Sophie could take in. She had no idea what he was thinking as he stared at her, but her entire body felt as though it had come alive. Their eyes locked onto one another and didn't let go.

Raff stared back. Wow. Just… wow. Who was this girl? Was she French? Maybe not… English, perhaps? She was stunning… exquisite. Those eyes, that long mane of hair. That figure… but she was so much more than that. There was simply something about her. Raff caught his breath. The French called that having a certain je ne sais quoi. And this girl, she had it in truckloads.

'Soph. What are you having?'

Him, Sophie thought to herself. Him. All. Day. Long.

Raff half-smiled at the girl. Hah he imagined that? It hadn't been uttered out loud but he had strongly sensed what was going through the girl's mind. Because he felt the same. What on earth was happening to him? They had only just met and Raff wasn't prone to such thoughts. Raff tried hard to get a grip of himself with some sensible rationale. He'd been in a few relationships… one significant and destructive, plus a few others that hadn't affected him much at all. But he was hardly new to all this. But still… this was intoxicating.

Eloise glanced at Sophie and then at the guy, realising they were having some sort of a moment.

'*Raff,*' *the guy said, holding his hand out.*

'*Sophie,*' *Sophie said, holding her hand out.*

Their fingers touched, their hands entwined, their bodies leant in towards one another and their eyes locked. Sophie fell desperately in love. And so did Raff. And that, as they say, was that.

Chapter Five

Sophie shook herself out of her reverie. Raphael Lussier. Raff. How could this be happening? This was the person responsible for shattered dreams and a broken heart. The person who had given her the fluttery heart and the spinning head and all the excitement and passion she could ever handle. And this was the person who was the very reason Sophie had fled Paris five years ago.

She met Raff's eyes and was startled to see that he looked as shocked as she probably did. He looked tortured, in fact. But he looked good. Tall, dark and handsome. He wore jeans with a pale grey sweater, with a scarf thrown around his shoulders and jeans tucked into brown boots. Eloise always used to joke that Raff would look at home in London, the way he dressed, but regardless, he had a certain style and he wore it well. He looked older, because of course he was and he was a little rugged around the edges, but again, he wore it well.

Sophie was conscious of the fact that she was wearing yesterday's outfit, the clothes she had travelled in and slept in: smart enough skinny jeans, with black ankle boots and a white fitted shirt that probably now resembled a crumpled tea towel. She knew she must also look older, but she had no idea if she looked better than she had the last time Raff had seen her, or worse. Not that it even mattered.

Raff stared at Sophie. What on earth was she doing here? Sophie hadn't set foot in Paris for five years. Even though Mariele was missing, Raff wasn't sure he was expecting Sophie to turn up in Paris. That said, Sophie had always been devoted to her mother, so maybe it wasn't so shocking after all that she was standing in front of him.

Raff stared at her. She looked... beautiful. Tired, admittedly, but still gorgeous. Her hair was longer and more groomed than he remembered it being back in the day, but her figure was... she still looked...

Raff was rarely lost for words. But today, right in this moment, he knew he would struggle to articulate the thoughts that were racing through his mind.

'R-raff.' Sophie was furious that her voice wobbled when she spoke. She was cross with herself.

'Sophie.' Her name came out as a whisper. Raff was equally cross with himself. Why had his voice sounded like that?

Sophie felt jolted. The way Raff said her name, his accent... it was... no. She mustn't think about that. 'What are you... what are you doing here?' she managed. Her heart was thumping like crazy. *Stop sounding like an idiot*, she scolded herself.

Raff gestured behind him without turning, not wanting to sever the connection. 'The macaron shop...'

Sophie was puzzled. What did Raff mean? That he was the one helping her mum run the shop? How on earth had that come about? When had he started working here again? Why hadn't her mum mentioned something? Why hadn't Eloise, come to think of it? Raff was a pastry chef;

Sophie knew that. He had worked in her mum's shop for a while, years ago. But he had left… he had left to work somewhere else before Sophie had left Paris.

'I… came back a few months ago,' Raff explained haltingly. 'Your mum asked me to come back.' It was true: Mariele had got in touch with him some months ago, but Raff had only been able to start recently. Mariele had been really persistent, which had been odd, but it had suited him to work closer to home again.

Sophie was flabbergasted. What on earth was going on? Her eyes flickered towards Eloise accusingly, but her anger dissipated when she saw how upset Eloise looked. Turning back to Raff, Sophie tried to get herself together. She wanted to run away. She wanted to turn around and just run. To the airport preferably. Onto a plane that would take her as far away from here as possible. Well, home preferably. But she was rooted to the spot, unable to move. After all, what sort of idiot would she look like if she did that?

Sophie felt panic rising inside her. What the hell was she supposed to do now? She was here to track her mum down; she didn't want to have to deal with Raff. How could he be working here again? Why would her mum have asked him to? Sophie felt a myriad of emotions charging through her. Anger, confusion, hurt. And… memories. Loads of memories hitting her left, right and centre. Good ones, bad ones, amazing ones. Amazing ones.

She looked back at Raff and was disarmed to see that he was smiling at her. Like, really smiling at her. Smiling in a totally unselfconscious way, as if he couldn't help it. Because he was just happy to see her or something. Which

Sophie felt sure couldn't be the case, but before she could stop herself, she felt herself smiling back at him. Just for a second. And then she pulled herself together. Why was she smiling at Raff after everything that had happened? Five years ago, this guy broke her heart into tiny pieces.

Raff realised he was smiling at her and he hadn't meant to. Not because he didn't want to, but because it didn't seem right in the circumstances. Mariele was missing and none of them knew where she was or what had happened to her. And as for Sophie… words couldn't even begin to describe how she had shattered his whole world all those years ago.

'Listen,' he started, throwing his thumb over his shoulder. 'I need to get the shop opened up…'

'Yes, of course,' Sophie nodded rapidly, her stomach suddenly feeling tight.

'I'll… I'll see you later,' he said. He threw Eloise a look before taking his leave, wanting her to know how furious he was with her for not letting him know about Sophie arriving.

Eloise shook her head and put her finger to her lips before going to close the lounge door.

'Why didn't you tell me?' Sophie burst out.

'I couldn't… I wanted to… I was scared you wouldn't come…'

'Of course I wouldn't have come!' Sophie started to pace across the room. 'And you know that, Eloise. So you know you should have told me about him. You know.'

Eloise looked distraught. 'I'm so sorry, Soph. I just needed help finding mum and I didn't know what else to do. I wanted to speak to you about it before you saw him, but he got here early to open the shop and came in and I didn't know he was going to do that and I…'

'Ok, ok!' Sophie held her hand up. 'Ok, Ellie. I get it.' She sank down into an over-stuffed armchair. 'Oh man!'

Eloise sat next to her. 'I know.'

'This is… huge.'

Eloise nodded. 'Yep. Are you ok?'

Sophie let out a jerky breath. 'I don't know. I was freaked out enough by mum disappearing, but this…'

'Yes.' Eloise nodded again. 'I understand. Why don't we get some air?'

'I should get some air,' Sophie agreed vaguely. 'And I probably need to have a shower and get changed…'

'Later,' Eloise said. 'Let's… leave those croissants and go out for breakfast.'

'Ok,' Sophie said, getting to her feet. 'We need to talk about mum…'

'We need to talk about Raff,' Eloise said firmly, grabbing Sophie's handbag. 'Let's go.'

–

Raff leant against the door. Christ. What had just happened? He hadn't thought he would see Sophie ever again. She disappeared… well, left, for England five years ago and Raff hadn't heard a word from her since. He had tried to get in touch – so many times – but she hadn't wanted to see him. Eloise had tried to talk Sophie out of her decision and so had Mariele, but to no avail and Raff had been distraught. He had wanted to dash over to England to drag her back again, but when she had refused to take his calls and answers his letters for a few months, he had conceded defeat. And he had missed her ever since.

Raff had never felt so hurt and devastated in his life. Sophie had meant everything to him. Everything. He had never felt about anyone the way he had about her... not before and not since. And Raff still didn't really understand what had gone wrong between them. He knew it was something to do with Coco, but beyond that, he was still baffled after all these years.

Raff tried to pull himself together and he headed over to the counter. The shop was still empty as he had put the CLOSED sign up, so he went to the door and flipped it over.

What on earth was he supposed to do now, he thought as he stared through the door? Paris suddenly felt very different with Sophie back in it, but Raff couldn't possibly have said why.

'Why did you shut the shop, you idiot? You'll send all your customers over to the competition.'

Raff looked up and found himself smiling. God, his best mate had the best timing in the world. He was also wearing the most grotesque mustard-yellow shirt that resembled something a cat had vomited on.

'Why do you look as though you have the weight of the world on your shoulders?' Louis asked with a frown.

'Why do you look as though you've been buying clothes from a second-hand shop?'

Louis mock-punched Raff's arm. 'This is fashion, *mon ami*. You wouldn't know it if you saw it.'

Raff rolled his eyes, glad for the moral support nonetheless. Tall and gangly, Louis was a musician and a self-confessed former reprobate whose reputation for womanising and partying had been – in Louis's opinion only – legendary, but he had finally settled down with a lovely girl called Anne-Marie who was stable but apparently naughty enough behind the scenes to keep Louis on the straight and narrow. They had always both assumed that Raff would get hitched first – to Sophie, actually – but ironically, and due to Sophie's abrupt disappearance all those years ago, Louis had unexpectedly got there first, having met Anne-Marie at around the same time as Raff and Sophie had got together. Their wedding had been a typically bohemian affair with wild flowers everywhere and a live band who had played jaunty jigs all night long. Raff had made them two beautifully unusual cakes rather than the traditional *croquembouche* – one in the shape of a white guitar for Louis and one in the shape of a giant, red handbag as Anne-Marie designed and sold bags for a living. It had been a wonderful day and Raff remembered his heart aching throughout for Sophie; her absence had torn a gigantic hole in his life.

Raff stood aside to let someone else in. Madame Tournier, one of their best customers, wore a faux-fur coat all year round whatever the weather, and her hair resembled a coronet of sandy-coloured candy floss. She also consumed more macarons than any woman of a certain age would be willing to admit to.

'You look as though you have seen a ghost,' Madame Tournier commented, patting him on the arm as she waddled past.

Raff nodded ruefully. Madame Tournier was more accurate than she might imagine. That was exactly what had just happened. He had just seen a ghost. And even though he had only seen that ghost for a few minutes, Raff knew he was slowly unravelling inside.

'What's she on about? What ghost have you seen?' Louis asked, checking out his reflection in the shiny glass of the counter. 'Charity shop? Seriously!? I look amazing.'

'Sophie's back.'

Louis gaped. 'What?'

'Yep. She's back.'

'But… but…' Louis was almost as speechless as Raff had been ten minutes earlier. And Louis was rarely lost for words.

'Close your mouth; we have hygiene rules in here.'

To distract himself, Raff ducked behind the counter and grabbed a large pink box. He knew Madame Tournier's order and he set about filling up the box. She favoured a classic selection of standard flavours such as vanilla, chocolate and coffee, but she also liked Raff to surprise her with some new concoctions. She was a great taste tester in fact, and normally he'd carefully select some of his fresh efforts based on her preferences. Today, however, he randomly selected one from each row, closed the box and handed them over, promising to add the order to Madame Tournier's account. She was one of the few customers he gave credit to because she always paid on time and she spent so much money; it was worth the risk.

'Right, now that she's gone, tell me everything,' Louis said, going behind the counter and half-heartedly pretending to fire up the coffee machine.

'Stop it,' Raff ordered. 'You'll break it.'

Louis held his hands up in agreement. He was useless at anything technical that wasn't attached to a musical instrument of some kind. 'Aah… Sophie is here to find her mum,' he guessed, throwing himself into a chair.

Raff nodded, rubbing his hands over his face as he took stock of his thoughts. He started to make two coffees. 'She looked as shocked as I felt. I'm assuming Eloise didn't tell her about me working here either. I don't blame her for that; I suppose she thought Sophie might not come if she knew I was here.'

Louis shook his head. 'I still have no idea why she even ran out on you all those years ago. Does she know what state she left you in?'

'I shouldn't think so,' Raff shrugged. 'Not unless Eloise told her.'

'God.' Louis eyed his friend with concern. 'Well, I hope she finds Mariele and heads back to England immediately.'

Raff sighed. Louis used to love Sophie before she left, but since then he hadn't exactly been her biggest fan. It was all so long ago and not something he and Louis talked about these days, but Sophie's arrival had brought his old thoughts and feelings crashing back.

'How does she look?' Louis asked, sitting back in his chair.

'Good,' Raff replied, without missing a beat. 'Really good, in fact.'

'*Merde*,' Louis said.

'*Merde*,' Raphael agreed, turning back to the coffee machine. He handed Louis a coffee.

'So now what?' Louis said, turning back the cuffs of his ugly shirt.

'I have absolutely no idea,' Raff replied honestly. He stared past Louis and contemplated the Parisian skyline. How come Paris suddenly felt different now that Sophie was back in it? 'I genuinely don't know what to think or feel, let alone what to do.'

'I'm not surprised,' Louis said sympathetically. 'Good job I'm here to sort your life out for you.'

Raff privately pulled a face. Louis was good at many things, but Raff wasn't sure he was the best person when it came to relationships. Louis had got incredibly lucky with Anne-Marie; she clearly wore the trousers, running their relationship effortlessly and taking control of everything, and Louis, whether he realised it or not, simply went along for the ride.

Still, Raff was glad of the support. Because right now, he sure as hell needed it.

Chapter Six

'Right.' Eloise pushed a strong coffee across the table; she had regained her composure after Raff's sudden arrival at the cottage. Sophie wished she felt the same. But she didn't. She was jolted beyond belief.

Eloise took control. 'Firstly, drink that. Secondly, talk to me.'

'What about?' Sophie said rather sharply, sipping the coffee.

'About Ryan. In the first instance.'

Sophie shook her head, still annoyed with Eloise. Her twin had taken her to a cafe called the *La Ville de Provins* near the *Gare de l'Est*. It was a traditional brasserie with a sunny terrace and its decoration was typically 'bistro' in style. It also brought back yet more memories of Sophie's childhood; Mariele would take them to this cafe as a treat and also when she didn't want to cook. It didn't have the familiarity of *Chez Josephine*, but it had a certain style and elegance of its own.

Sophie glanced out of the window. She loved this corner of Paris. It was located on the right bank of the River Seine and the borough was called Warehouse. It was home to two of Paris' six main stations – the Gare du Nord and the Gare de l'Est, amongst the busiest in Europe.

Sophie felt quite overwhelmed at the childhood memories the views from the window were bringing back.

Eloise swiftly ordered two croques-monsieurs and a *tartine* bread, butter and jam, her favourite.

'I can't eat all that,' Sophie protested.

'You're not.' Eloise took off her jacket. She dressed very differently from Sophie normally, but today, in a black shirt and belted jeans, she didn't look dissimilar. They actually looked like twins for once, albeit by accident. 'So. Ryan.'

Sophie tore a corner off a croque-monsieur, aware that Eloise was stalling. But seeing as she wasn't sure she was ready to talk about Raff, Sophie allowed herself to talk about Ryan instead.

'I've told you everything about Ryan, I'm sure.'

'Have you heard from him?' Eloise emptied three packets of sugar into her coffee.

Sophie didn't comment on the action, knowing Eloise would call her a sugar-Nazi if she did. She and Eloise wouldn't ever agree about Eloise's sugar addiction so it was best left alone. 'Now and then,' Sophie said. 'I can't just switch my feelings off, but I feel so hurt about the whole thing. I don't know if there is a way back from it.'

Eloise pulled a face. 'I don't blame you. It's a pretty callous thing to do. Why not just get engaged and do the long-distance thing for a year?'

'I know.' Sophie nodded. 'I was so gutted. Whenever he calls, those old feelings come back, but I just don't know if I feel the same about him now. It's confusing.'

Eloise tucked into the bread and jam. 'Oh my God, so good. I limit myself to this once a week now that I've had children.'

Sophie smiled. Eloise had an amazing figure – in spite of her sugar addiction.

'But I get that it's confusing,' Eloise continued. 'He's gone, but he hasn't gone.'

'Exactly.'

'I liked Ryan,' Eloise mused. 'But I wasn't altogether sure he was the best person for you if I'm being perfectly honest.'

Sophie raised an eyebrow. 'Why are people only saying this to me now that he's dumped me to move to Dubai? Pinter said all this before I left England. I really loved the guy.'

Eloise looked apologetic. 'Oh ok. I suppose I just thought he was a bit… perfect. A bit safe. And maybe not quite right for you. A bit…'

'If you say prissy…'

Eloise grinned. 'That's a good word.' Her expression became sober. 'Ok, listen. Let's just see how it pans out on the Ryan front. But I *will* say this: I don't think he deserves you after what he's done.'

'Fair enough. I'm not sure he does either.' Sophie faltered inside. She knew that was probably true, but she couldn't help still loving him at the moment. She couldn't just switch her feelings off, could she? He had been amazing for the entire time they had been together; maybe it wasn't so terrible that he wanted to focus on his career for a while before settling down.

Sophie frowned, confused all over again.

'So. Raff.'

Sophie winced at his name and at Eloise's typically abrupt, shotgun delivery. 'Raff. Yes. Thanks for that, by the way, El. A heads-up wouldn't have gone amiss.'

'I know, I know.' Eloise looked shame-faced. 'Listen, Sophie. I really do want to apologise for not warning you about Raff. He's only been working at the shop for a few months and I wasn't even sure he was staying and then mum disappeared and…'

'Ok, ok.' Sophie held her hands up. 'I get it. But you should have warned me. It's Raff, Eloise. *Raff!*'

Eloise cast her eyes down. 'Yes.'

Sophie took pity on her sister.

'But you know what I think about the whole situation, Soph,' Eloise said, lifting her head again. 'And I still think it now.'

Sophie shook her head irritably. Eloise had been Team Raff after the break-up for a while and it had incensed Sophie. She had no idea why Eloise hadn't immediately jumped to her defence rather than Raff's, but that was the way it had been. Eloise seemed convinced that Sophie had made a mistake and they had fallen out for a while, but they were sisters and they were twins and they were close and they had found a way back.

Sophie sighed. She would deal with the Raff situation later. They needed to find their mum. That was why Sophie was in Paris.

Eloise was checking her watch. 'I need to phone Georges shortly; he dealt with the boys this morning, but God knows if they turned up at school with their lunch boxes or in the right clothes.'

Sophie smiled. She wasn't quite sure how Eloise put up with Georges, the lazy so-and-so, but she assumed her sister must love him very much. 'Ok – so, mum. Do you have any idea at all where she might be?'

Eloise immediately looked worried again and she rummaged in her handbag, finally fishing out a piece of paper. 'No idea at all. I've phoned everyone in her address book and I've spoken to all the neighbours. No one knows anything. She was last seen on this date.' She handed the piece of paper to Sophie. 'I've written it all down: the people I've spoken to, when she was last seen, what she might be wearing.'

Sophie scanned through the notes, seeing that each one was marked with a neat bullet point. Eloise was the precise, organised twin and Sophie was creative and spontaneous. Eloise's notes were thorough. She had checked all the obvious points and people, and had documented each one meticulously.

'What do you think she means by this note?' Sophie said, taking it out of her pocket.

Eloise held her hands up. 'I don't know! I'm not sure if she's just being dramatic. "My heart isn't happy." What does that even mean?'

Sophie stared at the note. Their mum could be prone to drama at times, but Sophie didn't think this was the case here. Mariele surely wouldn't want to worry them; she had presumably left the message to reassure them both, not stress them out. So, if she mentioned her heart, it was relevant in some way.

'Well, it can't be our father at any rate,' Sophie offered. Their mother never talked about their father so she and Eloise had assumed he was a waste of space.

Eloise shrugged. 'I guess not.'

'So…?'

Eloise shrugged again. 'God, Soph! Who knows? There's never been anyone serious, has there?'

Sophie devoured the rest of her delicious croque-monsieur, suddenly realising how hungry she was. It was true though; Mariele had never settled with anyone. She wasn't exactly flighty when it came to men; there had been the odd guy on the scene on and off. But they didn't seem to last very long and Mariele always said she had plenty to be getting on with looking after the twins and with her macaron business.

Sophie remembered Mariele talking about true love a lot when she and Eloise were younger and about following your heart, but there wasn't much evidence of such things in Mariele's life. She was a bohemian, creative woman who seemed to have left that side of her behind and immersed herself in the lives of her children and grand-children, and in her work.

'I miss her,' Eloise blurted out.

Sophie grabbed Eloise's hand. 'Me too. We'll find her,' she said more confidently than she felt. 'We have to.'

Eloise looked tearful. She was always the more emotional twin. 'I'm so glad you're here,' she said. 'And I'm so sorry I didn't tell you about Raff.'

Raff. Sophie took a deep breath. Raff was a whole different ball game. 'Go check on Georges,' she said. 'I'll get this.'

Eloise stood up gratefully and kissed Sophie's cheek. 'Thank you. I need to get back to the nursery as well... I've missed nearly a week of work. I'll call you later, Soph.'

Sophie nodded. Settling the bill, she stepped outside and walked back towards the cottage. The sun sat high behind the Sacre Coeur, throwing light out across Mont-martre. Sophie was desperate to start searching for her mum, but first of all, she had to speak to Raff. Her heart started hammering at the mere thought of it, but she headed back to the macaron shop. She was determined not to lose her nerve.

–

Sophie reached the shop and promptly lost her nerve. Realising that she hadn't had a shower since yesterday morning, she swiftly bypassed the macaron shop and went into the cottage instead. A long, hot shower that reminded her of her childhood as it hissed and spat for a few minutes before bursting into a fresh cascade of warm water felt like home.

Unpacking, Sophie threw her clothes into the drawers, not sure she needed to waste too much time being neat. Eloise was the neat one out of the two of them anyway; Sophie was a little more 'fly by the seat of her pants'. And for all she knew, she could be back in London by tomorrow evening. Her mum might just turn up out of the blue or Sophie might get lucky and just find her immediately. But either way, it was easier to work out what to wear when everything was out of the suitcase.

God. Sophie slowed herself down. Eloise had always been the one to organise herself and well, basically control everything. Sophie wasn't used to being in charge of anything... let alone finding their mother. She finished putting her clothes away and at the bottom of one of the drawers, she found a large, ornate box decorated with brightly coloured mermaids and octopuses and fish.

Sophie's heart began to thump. She recognised this box. It had been her treasure box as a child... somewhere she would hide or keep things that meant something to her. She sat down on the bed and slowly opened the lid.

She caught her breath. It felt as though time had stood still for a moment. Inside the box were a collection of special things from her past. Crinkled-up, peach-coloured rose petals from her grandmother's garden that she used to make rank perfume with. There was the bunny she used to cuddle in bed, imaginatively named 'Bunny', silk flowers her mum had given her to wear in her hair at a party, garish costume jewellery she used to parade around in. And a pile of shells from the beach in Trouville-sur-Mer they used to visit as a family when Sophie and Eloise were kids. Sophie held them to her nose and was immediately transported back in time…

Nineteen Years Ago

'*Catch!*' *Mariele threw the ball to Sophie.*

Laughing hard, an eleven-year-old Sophie leapt up but missed the ball.

Eloise standing behind her caught it neatly. 'Oui!' she yelled, punching the air with her fist.

Sophie hid a smile. Eloise was so competitive, always had been. She watched her sister tugging at her ill-fitting bikini, clearly uncomfortable with so much skin exposed. Sophie, however, loved her new canary-yellow two-piece.

Mariele held her hand up. 'No more,' she implored with a smile. 'We've been playing for over an hour.' She ran her hands over her stylish black and white swimsuit and strolled to their messy row of striped, jewel-coloured beach towels — emerald-green, ruby-red and bright blue. 'It's tan time. I want to get brown.' Flopping down, Mariele beckoned the twins to her. 'Come. You need some sunscreen on.'

'It's so beautiful here,' Sophie sighed, sitting down and moving her hair to one side to expose her shoulders.

Mariele pulled a huge, wide-brimmed sun hat onto her long swathe of dark, wavy hair and started to rub cream into Sophie's skin.

'It's loud,' Eloise grumbled, straightening their towels primly before tugging her bikini out of her bottom and taking a seat.

Sophie and Mariele exchanged a glance. Eloise didn't really enjoy the beach. To her, it was messy and noisy and the fine dusty sand got everywhere; it just wasn't tidy or ordered. Whereas Sophie and Mariele loved it, especially Trouville. The beautiful stretch of pale sand, the lovely boardwalk, the huddle of pretty, hundred-year-old villas at the edge of the beach. More family-friendly than its glamorous neighbour Deauville, Trouville had retained its authentic charm and it had a cultural, bohemian air that Mariele in particular adored.

'We'll go in an hour or so,' Mariele assured Eloise as she rubbed sun cream onto her daughter's pale shoulders. 'Just a little cooking time.'

'We're not macarons,' Eloise moaned, lying down and putting her cap over her face.

'I'm aware of that,' Mariele smiled, winking at Sophie. 'But if you were, you'd be… a rose and vanilla one.'

Eloise lifted her cap and frowned. 'Really? Why?'

Mariele laughed. 'I don't know! You just would be. Well, let's see. Maybe because roses are fragrant and beautifully perfect and delicate. And vanilla, because it's sweet and warm and everyone loves it.'

Despite her grumpy mood, Eloise giggled.

'And me?' Sophie asked eagerly. 'What would I be?'

'You…' Mariele took Sophie's chin in her hands and turned her face this way and that way. 'You would be… a pistachio with white chocolate ganache.'

Sophie clasped her arms around her knees gleefully. 'Why?'

'Pistachio because it's buttery and smooth and classic, even though I see it as rather quirky,' Mariele stated. 'Just like you. And white chocolate because it's sweet and creamy and indulgent… an absolute treat.'

'And because she's cinglé,' Eloise chuckled. 'Like a nut… nutty… crazy.'

Sophie broke into laughter. Only her mum could make her and Eloise feel this way.

Mariele gathered them both into her arms and hugged them both. 'Mes filles,' she said, holding them tightly. 'My everything.'

Sophie and Eloise squealed as she squeezed them too hard.

'Now, while I cook like a little macaron, can you find us some pretty shells?' Mariele said, letting them go and lying back on her towel. She wiggled her toes, the red polish she always wore glinting in the sunlight. 'The most beautiful shells you can find… for your rooms and for the shop. Go!'

Shrieking with delight, Sophie and Eloise ran to the shore, all gangly legs and dark hair flying out behind them, hell-bent on finding the best shells on the beach…

–

Sophie came to and stared down into the box of treasures. God, she missed her mum. And she wanted her back right now. That memory… it summed her mum up completely. The fun and the laughs and how… free she always was. How glamorous.

Feeling emotional, Sophie delved into the box again. At the bottom was a bunch of photographs. She pulled them out. There were photos of her mum looking stylish in various party dresses, and some of her as a child. She looked serious and cute. There was a black and white one of Mariele sitting on the bonnet of a Mini in a little dress with her long legs crossed and her dark hair streaming out behind her in the wind. Sophie had no idea who had taken the photograph or what it meant, but her mum used to look at it sometimes with a sad look on her face.

Sophie inhaled. And then there were all her photographs of Raff. Photographs she had taken of him. Like a besotted idiot seemingly, as there were many, many photographs, with a crappy camera she had been given for an early birthday or with a more expensive one her mum had saved up for and bought when Sophie was older.

Sophie pulled the photographs out. There were colour photographs, black and white and sepia. All the different mediums Sophie had been experimenting with when they were together. Sophie stared at them. The black-and-white mock-moody one of Raff pretending to stare into the distance at something fascinating, before cracking up into laughter and turning back to her, his head thrown back. The full-on colour version of him with his chocolate eyes staring into the lens, his mouth breaking into a wide smile. The clumsy half-shot of the two of them wrapped around one another, long before selfies were in fashion.

Wow. Sophie felt overwhelmed by a rush of emotions. Raff was *that guy*. That guy who had come along and changed her life. Who had taught her how to feel and how to love and who she wanted to be. Raff had been everything to her. Everything. He had been passion and love and addiction and intoxication and he had been all-consuming and it had been amazing. And then it had been devastating and heart-breaking and all-consuming in the non-amazing way that a broken heart had a tendency of being.

The thought of Raff sent her reeling – but she had to put all of that aside. There were more important things to worry about right now and she was in Paris to find her mother, not reminisce about Raff.

Sophie leafed through the rest of the photos. She found some of her French grandmother, Fifi, looking flamboyant in a variety of bright, outrageous or downright bold outfits, including one controversial one in what was clearly a real, floor-length fur. There were a few of her English grandparents who had passed away some years back, looking alternately serious or happy. There were lots of black and white ones of people Sophie didn't recognise, perhaps more distant relatives of her mum. There were a few of a handsome man who was vaguely familiar to Sophie but she had no idea why. He had dark hair and rugged features and he was smartly dressed in each of them; even when he was wearing more casual clothes, he had the air of someone who was both stylish and proper.

Sophie shrugged and put everything back in the memory box. Why had her mum kept all those photographs? She was a bit of a hoarder at the best of times, but she tended to put photographs in frames and out on display if they meant something to her. As for the ones of Raff... it was odd that her mum had kept those. Sophie had left them behind on purpose, because she knew it would make it easier to forget him; if she'd had photographs to look at, Sophie had been worried she might cave and run back to Paris... back to him and that was something she simply couldn't do, not after everything that had happened. But Sophie hadn't meant for her mum to keep them as mementos. But anyway. He was downstairs running the macaron shop, so for the short time she was here, she was going to have to get on with it. She had got over him once before, so coming face to face with him wasn't going to break her.

Sophie pulled herself together. She selected a cream, silky top and a pair of skinny jeans and got dressed. Brushing through her long hair, she felt her heart hammering in her chest at the thought of coming face to face with Raff again. She was also furious with herself for even feeling that way. It was absurd. It was just Raff. Raff had been significant in her life at one time, but that was a long time ago. Now, he was just her mum's business partner; god alone only knew why him, out of all the people her mum could have chosen, Sophie thought, feeling a flash of exasperation, but that's how she needed to think of Raff: as her mum's business partner.

Heading downstairs, Sophie took a deep breath and went into the macaron shop. Raff was serving a stream of chattering customers and appeared stressed out. He looked up and gave her an awkward head nod. Without pausing for thought, Sophie headed behind the counter, tied her long hair up with one of the bands she always kept on her wrist and washed her hands. Turning back to the line of customers, Sophie started attending to customers. She hadn't worked in the macaron shop in a long time, but it was straightforward enough, unless it was super-busy. Like now. She felt flustered all of a sudden.

Raff looked relieved and carried on serving. 'Thank you,' he mouthed.

Sophie ignored him. She wasn't doing this to be nice to Raff; it was her mum's shop. She ran her eyes over the perfectly round macarons; they came in the standard size and also a mini-sized version, which Sophie had always loved as a child because they were so cute. There were new flavours too. When Sophie had left Paris, her mum specialised in the classics: chocolate, raspberry, coffee, vanilla. All of those were still present, but there were so many others: lavender and honey, crème brûlée, orange blossom, caramel apple and several more. Sophie suspected Raff had something to do with the innovative new colours; he had always been fairly avant-garde when it came to his craft. Sophie also guessed it was to move with the times; most of the macaron shops in Paris sold quite out there flavours in rich, bold colours. She sensed Raff's eyes on her as she familiarised herself with the new flavours and it was making her feel edgy, but she kept her mind focused on what she was doing.

'*Au Champagne et framboise?*' she said, picking up the silver tongs with a flat scoop they always used to make sure the macarons didn't get dented. '*Huit? Douze?*' she added, picking up the correct sized pink box when the customer answered. It was lined with a puff of ruby-coloured tissue and Sophie took care to tie the white ribbon neatly around the box.

'*Merci beaucoup,*' she smiled as she handed the beautifully presented box across the counter. Dealing with the euros swiftly, she turned to the next customer in line and started to serve again. Raff got on with replacing macarons as they were sold and busied himself at the back, presumably baking more trays or prepping for the following day.

The line gradually died down and Sophie leant against the counter. Only two people had come in for coffee so far, but she assumed that could change as the lunch hour progressed. Sophie wanted to ask Raff about the cafe side of the business, but that would mean talking to him and she wasn't sure she was ready to do that. Well, she would have to eventually of course, but Sophie wasn't sure today was the day for that. Or tomorrow, for that matter.

Raff emerged from the kitchen wiping his hands on a towel. He looked rather more dishevelled than he had earlier that day – his hair was sticking up as if he had clutched it a few times and his top had a streak of blueberry-coloured ganache across the front – but he also looked less grumpy than he had earlier.

'Thank you,' he started to say again, but he didn't continue as the door opened once more. A ravishing teenager wearing tight jeans, over-the-knee boots and a baggy jumper strolled in.

Raff shot a worried glance at Sophie.

Sophie started. Oh wow.

Coco strode through the shop and kissed Raff's cheek before turning to Sophie. '*Bonjour.* I'm Coco. I am Raff's daughter.'

Sophie nodded wordlessly. Coco was indeed Raff's daughter. She was also the very reason Sophie and Raff had imploded and split up five years ago. The very reason, in effect that Sophie had left Paris and never returned. And here she was, standing right in front of Sophie.

Chapter Seven

Sophie tried to pull herself together. She had to get it together.

'H-hi,' she managed finally, feeling as though her mouth was full of cotton wool.

'Hi,' Coco returned confidently.

Sophie stared at Coco, watching her wordlessly as she snatched a macaron from behind the glass case and started munching on it. Coco then threw herself into a chair, still eating.

She really was beautiful, Sophie mused, feeling shocked at the sight of her. Coco had long, dark hair almost to her waist and eyes like Raff, with the same long lashes. The same small gap in her front teeth, Sophie noted, remembering it from before. Coco had petite features and an astonishingly pretty face.

Coco was leggy and tall and exuded a confidence far beyond the fifteen years she had lived so far. Sophie wondered how much Coco resembled her mother… Estelle. Sophie distinctly remembered Coco's mother's name and what she looked like. Estelle was a model. Stunningly beautiful, brimming with confidence and sass. She didn't have the 'blank canvas' model look that many girls had; Estelle was beautiful, even without make-up and she had a cheeky, confident look Sophie was sure had sold lingerie, shoes, clothes, gloves, jewellery and whatever else Estelle had been chosen to represent.

Sophie felt rather sick thinking about Estelle. She remembered feeling threatened by Raff's ex-girlfriend even before meeting her, because of the amount of time she had been in Raff's life and of what Sophie had suspected Estelle meant to him. And when she had arrived out of the blue the way she had, with Coco in tow, Sophie's world had imploded.

Sophie swallowed and re-focused her attention on Coco. Coco wore a fair amount of make-up she didn't really need, but Sophie guessed that was down to her age. Fifteen-year-olds wore lots of make-up, didn't they? Sophie was pretty sure she had caked on the eyeliner at that age too, even if she hadn't been a fan of the pale, powdery cheeks and red lipstick. Coco didn't need it, but she still pulled it off; the overall effect was fairly breath-taking.

'This is Sophie,' Raff said, turning to her.

Coco threw her a brief sunny smile before frowning. 'Have we met before?'

Sophie caught Raff's eye. She and Coco had met before... just once when Coco had been ten years old. She had been gorgeous then – a perfect, leggy doll of a child with a mop of dark hair and huge eyes. – and Sophie hadn't been able to get the image of her out of her head for many years to come.

'Just once,' Raff said haltingly, not taking his eyes off of Sophie.

Where was Coco's mum, Sophie wondered, wishing Raff would stop staring at her. Was Estelle on the scene these days? Was she being a mum to Coco now? And were Estelle and Raff together? Sophie was surprised to feel a stabbing pain at the thought and she brushed it aside impatiently. How ridiculous! She wouldn't have the first idea what was going on in Raff's life these days. They hadn't spoken since she had left Paris. Raff had contacted her several times – she still had all the letters he had sent her – but she hadn't responded to them, despite her mum and Eloise berating her and telling her she was making a mistake. Sophie had conceded and read them – just once – and then she had tucked them away out of sight. She hadn't been sure if it was because, having read Raff's words, she doubted herself or because she didn't believe any of it. Either way, Sophie had been so broken, it was all she could do to pull herself up and start over. It had been the hardest thing she had ever done.

Sophie realised Coco was talking to her. '*Pardon?*' she said. 'Sorry, I didn't hear you.'

Coco turned her head on one side. 'You have a lovely face,' she commented. 'You could be a model.'

'Me?' Sophie laughed. She felt momentarily flattered. Coco was beautiful; such a comment was a huge compliment. 'No way! I was about to say the same to you.'

'I don't want to be a model,' Coco said dismissively, lounging back in her chair. 'My mum is one and I don't want to be like her. I want to be an artist.'

'No money in that.' Raff shot Sophie a glance. 'Actually, I could be wrong. You should speak to Sophie about that. She's an artist. A very good one, in fact.'

'Are you?' Coco looked at Sophie with renewed respect. 'That's brilliant.'

Sophie's eyes flickered to Raff. Did he think her work was good? He certainly used to. 'I'm actually more of a photographer these days,' she said to Coco. 'But I still paint when I have time.'

'You must tell me more about this,' Coco exclaimed excitedly. She straightened in her chair. 'We must spend some time together. You can tell me all about it: what I need to do, the kind of thing you do. Did you study? Where did you study? Have you brought some of your work with you?'

'Coco!' Raff halted her barrage of questions. 'Take a breath. Give Sophie a chance to think.'

Coco looked contrite and she stuck her bottom lip out. 'Sorry, *Papa*. Sorry, Sophie.' She stood up. 'But I really would enjoy talking to you if you have some time.'

Sophie caught her breath. How ironic. Raff's daughter was asking to spend time together, seemingly wanting her advice. When she was actually the reason behind...

'That would be lovely,' Sophie said brightly, burying the thought. It wasn't Coco's fault – none of it was Coco's fault. 'We'll sort that out.' Sophie meant it; even if she wasn't in Paris for long and she found her mum soon, Sophie would spend a bit of time with Coco and give her some advice about her career... if she wanted it.

'Fantastic,' Coco said with a wide smile, scooping up her turquoise bag. 'It was great to meet you, Sophie. Bye, *Papa*!' Planting a kiss on Raff's cheek, Coco cheekily grabbed another macaron and then with a swish of her dark hair, she was gone.

Raff shook his head and turned to Sophie. 'Don't worry about the art thing if you don't have time. Your priority is to find your mum.'

Sophie took off her apron. 'That's ok. I'm sure I can spare some time for her, Raff.' She started to pick up her things. 'And I don't even know where to start with mum to be honest.'

'Yes, I can imagine. Anything I can do to help… ask me anything. Maybe she said something to me that might make sense to you…' Raff shrugged. 'I don't know. But I want to help. In any way I can.'

'Yes. Yes, I probably will do.' Sophie decided it was time to leave. 'Just… later.'

'Of course.' Raff nodded. 'I understand. And thank you for helping me out in here earlier. I really appreciate it.'

Sophie gave him a brief smile. God. How formal they were! How polite. How… awkward. Considering everything they had shared together, everything they had gone through together.

'No problem,' she threw back. 'Any time. Well, while I'm still here anyway.' She could feel Raff's eyes on her and it was unbearable. 'Is it ok if I leave you to it?' she said. 'I might get some air. See if I can work out where to start with mum.'

'Sure.' Raff looked away and started to tidy up. 'I can manage here for the rest of the day.'

Sophie walked towards the door.

'Did you bring your camera?' Raff asked suddenly. 'I just wondered.'

She nodded. 'Yes. I mean… I'm not sure I'll use it, but my boss at the photographic studio I work at suggested I kill two birds with one stone.' Sophie raised an eyebrow. 'But he's a bit of a sod like that.'

Raff smiled. 'He probably also knows how good you are. I don't blame him.'

Sophie felt awkward. She didn't want to, but Raff had always made her feel that way. Back in the day, it had been that exciting, squirmy, *alive* kind of discomfort. Today, it was an altogether different kind of discomfort and weirdness.

'Right. Ok, well I'll be off then.' Sophie pulled her jacket on. Leaving Raff in the shop, feeling his eyes burning into her back, she walked out.

Outside, Sophie took in a gulp of fresh air. She wanted to lean against the wall and slide down it, cry into her knees, but she knew she couldn't do that. She had cried far too many tears over Raff in the last five years, and she wasn't about to reignite those sad feelings. It was all in the past now. Sophie was in Paris to find her mum and she would just have to deal with the curveball that was Raff being inexplicably right under her nose again.

Raff. Sophie faltered and found herself clutching her chest. She had been so happy… *they* had been so happy. Sophie had naively imagined that she and Raff would be together for all eternity. She could never have envisaged anything tearing them apart. Until Sophie had found out about Coco.

Supressing a rush of emotion, Sophie started walking. Marching, in fact. She marched hard until she reached the *Gare de l'Est*. Hesitating, Sophie paused to take it in. Officially, *Paris-Est*, it was one of the six large SNCF termini in Paris. It faced the Boulevard de Strasbourg and it was one of the largest and oldest railway stations in Paris. Its entrance was vast and impressive and Sophie couldn't help pulling out her camera and taking a few shots. Strolling further, she came across the Gare du Nord and she took some more photos. She wasn't sure they were the kind of photos Pinter would want in an exhibition, but she didn't really care. It was like a rite of passage, rediscovering Paris, after so long. Like… coming home, but seeing it through new eyes again.

Realising she would end up in the *La Chapelle*, in the 18th arrondissement if she carried on walking, Sophie slowed down. Slumping onto a bench near the *Gare de Magenta*, she caught her breath. There were so many childhood memories here… so many memories of Raff.

Her phone rang and she took it out of her bag. It was Ryan. Sophie hesitated. She could do without another shouty phone call from a Dubai buffet that sounded as though Ryan was partying hard. It rang and rang and Sophie finally answered it.

'Soph.'

He sounded calm and sober.

'Hey.'

'You ok?'

Sophie sat back. 'Yes, I think so.'

'What's up?'

Ryan sounded concerned and Sophie came slightly undone. She couldn't handle anyone being nice to her right now. It had been bad enough when Raff had sounded all anxious and caring. But somehow, this seemed to be the right moment for Ryan to call.

'Just… I don't know where to start with my mum,' Sophie mumbled.

'God, yes. It must be a nightmare for you. Sorry, Soph.'

She felt tears pricking her eyelids. 'It's ok. I just want to find her.'

'Of course.' Ryan made a sympathetic sound. 'I prob-ably shouldn't say this, but I do miss you Sophie. I really do'

Sophie wasn't sure how that made her feel. Confused, that was for sure. But… good, perhaps? Good that he missed her. She was only human. And she felt so alone right now. No Ryan, no mum. And Raff, right here, in her face. Coco, too.

Sophie felt like crying all over again.

'What can I do to help?' Ryan said, sounding worried. 'I want to help, Soph. I could send you some money over if you need it? Hire a private investigator to help you track her down? There must be someone amazing in Paris we could enlist… whatever you need, it's yours.'

Sophie fell silent. That was the thing about Ryan. He had always made her feel so safe. So well looked-after. He was so practical and maybe that was what she needed right now.

For the first time in the last few weeks, Sophie wondered if she and Ryan might be able to make it back from this enforced separation. If it was maybe just a neces-sary rite of passage they needed to go through to find one another again. Or maybe she was just feeling vulnerable because Raff was back on the scene.

'Right. Listen, I have to go,' Sophie said, feeling that it was time to end the call. 'Thanks for your support. I'll keep you posted.'

'Ok,' Ryan sounded disappointed. 'Yes, stay in touch, Soph. I really hope your mum is ok. I meant it about the private investigator and the money, Sophie. Whatever you need. I… still love you and I honestly do miss you.'

Sophie rang off, not sure what to think. Her head felt as though it could explode thinking about Ryan and Raff and Coco and everything else. When really, her focus should be her mum. Finding her mum.

Mum, where on earth are you? Sophie thought desperately. *Why on earth have you disappeared like this?* Sophie felt nauseous. She had no idea where to even begin searching, and Paris was a huge place. Was Mariele still even in Paris? How was Sophie to know if she had hopped onto a plane and gone somewhere else?

The magnitude of her task dawned on Sophie as she watched tourists and Paris-dwellers walking in different directions. Where on earth did someone start looking for a missing person in a city of this size?

Chapter Eight

The following morning, Sophie woke up feeling groggy and exhausted. She hadn't slept well and had spent all night tossing and turning, feeling anxious about her mum. And Raff. And Ryan. God, this was all too much to think about. So many conflicting thoughts. It was difficult to make sense of it all.

Sophie stretched and sat up in bed. She had no idea where her phone was; she had a feeling she had left it downstairs somewhere. Sophie wasn't sure she wanted it near her in case Ryan had phoned again. She just wasn't in the mood to talk to him right now. All that 'I'm missing you' nonsense. What was all that about? What was she supposed to think? It was messing with her head and Sophie needed to maintain a clear mind. The engagement hadn't happened and their relationship was in limbo. Remembering how kind and practical Ryan had been on the phone the day before, Sophie felt flummoxed all over again.

Sophie pulled herself out of bed and had a quick shower. Throwing on a short red dress and grabbing a jacket, she headed downstairs. The cottage was in darkness, calm and quiet, but there was a buzz of low-level noise and activity coming from the macaron shop. Wandering into the kitchen, Sophie felt a prickle of discomfort at the thought of Raff on the other side of the wall, but she squashed it down and searched for her phone. She found it by the coffee machine and she glanced at it briefly, then started in shock: there, on her screen, was a message from her mum. After no contact whatsoever for the past few weeks apart from her cryptic note, up her mum popped with a text! It said:

> *Sorry I haven't been in touch, darling – hope you haven't been worried. Am so glad you are back in Paris... it reminds me of your childhood and all the wonderful things we did together. Speak soon, Mum X*

Sophie sat down heavily on a nearby chair, grateful it was there to catch her. She felt ecstatic knowing her mum was fine, but she was also confused. What did it mean? Sophie re-read the message. It was reassuring, but baffling all the same. Yes, it told Sophie that her mum was ok, but it didn't tell her anything whatsoever about her mum's whereabouts. Or what had caused her to need space in the first place. And why was she so happy that Sophie was back in Paris? Why had she mentioned all the childhood memories?

Sophie tapped her phone on her knee. Was there a clue there, perhaps? Had her mum revisited some of those places recently? Was it some sort of clue as to where she might be or... maybe one of those places had something to do with what had made her mum leave. That made more sense.

Sophie pondered. She didn't think her mum wanted her to jet off to Trouville-sur-Mer or anything like that. She had mentioned Paris, so Sophie was going to focus on that. Sophie realised she should tell Eloise about the text and also get her view on what it meant, but she called her sister and got no answer. School run, probably. Damn. Sophie needed to talk to someone about this. She felt happier though. Happier now that her mum had been in touch.

'Hey.'

Sophie looked up. It was Raff. He looked as though he hadn't slept well either and Sophie wondered why. Not that it was any of her business.

'You ok?' Raff asked, frowning. He looked concerned, and as though he was checking her out in her red dress. Or maybe not. Sophie inwardly shrugged. She used to be able to read Raff's mind a bit, but there no way she was able to do it now.

'I'm kind of ok, I suppose.'

Annoyed, Sophie decided that looking tired suited Raff somehow. He wore a brown shirt with the sleeves rolled up and slouchy jeans, but there were heavy bags under his eyes. He always spoke to her in English with the most ridiculous French accent, but his command of the English language was excellent, both in vocabulary and grammar.

'You look tired,' Sophie commented, before she could stop herself.

'Do I?' Raff rubbed a hand over his eyes. 'Just… family stuff.'

Sophie couldn't help wondering what he meant, but she didn't probe further. Coco presumably? Sophie wasn't sure what other family Raff still had around him. He had been very close to his parents back in the day, but she had no idea if they were even still around.

'Busy in there?' she said, referring to the shop.

'Kind of.' Raff half smiled. 'I've put the closed sign on the door. Just for a few minutes. I wanted to see how you were. It goes quiet after the pre-work rush anyway.'

Sophie wasn't going to read anything into that. Raff was probably just worried about her mum because he was running the shop solo. She held up her phone. 'I just heard from mum.'

'Really?' Raff broke into a proper smile. 'You must be so relieved. What did she say? Where is she? When is she coming back?'

Sophie opened the message and showed it to Raff.

He read it and looked perplexed. 'Ok. So we still don't know what's going on. Or when she'll be back. Or where she is.'

'No,' Sophie admitted. 'I was excited to hear from her and reassured that nothing terrible has happened. But then I thought… what does that message even mean? Where the hell is she? And what's going on?' She stood up. 'It's so frustrating.'

Raff handed her phone back and leant against the door frame. 'Well. I think it's great that you've had an update. And that Mariele seems alright. Maybe we're just not meant to know everything yet.'

Sophie let out a sigh. Raff had always had this way of looking at things. An almost spiritual perspective that explained or at very least made sense of things on some level. She had no idea why they shouldn't know the full story – yet – but she supposed Raff had a point. Maybe her mum wasn't ready to open up about what was going on in her life for whatever reason.

'Tell me about the shop,' Sophie said, changing the subject. 'About… how you're here.' She corrected herself;

she had been about to ask 'why' Raff was here. Which had nothing whatsoever to do with her… because it was none of her business, but also because Raff being back at the macaron shop could not have anything to do with Sophie at all.

'What about it?' Raff lead the way back into the shop and fired up the coffee machine. 'Fancy some breakfast? We should just about have time.'

Sophie glanced at her watch. 'I need to speak to Eloise but… yes, ok. Thank you.' She sent Eloise a text telling her the good news, promising to call after breakfast.

Raff headed into the kitchen and Sophie tended to the coffee machine. Raff hadn't asked what she wanted to eat but she was leaving him to it. He was a great chef in general, not just a great pastry chef; breakfast in bed had been Raff's favourite thing to cook for her. He'd been pretty inventive back in the day: omelettes with bell peppers, caramelised onions and sour cream, avocado and chilli with scrambled eggs before anyone put chilli on anything; Greek yogurt with stewed figs, pistachios and honeycomb.

Sophie's hand faltered on the coffee machine. Even the thought of those breakfasts overloaded her mind and body with sensations: the delicious food, what had happened before the breakfast, what would always happen afterwards. Sophie swallowed, feeling herself flush. No. Don't even think about it. There was no point. Randomly, Sophie thought about Ryan. He wasn't into cooking. And he didn't have the rampant sex drive Raff possessed, but he had his own sexily cheeky way of doing things, which Sophie had been grateful for. The more different Ryan had been from Raff the better it was, in her opinion.

'Coffee ready?' Raff appeared with two plates.

'Er, yes.' Sophie fumbled around with the machine and managed to produce two fairly good coffees. She took the coffees over to a table while Raff grabbed some cutlery.

Eggs *en cocotte*, eggs baked in little ramekins, with a sprinkling of crispy pancetta on top. They looked and smelt amazing.

'There are mushrooms in there too,' Raff told her, sitting down. 'Porcinis and chestnut mushrooms. Your favourites.' He looked away. 'Well, maybe they are not these days.'

'No, they still are my favourites.' Sophie felt the eggs melt in her mouth and tasted an earthy burst of sautéed, buttery mushrooms. She wasn't going to read anything into Raff having a good memory. Especially not when it came to food. 'Wow. So good.'

'Thanks.' Raff nodded as he munched thoughtfully on a mouthful, always hyper-critical of his own efforts. 'Not too bad.' He eyed her. 'So, now that we can relax a bit after Mariele's text, tell me. What's new with you?'

Sophie carried on eating, giving herself some time. Half of her wanted to open up to Raff and tell him everything because, even though she hadn't seen him in five years, that closeness between them that had always existed still felt almost tangible, but the other half of her just wanted to shut down and protect herself and not tell Raff a single thing, because anything concerning Sophie had ceased to be his business after Coco arrived and after everything that happened as a consequence of that.

'Not much,' she offered finally, closing her feelings off.

Raff lifted an eyebrow and said nothing, as if he realised she had chosen to shut down.

Sophie cast her eyes down. She had always liked the way Raff did his sexy, single eyebrow lift thing, but she wasn't about to allow it to affect her now. Thank God Pinter wasn't here; Sophie had no doubt he would make huge things out of the body language between her and Raff, let alone out of anything else he might pick up on. Sophie steeled herself, and remembered exactly why she left Paris – and Raff – in the first place.

Feeling breathless for a moment, Sophie consciously pulled herself together. She wasn't sure what she would say to Raff about her life anyway. Certainly nothing about her relationship stuff at any rate. Sophie didn't exactly want to admit that her boyfriend of two years had ended their relationship and jetted off to Dubai instead of proposing to her. Even if that might not completely spell the end of them.

Sophie was shocked at herself: was she thinking of taking Ryan back when in her heart, she had told herself things should be completely over? She hadn't thought about taking him back before coming face to face with Raff. And Coco.

'What do you want to know about the macaron business?' Raff asked, clearly sensing that Sophie didn't want to talk about herself, shifting to a more business-like tone. 'Ask me anything you want to.'

Sophie relaxed slightly. Safer territory. 'Just… what's changed since I was last here, I suppose. How you and mum work together.'

Raff cradled his coffee. 'We work really well together. She's very traditional and I'm more of a… modern thinker, I guess.'

Sophie put her knife and fork down. Yes. She remembered that from her time in Paris all those years ago. Raff was very creative and forward-thinking. He had helped out in the business back then, while he was training.

'So I've been trying to get your mother to think about new flavours,' Raff was saying. 'Nothing too wild, but just… some fresh ideas.'

'And how has that gone down?'

Raff let out a short laugh. 'Sometimes great, sometimes not so much.'

Sophie couldn't help joining in the laughter. Mariele could be the most stubborn woman on the planet at times, but she also possessed a real bohemian streak and could be open to change and new ideas. When she wanted to be.

Sophie's mouth twitched. She and her mum were very alike in many ways. Her mum had always told her that she was the second most stubborn person in the world after herself.

'I've managed to get her away from just selling the really basic flavours,' Raff said, jumping up and heading to the glass cabinet.

'I noticed that the other day,' Sophie commented. 'A few new concoctions.'

Raff lifted a mini macaron out with the tongs. 'Try this. Salted caramel.'

Sophie bit into it. 'Amazing.' It really was. It melted in her mouth, and the strong, sweet caramel flavour faded into a salty stickiness that somehow cleansed the palate of the sweetness.

Raff took out a box and put a few more macarons into it. 'These are all the new ones.' He brought them over.

'Champagne with gold leaf. Lavender and coconut. Black vanilla. Blueberry and cream cheese. And that's as much as I've managed to get away with so far.' Raff grinned. 'But I have plans for several more, which I'll tell you about another time.'

'All gorgeous,' Sophie said, meaning it. She sampled the champagne with the speckles of gold leaf, which looked ridiculously pretty. 'It's so delicate. I would get so fat if I still lived here.'

'No way. You're… you look so…' Raff stared at her then tore his eyes away. 'Anyway. That message from your mum. I wonder why she was talking about the childhood stuff.'

'Yes, me too.'

Raff narrowed his eyes. 'I'm trying to think of anything she might have said that will give us a clue as to where she might be. I mean, I know we don't need to panic as much now that we know she's ok, but still.'

Sophie picked up the breakfast plates. 'I know. Seriously, anything you can remember would be great, Raff. I still want to find her.'

Raff helped her. Sophie caught a whiff of Raff's aftershave. It was the same one he had always worn back in the day and she had always loved it. Woody, masculine and very Raff. Sophie wore a different perfume these days, but she was sure Raff wouldn't remember or even notice.

'Hang on.' Raff thought for a second. 'A while ago, just before she disappeared, Mariele was talking about some art gallery. Some photographer she wanted to see.'

'Ok…' Sophie wasn't sure if it was important, but it was a start and better than nothing. 'Which gallery? Do you know remember the name?'

Raff screwed his face up. 'No. God. No, I can't! How annoying. But I would know it if I saw it because Mariele showed me a flyer thing for it. It's near the Pompidou centre.'

Sophie hesitated. She wasn't sure she wanted to hang out with Raff, but if it was the only way to find this gallery and her mother...

Maybe Raff could just show her where the gallery was and he would leave her to it. That could work.

'We could go later, when the shop closes?' Raff offered. 'I... won't stay once we've found it. Not if you don't want me to.'

Sophie gave a vague shrug. She turned towards the door of the shop. 'I think there are customers...'

'Oh, ok...' Raff nodded. 'No problem. I'll go and let them in. I'll see you later, ok?' He headed towards the door.

Sophie stared after him. It was so strange being around Raff again. It felt familiar yet strange and she wasn't sure how she felt about it. Her phone rang and she answered it.

'Eloise... Yes, I know! I'll talk you through the message...'

Chapter Nine

Back at his house later, Raff had a shower and got changed into a fresh shirt and jeans. Throwing on a smart suit jacket, he decided he wasn't sure whether he had done the right thing by telling Sophie about the art gallery, let alone offering to take her there. She genuinely seemed to find his presence difficult and Raff didn't want to make things harder for her. But it was done now and he couldn't back out of it. Besides which, he hadn't done anything wrong! But Sophie clearly still didn't know that. Raff wondered if he should feel angrier with Sophie, but for some reason he couldn't. He still felt disappointed and sad and confused about how it had all gone wrong five years ago, but he was also worried about Mariele. And he owed it to her to focus on her disappearance and help Sophie.

Raff headed downstairs. He could hear Coco roaming around upstairs and he wondered if she was going out somewhere. Drifting to the floor-to-ceiling window in the lounge which overlooked the garden, Raff sucked his breath in. The house was only twenty minutes or so from the macaron shop via some twisty cobbled streets, but it was a little haven away from the hustle and bustle of Paris. It was actually a ground-floor flat and a first-floor flat combined, but it had a country feel to it and a good-sized garden; Raff had always loved living here. It was actually his father's house. Henri still lived there but in a spacious annexe to the side of the property.

Raff bit his lip. He was almost as worried about his father as he was about Mariele, but for very different reasons. Henri hadn't disappeared as such; he just wasn't the man he used to be. After Sophie had left, Raff had moved out with Coco and into an apartment nearer the Seine; however, after everything that had happened with his parents, he had moved back in again, bringing Coco with him as there were plenty of spare rooms.

Raff checked his watch. Sophie would be here at any second. Staring out into the garden, Raff caught sight of the pond at the end. The location of their first kiss all those years ago. It was a week after they had first met…

Six Years Ago

'*This garden is so pretty,*' Sophie said, rubbing her shoulders.

'*Here, have my jacket.*' Raff pulled his leather jacket off and wrapped it round her. It was chilly and dark, but there was light shining from all the stars in the inky sky above them and from inside the house.

'*What a gent,*' she said, pulling his jacket around herself even more. '*Thank you. I'd like to photograph this place.*'

'*Really?*' Raff raised his eyebrows. He liked the fact that they switched between French and English. Her English was obviously far better than his being her first language, but Raff liked to think he could hold his own. '*Surely there are better things to photograph.*'

'*Like you, perhaps?*' She looked mischievous.

'*Ha. I didn't mean me. I meant that there are so many beautiful parks we could go to.*

She eyed him with her head to one side and broke into a full-on smile. 'We could but do you have the time to spare with your busy pastry-making career?'

Raff turned to face her. 'I would always make time to see you.' He loved how he felt when he was with her. He had never felt like this before. Excited, hopeful, happy, all at once.

Sophie remained quiet, but he thought she looked pleased. A light breeze lifted her dark hair from her shoulders and Raff took the opportunity to study her profile. She had a chiselled nose and her eyes were set wide apart. Her mouth… Raff lingered. It was beautiful. Kissable.

There was a pause and she spoke again. 'I would like to photograph you actually. You have good cheekbones.'

Raff pulled a face and laughed. 'I'm a guy. I don't even know what that means. But anyway. I love that you're into photography. Baking and crafting: that's art. Photography: that's art too. Is it a hobby or a potential career?'

'Definitely career.' She was clear on this topic. 'People, places… capturing a moment in time is such a special thing.'

Raff considered her, loving the way her eyes lit up when she was passionate about something. 'And at least you create something that is timeless. I create something and then it gets destroyed.'

She gave him a sideways glance. 'Yes, I suppose it does! Does that bother you?'

'Not at all. I love what I do. As long as it looks amazing, because we all eat with our eyes first, you know?'

She nodded then lifted her head to stare up at the Parisian night sky, surely the most beautiful in the world? 'Look at those stars. I wish I knew more about all the formations. No. Not formations. Constellations?'

'I have no idea, I'm afraid,' Raff confessed. He couldn't stop staring at her, but she was rather beautiful. Not classically so, but she definitely had something. 'Oh dear. Romantic moment failure. Ask me about pastry. Or macarons.'

Sophie shook her head. 'I probably know almost as much as you do about macarons! You should come to the shop. My mum will probably love you.'

'Will she?' Raff raised an eyebrow. 'I'm more interested in how you feel about me, if I'm honest.'

'I'm not sure yet,' she replied, her eyes flirting with his.

'Well, I know how I feel about you.'

'Is that so?'

Raff nodded. 'Yes. I've seen you almost every day since we met in the shop the other night. And all I want to do is see more of you. I think something huge has happened here. I saw you and just… fell.'

He heard her gasp. 'Me too,' she said.

He pulled her closer. 'Kiss me,' he said.

'Since you asked so nicely,' she whispered.

Their lips met and they kissed. Sophie wound her arms around Raff's neck. He put one arm around her waist and the other arm came up so he could sink his hand into her hair. They kissed and kissed and kissed. Until they could barely breathe. And from that point, they were intrinsically linked…

The doorbell rang and Raff was yanked out of his memory. He walked to the door and opened it. Sophie stood there, wearing a sleeveless cream dress with a black pashmina wrapped around her shoulders.

'Hey.' She remained on the doorstep as if she wasn't sure what to do.

'Come in,' he said, standing aside. Wow. It was harder than he had thought it would be, seeing her here. How many hours had they spent here? Hanging out, talking, kissing… everything else…

Sophie felt jolted to be back at Raff's house. Well, his parents' house. She had spent so much time here when she lived in Paris. She knew every inch of it; it was like her second home.

'Where are your parents?' she asked, stepping into the house. God, the memories. It looked similar; the book-cases were still loaded with books as Raff's father was such an avid reader, but the old-fashioned record player his mum had loved so much was absent. She took a quick look around. Not only were some of the things she remem-bered missing, but there seemed to be little in the way of feminine touches. No cushions or flowers or anything… pretty.

Sophie couldn't help feeling oddly pleased that perhaps Raff wasn't living with someone. But she had no right to think that.

Raff stared at her. 'My mum died. A year ago. But I guess you wouldn't know that.'

'Oh no! Raff!' Sophie was shocked. Raff's mum had been absolutely wonderful. So kind and caring. A lovely, motherly figure. Not as glamorous as her mum probably, but calming and reliable.

Why hadn't Mariele told her that Raff's mum had passed away, Sophie wondered? Maybe she simply thought Sophie wouldn't be interested. She had cut Raff out of her life unequivocally when she left Paris.

'I'm so sorry to hear that, Raff.' Sophie meant it. 'I loved your mum. She was amazing.'

'Yes.' Raff wasn't sure what else to say, but he felt irrationally angry. Why didn't Sophie know this? It had been the worst time for all of them. Worse than when Sophie had left Paris, but only just.

'Is Henri ok?' Sophie asked after Raff's dad.

'Not really,' Raff replied shortly. Half of him wanted to confide in Sophie and tell her everything, because he always used to tell her everything. But the other half wanted to shut her out because they hadn't spoken in years.

'Oh hello, Sophie,' Coco said, appeared on the stairs. She was wearing a short black skirt, with black tights and heavy-looking ankle boots.

'Where are you off to?' Raff demanded with a frown. What on earth was she wearing? She was far too young to be dressed like that!

'Just out to see a friend,' Coco replied airily.

'A friend?' Raff didn't believe her. She looked as though she was dressed to go and see a boy.

'Yes.' Coco sailed past him and kissed his cheek. 'I have my phone; I'll be in touch, I promise.' And with that, she was gone.

Raff shook his head. 'I worry about her so much. I want to trust her, but I suspect she has a boyfriend. She's too young. Do I sound old saying that?'

'No. It must be... tricky.' Sophie wasn't sure what to say. She didn't hold anything against Coco; it wasn't her fault. She seemed sweet. But seeing Coco made her feel angry towards Raff again because of everything that had happened just before Sophie had left Paris.

'Let's go,' Raff said, grabbing his car keys. He ran upstairs to the annexe and checked on his father; he was asleep and looked peaceful. Raff was glad. Coming back downstairs, he decided he would do this art gallery thing with Sophie and then he would come straight back to check on his dad and to make sure Coco got home at a reasonable time.

Chapter Ten

Sophie had always liked Raff's car. It was a cream, rather battered, but very stylish convertible Citroen. The roof was up tonight as it was chilly, but Sophie remembered how fabulous it had felt with the roof down, driving out of Paris to find restaurants in the country and pretty places to have picnics. Sophie was half surprised to see it, but she supposed Raff didn't drive that much. She knew he loved this car with a passion. And generally, when Raff loved something, he looked after it and didn't let it go.

The same couldn't be said about how he'd behaved with her all those years ago unfortunately, Sophie thought to herself as she glanced out of the window. Raff had looked after her and then he hadn't and then he had let her go. Sophie caught her breath. How could this still affect her so much after all this time?

Sophie shrugged the thought off. She needed to focus on her mum. In the distance, she could see the Seine and the back of Notre-Dame. Heading away towards the Georges Pompidou centre, they didn't speak, but Sophie could tell that Raff was on edge. She wasn't sure if it was because of Coco or because of her, but she said nothing. She just wanted to see if they could find a clue as to where her mum had got to.

Raff found a parking space and expertly reversed his car into it.

'Ok. It's along here somewhere,' Raff said as they walked down Rue Saint-Martin.

Sophie loved Rue Saint-Martin and she paused for a moment to take it in. It was old Paris at its best: beautiful, historic architecture, a grand old church and a sweeping arch at the north end. There were loads of places to eat and it felt arty. Not in the way Montmartre did in all its bohemian glory, but with its high-ceilinged galleries and cool shops, it had a lovely, chilled vibe.

Raff was frowning. He couldn't for the life of him remember what the gallery was called. He caught sight of Sophie and he could tell she was drinking the atmosphere in. She always had a particular look on her face when she appreciated something; her nose crinkled up and a slight smile would play on her lips.

God, she was gorgeous from this angle, Raff thought to himself. From all angles actually.

'I love this area,' Sophie said suddenly, turning to look at him. 'Don't you?'

'Yes.' Raff looked around, taking his surroundings in more, properly looking rather than just… being there. 'It's cool. Not beautiful, but cool.'

'Yes. It is cool.' Sophie smiled at him. Then turned away.

Raff cleared his throat. 'Ok. The gallery is called… it's…' he stopped outside a small well-lit gallery, nestled among larger ones. 'It's this one,' he said decisively.

There was clearly an exhibit going on inside. The gallery was full of people pointing at the walls and holding glasses of champagne and loud chatter could be heard even with the door closed. Sophie wasn't sure if they should go in, but Raff just pushed the door and held it open for her to follow.

A stylish woman dressed in a hot-pink suit approached them immediately. 'Well, hello. I'm Ines, the owner of the gallery. Are you here to see the work of our brand-new artist Jerome Bouvier?'

'Absolutely,' Raff said smoothly. 'We're both really excited. Nice to meet you, Ines,' he added, holding his hand out.

Sophie couldn't help feeling amused at how easily Raff had slipped into his role. 'Hello, Ines,' she said. 'I'm Sophie.'

'Sophie…' Ines stared at her. 'You look so familiar to me.' Her eyes lit up. 'Are you Mariele's Sophie?'

Sophie shot a glance at Raff. 'Yes!' She felt her heart thumping. This had to be positive. Ines must know her mum fairly well, surely?

'I know Mariele well,' Ines confirmed, guiding them towards the first painting. It was a large canvas, covered in violet and clashing yellow paint in a style that might be described as 'abstract'.

Sophie detested this kind of art, but she wouldn't dream of saying so tonight.

'How is Mariele?' Ines continued, considering the art proudly. 'She was in here a few weeks back, I think. No, maybe a month or more ago.'

Sophie nodded. The timing sounded right with what Raff had said. 'She's er…'

'Very well,' Raff chipped in. He met Sophie's eyes. Clearly Ines didn't know that Mariele was missing.

'She talks about you a lot,' Ines said, smiling at Sophie. 'You and your twin sister, but especially you. She showed me photos… that's how I recognised you.'

Sophie caught Raff's eye. Was that weird? Why had her mum been talking about her so much when she was here? Sophie was confused. She felt as though there must be a clue here, or something significant, but she wasn't sure what it was.

'What do you think?' Ines gestured grandly to the canvas.

'Er…' Sophie wasn't sure what to say. The painting was awful in her opinion, but she couldn't possibly say that. And she wanted to get the conversation back to her mum.

Raff swiftly stepped in. 'It's very bold,' he said sagely, putting his head on one side. 'I love the way the artist has used such sweeping strokes to… er… convey his feelings. His inner emotions.'

'*Absolutement!*' Ines exclaimed enthusiastically, clearly impressed with Raff's 'knowledge'.

'Mariele doesn't really like this kind of art, does she?' Raff said, going out on a limb. 'She's into more classical stuff.'

'Yes, yes.' Ines didn't sound too sure about Mariele's art preferences. 'Would you like some champagne?' Sophie took a glass, and Raff did too.

'Mariele was talking about that English bookshop when she was here last,' Ines said out of the blue.

'Shakespeare and Company?' Sophie asked, hopefully. It had to be!

'That's it,' Ines nodded. 'She mentioned it quite a lot. I think it must have been special to her?'

Sophie clutched her champagne flute. The quirky bookshop near Notre-Dame was her mum's favourite shop. She called it 'her little piece of England' and she used to take Sophie and Eloise there a lot when they were younger. Sophie had no idea what it meant for their search, but it was something at least.

'Did she say anything else?' Raff asked, keen to get all the info they could.

Ines shrugged. 'Not that I recall. She wasn't drinking though, I remember that. And she loves champagne, I think!' She caught someone's eye. 'I must go. It was lovely to meet you... please, enjoy the rest of the exhibition.' She wafted off in the other direction, about to launch into another big speech about their star artist.

Raff raised his eyebrows at Sophie. 'Well, I suppose we've got something.'

Sophie nodded and leant her chin on her champagne flute. 'Yes. Not much, but something, I guess. Mum loves that bookshop.'

'Shall we check it out? Maybe tomorrow?'

Sophie was taken aback. 'Oh, you don't have to accompany me to everything, Raff. I can do this on my own.'

'Of course you can. But I'd like to help you. I'd like to help you find Mariele.' Raff necked his champagne. 'Or maybe Eloise will be free. But anyway, my car... and I, are here to help. If you need us.'

Sophie bit her lip. It was oddly reassuring having Raff there. He seemed far better at the detective stuff than she was. But did she want to spend that much time with him? Sophie wasn't sure.

Raff watched the emotions flitting across Sophie's face; he was still able to read her thoughts clearly. She was like an open book to him – always had been. He could tell that she felt at home with him and hadn't been expecting that, but she wasn't sure she wanted to hang out with him. The only thing Raff couldn't work out was why. Did she hate him? Still blame him for Coco? He watched her check and phone and was suddenly gripped by a thought. Was there a boyfriend back in England? A fiancé, God forbid?

Of course there was someone, Raff thought to himself. Sophie was stunning. And lovely. She wasn't going to be single, was she? Not after all this time.

'Boyfriend?' he asked, before he could stop himself.

'What?' Sophie's head snapped up.

'Boyfriend. On the phone. Back in England.' Raff was furious with himself. 'Sorry. None of my business.'

'Oh. No.' Sophie wondered why he had asked her that. But she wouldn't mind asking him the same thing. She didn't have a clue about how to broach it, however. And she didn't even know why she wanted to know. 'I was just checking if mum had been in touch again,' she added honestly. 'I've sent her another text, even though I have no idea if she's receiving them or reading them.'

'Right. Of course.' Raff checked out the bottom of his empty champagne glass. 'Shall we make a move?'

Sophie nodded. Leaving their glasses on the side, they said goodbye to Ines and headed outside. Getting into the car, Sophie let out a jerky breath.

'Thank you so much for your help in there. I didn't even know what questions to ask.'

Raff shrugged and started the car. 'Of course. Not like you, though. You're usually the chatty one.'

'True.' She half smiled in the dark. Raff always used to joke that she told him every intricate detail of a situation to the point where he felt he had been through it with her.

'I hope Coco is home when I get back,' Raff said, worriedly.

Sophie nodded. 'Yes, I get that. It must be hard to have someone you love that much. That you worry about where they are all the time and if they're safe.'

Raff glanced at her, but said nothing. They drove along in silence and once again, Sophie was struck by how beautiful Paris was at night. How breathtaking. The lights made it look so romantic and gorgeous. God, but she had missed this place! The only thing that felt wrong was that her mum wasn't here.

'There you go,' Raff said, pulling up outside Mariele's house.

'Thanks for the lift. And for coming with me.' Sophie got out of the car, but put her head back inside. 'Let me know about Coco later? That she's safe? I can see how worried you are about her.'

Raff was surprised that Sophie had said that about Coco, but he corrected himself. Whatever had gone on in the past, Sophie was a caring person, always had been. 'I will. Thank you. Could you put your new number in my phone please?' He realised he sounded formal, but he couldn't help it.

Sophie tapped her number into Raff's phone quickly. He dialled it so she had his number too.

'You wear a different perfume,' Raff commented out of the blue.

'What?'

'Your perfume. It's… different. To what you used to wear.'

Sophie was stunned. Had he really noticed such a thing?

'I mean… it's lovely… what you wear now. But it's not the same as before. That quirky one you used to love.'

'No.' Sophie swallowed. How odd. And how odd that Raff noticing affected her so much. It was such a small thing and yet… Sophie thought for a second.

'And no, there isn't.'

'Isn't what?' Raff frowned.

'A boyfriend. Back in England.' Sophie felt her cheeks turn hot. God, she was blushing. Why was she even telling Raff this?

'Oh, ok.' Raff felt absurdly happy about that. For no apparent reason.

'There was. A boyfriend. Almost a fiancé, but there isn't now.' Sophie was rambling. 'He's in Dubai. And not my boyfriend. And definitely not my fiancé.' She stopped talking. 'I'm going to go now.'

'Ok. Good night,' Raff replied as she shut the car door. He watched her walk quickly into the house. He pulled away once he knew she was inside.

Wow. So there had been a boyfriend. Of course there had. Almost a fiancé? Why did that make him feel sick? Raff shook his head. He had done his best not to think about Sophie for the past five years. Who she was with, what she was doing, whether or not she was married or living with someone or had kids or was in love with someone the way she had been in love with him… any of the things Raff knew would kill him to find out. He had wanted to know, but he hadn't wanted to know. When he had started working with Mariele, he had tried to find out what was going on with Sophie, but she had been fairly coy on the subject.

A message flashed up on his phone.

> *I'm home, Papa, so you can stop worrying about me. Coco X*

Raff instantly relaxed. Thank God for that. What a relief. Maybe he was being silly about Coco. Another message popped up.

> *Thanks for helping me. What ugly art! See you tomorrow for English books and detective work. Sophie.*

Raff found himself grinning like an absolute idiot all the way home.

Chapter Eleven

Sophie and Eloise stopped when they reached the Notre-Dame Cathedral.

'It's so... imposing,' Sophie commented, staring up at it. Midday sunshine was blazing down on the monument making the beautiful, coloured windows sparkle. Sophie could only imagine how ethereal it must look from the inside today with the natural light doing its thing.

'I'm so used to seeing it,' Eloise said, looking unimpressed by the Gothic monument.

Sophie rolled her eyes. Eloise had never been into architecture. Sophie drew out her camera and took some quick photographs. The Notre-Dame Cathedral was known as 'Our Lady of Paris' and it was a medieval, Catholic cathedral considered to be one of the finest examples of French Gothic architecture. It was the most visited monument in Paris, so Eloise was way off beam with her ambivalence.

Sophie walked around the outside of the cathedral. She especially loved the three circular rose windows with their lovely stained glass. The south window in particular was huge and more artistic than the others in Sophie's opinion. She would love to go in and see the beautiful organ at the back and the bells but she would have to come back another time. Taking a few more photographs, she turned back to Eloise.

'Was Raff ok about me coming to the bookshop instead of him?' Eloise asked.

'Yes, of course. And he was busy in the macaron shop.' In truth, he had looked slightly disappointed, but he was working and Eloise was free and she wanted to be involved in the search for their mum. Sophie felt slightly awkward about the text she had sent him the night before anyway. Too much? Too friendly? Rather… forgiving? A tad flirty? Sophie cringed inwardly. God, she hoped not. That wasn't the way she wanted to come across.

'I told him about Ryan last night,' she added, as they walked towards the book shop.

'Did you?' Eloise looked surprised. 'How did that come about?'

'He asked me. If there was a boyfriend back in England. So I just… told him the truth.'

'Fair enough. I mean, that doesn't surprise me, because I know he'd want to know. But I didn't think you'd open up and tell him.'

Sophie frowned. 'Why not? Me and Raff used to be really close.'

Eloise pulled a face. 'You used to be close, yes. But you're not now. Not after five years. Besides, you can be really cagey at times.'

'What?!'

Sophie felt affronted. She was a great big open book with her emotions written all over her face, with her heart plastered on her sleeve most of the time. Well, she used to be. Maybe she wasn't so much now. Sophie wasn't sure how she felt about that realisation. Since when had she become cagey? After Raff? During Ryan?

'Here it is,' Eloise said, coming to a halt.

Sophie paused, staring up at the bookshop.

The Shakespeare and Company bookshop had been opened in 1919 by Sylvia Beach, an American. Back in the 1920's, it had been a gathering place for many then-aspiring writers such as Hemingway and James Joyce. The second version of the shop, in the 5th arrondissement was opened in 1951 by George Whitman, another American, and it was originally called 'Le Mistral' but it was renamed Shakespeare and Company in 1964 in tribute to Sylvia Beach's store and the 400th anniversary of William Shake-speare's birthday.

'God, this reminds me of when we were kids!'

Sophie exhaled as she took in the green and yellow exterior with the bright red front door. There were little stands outside, loaded with books and the new, to Sophie, cafe next door sold coffee and mostly vegetarian food as well as vegan and gluten free, according to Eloise. The aroma coming from the shop was delicious. Waves of memories washed over Sophie and she knew that when she and Eloise went into the bookshop, the smell would be evocative of her childhood.

Why hadn't she been back to Paris before now? Sophie wondered. Because of Raff, yes, but still. Sophie adored Paris, and before Raff had come back to work for her mum, why would she even have bumped into him? She had *missed* Paris. And she hadn't even realised that. She had become so deeply entrenched in her life in England and, over the past few years, with Ryan, that she had pushed Paris from her memory completely. But now she was back, Sophie realised how much Paris was part of her.

Eloise's face lit up and she linked her arm through Sophie's. 'Let's go in and see if we can figure out why mum was going on about this place.'

They stepped through the door and into a place of history and childhood memories. It smelt of new books and old books which were stacked away haphazardly in floor-to-ceiling wooden bookshelves. The shop's motto, 'Be Not Inhospitable to Strangers, Lest They Be Angels in Disguise', was written above the entrance to the reading library, which was free and open to the public. The shop was famous for housing aspiring writers and artists in exchange for helping out at the store.

Eloise and Sophie perused the shelves, checking out the books. They grinned at each other as they felt all sorts of memories from their childhood come rushing back.

'Mum used to love this section, do you remember?' Eloise said, pointing. It was the rare book area and it contained different versions of classic novels, unusual books, funky little children's books and collections of poetry.

Sophie nodded. 'But why would she have been talking about this place so much at that art gallery? Do you think we should show a few people mum's photo?'

'It can't hurt,' Eloise agreed.

Sophie started showing Mariele's photo to the staff in the shop, but no one seemed any the wiser. Sophie began to feel downhearted. She checked her phone in case her mum had come back to her on her last message, but there was nothing. There was however a message from Ryan.

*I miss you so much, Soph. Dubai is crazy and I
really wish you were here. Call me?*

Sophie showed it to Eloise who rolled her eyes. 'Still
trying, I see,' she commented.

'Yep.' Sophie wasn't sure how she felt about Ryan's
texts. He was cranking in up the 'missing you' angle quite
a bit and she wasn't sure why. Did he assume they might
get back together or something? She turned to find an
elderly gentleman touching her arm. 'Oh, hi. Can I help
you?'

'I think you were showing a photograph of someone I
know,' the man said in stilted English.

'We can speak French,' Sophie smiled, reverting to it
smoothly.

The man looked relieved. 'Ok. This is Mariele, yes?'

'Yes,' Sophie said, immediately feeling excited.

'She used to come here a lot. Not recently,' he said, his
eyes meeting Sophie's.

She shook her head, but didn't comment.

'But she loves books and art. The *Louvre*,' he said
randomly. '*Les Deux Magots*,' he added. It was the historic
little cafe in Saint-Germain-des-Pres that artists and
writers used to frequent back in the day. 'Try there,' he
said, nodding rapidly.

Sophie watched him leave, bemused. What on earth
did any of that mean?

'Ok, so we know that mum is an "arty" type",' Eloise
said with a frown. 'We keep being directed that way. I just
haven't got a clue what any of it mans.'

'Me neither.' Sophie shook her head. 'This feels like a
wild goose chase, Ellie. I honestly don't know what any
of it means.'

Eloise checked her watch. 'I need to go shortly. Let's go for a coffee. Lunch maybe?'

Out in the fresh air again, Eloise suggested they walk to *Les Deux Magots*, just in case it meant something. Fifteen minutes later, they were ensconced in the corner, outside.

'It reeks of history here, doesn't it?' Sophie said, inhaling the air.

Eloise nodded and ordered some coffees, perusing the menu as she did so. Sophie admired her ability to multi-task; Eloise had become even better at it since having kids. Out of necessity, no doubt.

Les Deux Magots. Sophie looked around. She knew that loosely, it translated as 'The Two Chinese Figurines' and that the cafe had been founded in 1812. Back in the day, the cafe was a meeting place to the likes of Hemingway, Simone de Beauvoir and Sartre, whereas these days, it was a mishmash of fashionistas, artists, writers and politicians. There were some very colourful characters here, as well as many business types, suited and booted.

Sophie had always found it a really cool place to hang out and she especially liked the fact that the *Deux Magots* literary prize had been awarded to a French novel every year for… well, Sophie didn't know exactly how many years.

'So, how are things with Raff?' Eloise asked, stirring the usual huge amount of sugar into her coffee.

Sophie shrugged. What could she say to that? Things were… fine with Raff. In as much as they could be, she supposed, considering the bad blood between them. Sophie stared past Eloise, enjoying the Parisian chatter surrounding them as she watched the eclectic mix of arty people strolling past. The sun was high in the sky and it was leaving a golden sparkle on every surface as it shone down on Saint-Germain-des-Pres.

'I'll have the fish stew,' Eloise told a waiter efficiently as he cruised past.

'Me too,' Sophie said. She was desperate for a good *moules-frites*, but there were so many good places in Paris for that. It was something she had always eaten with Raff, actually. Ryan had hated shellfish, which Sophie had found disappointing; something she had never mentioned.

Sophie frowned. She wasn't sure what to do about Ryan. He kept calling and texting and saying he missed her, but surely that ship had sailed, hadn't it?

'Have you asked him about Estelle?'

Sophie's head whipped round. 'What?'

Eloise met her sister's eyes unflinchingly. 'Estelle. Have you asked Raff about her?'

'Nope.' Sophie frowned at Eloise. Why on earth would she ask Raff about his ex-girlfriend? The woman he'd had Coco with. Estelle was probably the last person Sophie wanted to ask Raff about!

Eloise toyed with her sugar wrappings. 'It's just that… Estelle is an absolute nightmare from what I've heard. Pops up out of the blue every so often wanting to forge a relationship with Coco… before promptly disappearing off again and leaving Raff to pick up the pieces.'

'Sounds grim.'

Sophie wasn't sure what to think about any of this. Of course she had wondered if Raff and Estelle had gone back together after Sophie had left Paris. Probably more than she should have done. Estelle Dupres was a beautiful woman. She and Raff had serious history, and just before

Sophie left, Estelle had exploded into their lives creating havoc. And they hadn't survived it.

'How often does she come back?' Sophie asked, before she could censor herself.

Eloise smiled briefly, but hurriedly removed it. 'I would say every six months or so. Maybe once a year.'

Sophie raised her eyebrows. 'How long does she stay?'

'A few weeks at a time, I think.' Eloise drained her coffee. 'From what Raff has told me, anyway. And I've seen her once since he started working at the macaron shop.'

Sophie bit her lip and refused to ask if Estelle looked good. She was sure Estelle had looked good; she always did. Annoyingly.

Their fish stew arrived. It looked delicious and a spiral of steam was curling out of it. It was loaded with white fish, prawns, mussels and clams, and the aroma wafting from the orange, saffron and cayenne-loaded sauce was mouth-wateringly delicious. It wasn't a refined version; it had wholesome chunks of vegetable in it.

They both tucked in and for a good few minutes, there was no talking.

'I think you made a mistake leaving Raff like that,' Eloise blurted out suddenly.

Sophie stared at her, her coffee cup midway in the air. 'What? Why? You've never said this before!'

'I've tried,' Eloise said earnestly. 'Over the years, on and off, I've tried. You know I have. And I know there was evidence suggesting that Raff was lying, but still... I haven't ever been able to shake the feeling that you got it wrong.'

Sophie felt irritable. Where was all this coming from? Her phone buzzed, signalling a text. It was from Pinter; something about a photography job he had for her.

'Right.' Sophie rested her coffee cup into its saucer decisively. 'Tell me once what you think and then we're talking about something else.'

'Fair enough.'

Eloise knew her twin and she immediately accepted that Sophie would listen and hear her but then Eloise needed to let it go. Mostly so Sophie could process it and deal with it and put it in a box. Compartmentalise. It was the way she had always been, even when they were kids. Eloise remembered when their grandfather had died and Sophie had sat with a white, pinched little face whilst Mariele told them. She had asked a few questions and then she had shut down. Or rather, she had gone silent, she had rationalised it, she had cried and then she'd put it in a box and made peace with it.

'Ok.' Eloise pushed her coffee cup to one side. 'I think that finding out about Coco sent you spiralling. I think you felt threatened by Estelle and I think *you* think that Raff knew about Coco.'

Sophie nodded, her hands clasped tightly in front of her. That was all correct. She had assumed that Raff had known about his daughter and that he hadn't told her. *That* had felt like the ultimate betrayal. And so she had left.

'I think it was a knee-jerk reaction,' Eloise said gently. 'And I don't think you gave Raff the chance to explain or defend himself. He was shocked to the core to discover that he had a daughter. He honestly didn't know anything about her. I'm certain of that.'

Sophie blinked. 'Why didn't you say this at the time?'

'I did,' Eloise reminded her. 'Well, I certainly tried. And so did mum. And so did Raff. We all tried. At the time and afterwards.'

Sophie chewed her lip. God. She had definitely shut down when she had headed back to England. She had been so hurt she hadn't listened to anything or anyone. She had loved Raff so much, the thought that he had potentially kept something so huge from her had sent her into a dark place. But Estelle had told her that Raff knew about Coco. She had made a point of telling her that.

'Estelle told me he knew. That he had known for a long time.'

Eloise shook her head sadly. 'Of course she would say that, Soph. Of course she would. She's not a nice person!'

Sophie swallowed. Had she got Raff wrong? Had she believed Estelle when she should have believed him? Estelle had seemed so sure... so definite about it. She had given Sophie details, had shown her a letter she had written where she told Raff about it. A letter that looked as though it had been read over and over again.

'How long did Estelle stay that first time?' Sophie asked suddenly.

'Not long,' Eloise said. 'Enough time to get Raff on board with looking after Coco and then off she went.'

'Leaving Coco behind?' Sophie was aghast. 'I don't want to sound judgemental, but what kind of mother does that to their own child?'

Eloise took some money out to pay the bill, but Sophie waved her away. 'I don't know,' Eloise admitted. 'But I do know that she left to start up a whole new life without

Raff and without Coco. She may even have another family elsewhere, I'm not sure. Definitely another relationship.'

Sophie was shocked. And she felt terrible about Raff. She felt furious towards Eloise as well, but she knew she had no right to. Eloise had tried to talk to her when she had run off to England. Several times. And Sophie hadn't wanted to know. Jesus. Had she turned her back on something amazing? On the person she had thought was the love of her life? Had she simply distracted herself with Ryan so she could get over Raff? Sophie started to feel deeply uncomfortable.

'And you got together with Ryan a few years after you left, but I didn't think you were over Raff even then,' Eloise started. 'And I always thought that maybe…'

'Yes. Yes, I get it.' Sophie cut Eloise off. But not rudely. Christ. It was all too much of a revelation in one day. Sophie had no idea how she was going to feel when she saw Raff again now after this. But she still didn't know the absolute truth, did she?

'Shall we ask about mum?' Eloise said, stopping a member of staff. 'Sorry, but have you seen this woman in here?' She showed the girl the photograph. The girl shook her head. 'Ok… could you show the rest of the staff too please?'

'I'll leave them my phone number,' Sophie said, watching the girl show her colleagues the photo.

'I need to go, but let me know if they come back with anything won't you?' Eloise said, scooping up her bag and grabbing her sunglasses. 'Come for lunch on Sunday though. You and Raff, yes? And let me know if you hear from mum again, just in case she texts you rather than me.'

'Of course.'

Sunday lunch… with Raff? Sophie rolled her eyes. Surely Eloise wasn't matchmaking?

As Eloise left, Pinter phoned.

'Sophie, darling!'

'Pinter.' Sophie smiled.

'How is Paris?' Pinter asked grandly.

'Beautiful,' Sophie said honestly, getting to her feet. 'Far more so than I remembered.'

'You probably blocked it out,' Pinter pointed out reasonably. 'Knowing you.'

Sophie tutted as she walked along the street. Pinter knew her annoyingly well.

'I have a job for you,' Pinter said excitedly.

'I saw that. Is it that wedding you mentioned?'

Pinter laughed. 'Yes and no. Esther's sister is getting married so we're coming over for that and I'll get you to photograph it. But for this assignment, I just want to see… Paris!'

Sophie could imagine him spreading his hands out as if to say 'pizzazz!!' when he said that. If he hadn't been holding his phone at any rate.

'Just… Paris?' Sophie asked. She strolled past *Café Flore*, the other famous cafe in the area, well loved by writers and philosophers, with its cream and green canopy.

'Yes. The essence of the capital,' Pinter was saying. 'The style, the vibe, the…'

Sophie interrupted as she headed towards *Pont Neuf*. 'I get it, Pinter. Basically you're giving me an assignment which involves photographing the city on my travels just to keep me busy. Yes?'

'Exactly!'

Sophie could hear the grin in Pinter's voice. 'Ok. I'll do it, of course.'

'Get me some good shots. Nothing clichéd.'

'As if.'

Sophie rang off as Pinter enthusiastically sent his love, Esther's and, randomly but typically for Pinter, their French Bulldog Albert's. She jumped on the *Métro* at Pont Neuf and got off near the macaron shop. Raff was inside, but Sophie didn't want to disturb him. And after everything Eloise had told her today, Sophie wasn't sure she was ready to talk to Raff face to face. Not yet. She hurried indoors, left another message for her mum, ignored Ryan's text and started planning her photography assignment.

Chapter Twelve

'Dad! Wake up.'

Raff found himself rudely awakened by Coco and he wasn't happy.

'Coco! It's my day off,' he protested. He snuggled back into the sofa.

'Dad. I want to spend some time with you.'

Raff opened one eye and fixed it on his daughter beadily. What was she up to? He and Coco were close – why wouldn't they be? He had looked after her since she was a toddler… single-handedly. Well, his parents had been involved naturally – his mum had been fantastic and very hands on until her untimely death a year ago – but mainly because Raff still had to work. Apart from that, they had spent every moment together and most of Raff's happiest times had been spent with Coco. Sophie swam into Raff's mind then, but he pushed the thought away. She had been a bit distant recently, but he wasn't sure why.

'Come on,' Coco pleaded, grabbing his shoulders and jiggling him around.

'God.' Raff sat up, raking a hand through his hair. He had been looking forward to chilling out for the day unless Sophie needed him to help with the Mariele search. 'What do you want to do then?'

'I was thinking of the Louvre,' Coco announced.

'The Louvre?' Raff frowned. Coco had been to the Louvre dozens of times before. 'How come?'

'I have this project at school,' Coco said, waving a hand carelessly in the air. 'I need to study the Mona Lisa.'

Raff was definitely suspicious now. Coco had always said she hated the Mona Lisa and thought it was the most over-rated piece of art ever.

'You can't stand the Mona Lisa,' Raff told her, getting to his feet. 'So what's going on?'

'Nothing,' Coco said, looking innocent. She sat on the edge of the sofa.

Raff took a swig from a cold cup of coffee he'd forgotten about when he'd fallen asleep and studied his daughter. She was beautiful, and he knew that even though he was biased she really was. Endless, dark hair, chocolate-brown eyes and long lashes; the adorable gap in her teeth that Raff felt suited her far more than it suited him; petite, doll-like features and ridiculously long legs, today encased in pale grey jeans teamed with a black, edgy tee.

Back in the day, Raff had thought that he would find it unbearable if Coco had turned out to look too much like Estelle, but as luck would have it, she had grown into the perfect blend of both of them and it didn't matter one bit. Maybe that was because Raff felt differently towards Estelle these days. Either way, he certainly didn't begrudge her for giving Coco long legs and great hair.

'We need to check on dad,' Raff said, heading upstairs.

'I've been reading with him,' Coco said, bounding after him. 'He's ok.'

Raff pushed the door to Henri's room open. He was sitting by the window in his favourite seat. An open book lay on his lap, but Raff was fairly sure it wasn't being read now.

'Hey, Dad.'

'Raff.' Henri looked round. 'Coco. Back again?'

'Dad wants to check you're ok before we go out.'

A flash of anxiety flashed across Henri's face and it made Raff feel sad. He knew it wasn't because his dad felt edgy about them going out, but because he felt edgy at the thought of going out himself. Henri had practically been agoraphobic since Camille had died, not even setting foot in the garden, let alone venturing out into Paris.

'We're off to the Louvre,' Raff informed him, picking up his dad's book. Albert Camus's *La Peste – The Plague*, in English. 'Light reading there,' he joked. He had found the Camus novel heavy and turgid when he read it at school.

'Coco's choice,' Henri smiled.

Raff pulled a face. He couldn't stand Camus – far too serious and earnest. Raff much preferred Shakespeare, but it wasn't the done thing to say that in his native France.

'I have to read it for class,' Coco shrugged and pulled a sheepish face. 'Might as well read it with Grandpa.'

'I don't mind,' Henri said, turning back to the window.

Raff rubbed his neck. His father's grief was almost tangible and it was hard to witness some days. It was like a heavy dark cloak of sorrow and pain and anguish and heartbreak all rolled into one. It was etched across his face as furrows of misery and apparent in his drooped, beaten body language.

'I'll get you some lunch,' Raff said, supressing a sigh. He wished he could take his dad's pain away. He missed his mum every day, but he understood how much harder it must be for his dad. She had been his best friend and they had spent so much time together, it was clearly devastating to him that she was no longer around.

'I'm not hungry, son,' Henri replied.

Coco threw Raff a worried look.

'I'll bring you some anyway,' Raff insisted. 'It's boeuf bourguignon. Your favourite.'

'Ok,' Henri said disinterestedly.

Raff sorted some food out and a large cup of coffee for his dad and then he and Coco headed out into the sunshine.

'Car or *Métro*?'

'*Métro*,' Coco decided. She couldn't wait to learn to drive and it bugged her that she couldn't yet.

After the *Métro*, they started walking towards the Louvre.

'Why don't you phone that girl to see if she wants to join us?' Coco asked casually.

'What girl?' Raff frowned. Now they were getting to it. As much as Coco enjoyed spending time with him, this had all felt very contrived.

'Sophie, is it?' Coco smiled at him, the picture of angelic innocence.

Raff shook his head. What was his daughter playing at? Was she… matchmaking, for goodness's sakes? It hadn't occurred to Raff that his daughter would care if he was in a relationship or not. He had had a few girlfriends over the years, of course, but nothing really serious. Not since Sophie had left, in fact. His heart simply hadn't been in it. Either that, or he hadn't met the right girl, or whatever it was that people said.

'I'm sure Sophie's busy,' Raff told Coco. 'As you know, her mum is missing at the moment, although in touch now and again, so we hope she's ok. But still.'

'Just… phone her,' Coco suggested, flipping her dark hair over her shoulder. 'If she's busy, she's busy.'

Raff tutted and gave Sophie a call.

'Hey,' she said, answering after a few rings.

'Hey.' Raff rolled his eyes at Coco who was gesticulating wildly at him with her hands, as well as apparently trying to tell him what to say, mouthing like a goldfish. 'Coco wondered if you fancied joining us for a wander around the Louvre.'

There was a pause.

'That sounds…'

'I'm sure you're probably too busy…' Raff started, feeling that Sophie was about to bail.

'…lovely,' Sophie finished. 'And I'm not too busy. I've been taking some photographs for this project for my boss, but I'm free now.'

Raff felt stupidly pleased and he was annoyed with himself about it. It didn't mean anything. Sophie just happened to be free, that was all.

'Ok, well, we'll wait for you at the entrance then.' They said goodbye and hung up.

Coco clapped her hands like a child. 'Hurrah! That makes me happy.'

Raff ignored her and carried on strolling towards the entrance. He had no idea why Coco was so keen for Sophie to spend the afternoon with them, but at the same time, he could hardly say that he was unhappy about her impending arrival.

'You ok, Dad?' Coco asked. She looked absurdly happy and Raff didn't have the heart to tell her off for interfering.

'Of course.'

'I just… really liked Sophie when I met her,' Coco commented. 'And I think you really like her too.'

'I do.' Raff glanced over his shoulder, wondering which direction Sophie was going to arrive from. 'I just don't want you to get carried away and matchmake.'

Coco shook her head, her dark hair flying. 'I'm not really matchmaking. As such.'

Raff rolled his eyes. He could always tell when Coco was lying.

Sophie turned up ten minutes later. She was wearing a cute denim short dress and Converse trainers, and she looked amazing. Raff knew he was probably grinning at her, but he couldn't help it.

'Thanks for inviting me,' she smiled, saying hi to Coco. 'It's really kind of you.'

'Have you been taking photos of Paris today?' Coco asked, seeing the camera hanging from Sophie's shoulder. 'Show me?'

Sophie obliged by grabbing her camera and flicking through the photos she had already taken that day.

'Wow. You're good,' Coco said in awe. 'I would love to be able to take photos like that.'

Sophie shrugged modestly. 'I've been practising for years. But I do love it. There is something beautiful about capturing… beautiful things.'

Raff glanced over her shoulder and had a look at the photos. 'Coco's right. You've really caught Paris from interesting angles. It looks like the same amazing city, but from a different perspective.'

Raff lead the way into the Louvre and paid for their tickets. 'Ok. So apparently Coco has to be here for a school project.'

'Oh?' Sophie lifted her eyebrows.

Coco had the grace to look slightly embarrassed. 'Well, er, yes. Kind of. I need to look at…'

'The Mona Lisa,' Raff provided helpfully. It was his turn to look innocent.

Coco's mouth twisted up mischievously. 'The Mona Lisa,' she agreed with a giggle.

Sophie wasn't sure what they were getting at, but she quite enjoyed watching Raff with Coco. It was a side to him she wasn't familiar with and their jokey father-daughter dynamic was lovely to see.

'I think it's rather overrated,' Sophie said as they made their way towards the Mona Lisa.

'Me too,' Raff commented. 'But I like this…' he pointed at a painting he had always admired.

He and Sophie discussed art as they trailed around the Louvre. Coco was alternately on her phone or covertly watching them, but she more or less left them to chat and did her own thing. When they reached the Mona Lisa, there was the usual huge crowd of tourists surrounding it, oohing and aahing in different languages. Raff, Sophie and Coco waited patiently to shuffle into full view of the painting and they stood studying it for a few moments.

'Still overrated,' Raff decided unapologetically.

'It's so *small*,' Coco agreed.

'I think we're supposed to be describing it as enigmatic and that kind of thing,' Sophie said, amused. She hadn't seen the painting in years, but it always made her feel underwhelmed. The rest of the Louvre was fully worth it, however, and Sophie had always loved the building itself and many of the artefacts inside. She checked the information in the pamphlet Raff had acquired with the tickets.

The Louvre was staggering: the world's largest art museum and the world's most visited museum, it averaged 15,000 visitors a day. It was housed in the Louvre Palace on the Right Bank of the Seine in the 1st arrondissement, and it had been used by Louis XIV to display the royal collection of ancient Greek and Roman sculptures. During the French revolution, the Louvre became the perfect place to show off works of art. Over the years, many gifts from other countries, as well as works of art by the French had found a home in the Louvre. It contained more than 380,000 objects and 35,000 art pieces. There were sculptures, paintings, drawings, archaeological finds and much more. Michelangelo's Dying Slave, Lamassus, the Venus de Milo and the Great Sphinx of Tanis, amongst other things were here.

In 1983, Sophie read, French President François Mitterand proposed that the Louvre was renovated and the 'Inverted Pyramid' was added. Attendance had doubled since completion and Sophie personally really liked the modern addition.

'Shall we get some hot drinks?' Raff said, feeling rather bored of the Mona Lisa.

Coco nodded. 'Why don't we meet you at the cafe?'

Raff was surprised. Did Coco want to talk to Sophie alone? He wasn't sure he was comfortable with that. What if Coco started stirring things up and hinting that they should get together? He shot her a warning glance and she frowned and shook her head slightly as if to communicate that that wasn't her plan at all.

Raff relaxed and disappeared to get some drinks. Maybe it would be nice for Sophie and Coco to get to know one another.

Coco turned to Sophie. 'So. You've come back to find your mum?'

'Yes.' Sophie walked alongside Coco, dodging tourists clicking away with their cameras and chattering about the Louvre. 'I'm still so worried about her. I have no idea where she is… I just get the odd text from her saying she's alright. But I just want to know where she is and what's going on.'

'It would drive me insane,' Coco agreed. She hoisted her bag up on her shoulder. 'Well. I would if it was Dad at any rate. Not my Mum. I mean… she's never here anyway.'

Sophie bit her lip. Coco had inadvertently opened up the kind of conversation that could easily lead to Sophie asking questions about Estelle, if she was that way inclined. But Sophie didn't want to be nosy or pressure Coco by asking her about such personal issues. She needn't have worried; Coco was on a roll and didn't need to be asked questions. For some reason, she seemed to want to open up about it.

'I don't know what you know about my Mum, but she dropped me off with my Dad when I was really young.' Coco put her hand to her mouth. 'Oh. You know that bit. You were with Dad at the time.'

Sophie felt her cheeks turning pink. God. How awkward. She didn't want Coco to think it was her fault that she'd left Raff and Paris.

'It's ok,' Coco said reassuringly. 'I know you must have had good reasons for leaving.' She pulled a rueful face. 'Totally different situation, but I used to think that about my Mum. That she had good reasons for leaving.'

'Didn't she?' Sophie asked, intrigued.

'No, I don't think so,' Coco admitted, dropping her head.

Sophie came to a standstill and so did Coco. Sophie studied her. Coco looked so young at this moment in time. So vulnerable. Her mouth was full but looked sad and her eyes were downcast. Sophie wanted to ask what Coco meant, but she could see that it was a very sensitive issue.

'She used to say that she was a free spirit,' Coco volunteered suddenly. 'That she wasn't the type to settle down. That she needed her freedom.'

Sophie was shocked. She didn't have children herself, but she knew she wouldn't think that way if she ever had them. Losing one's freedom was part of the deal – right?

'I think she had me before she was ready,' Coco confessed. 'I think she had me and realised how hard it was, and when it got too much, she just dropped me off at my Dad's and didn't want to know.'

Sophie swallowed. Had Raff really not known of Coco's existence until that point? Eloise had hinted at this and Sophie hadn't been sure if she could believe her or not. After all, Sophie had made a fairly radical decision to leave both Paris and Raff, based on the fact that Raff had known about Coco and hidden it from her. Had she made the most terrible mistake?

'My Dad didn't know about me,' Coco said, as if reading Sophie's mind. 'He really didn't. My Mum had left him way before I arrived, and then she had me and stayed where she was for a while. I think she only got in touch with him because she couldn't cope anymore.'

'God. Are you serious?'

Sophie felt sick. How could she possibly have doubted Raff? He wasn't the type to lie and yet, she had been ready to believe that he had hidden a huge thing like having a daughter from his girlfriend. But… had Coco forgotten that she had told Sophie something very different at the time? Sophie felt totally confused. What the hell was going on? She wanted to ask Coco but she felt bad about it… Coco had been only ten at the time.

'Did you think he knew?' Coco asked, her eyes scanning Sophie's face. 'Is… is that why you left?'

Sophie nodded. 'Yes. I'm afraid so. I thought your Dad must have known. I thought there was no way your Mum would have kept this from him and just… turned up with you in tow. I genuinely couldn't believe someone would act that way, so I guess I doubted him.' She let out a jerky breath and felt close to tears. God, she felt absolutely wretched. Coco seemed totally innocent; as though she hadn't played a huge part in Sophie leaving, even if she hadn't meant to.

Coco put her head on one side. 'I can understand you thinking that though. I mean, who does that? As a mum… as a woman? I get how you think Dad must have known. But he really didn't. I think it was a huge shock when Mum dropped me off.'

'And when you left' were her unspoken words, Sophie thought. So Raff had to deal with discovering that he had a daughter he didn't even know about, and then on top of that, Sophie had left. To think Raff had coped with all of that on his own. Sophie had never felt more terrible in her life. She wanted to rush to Raff and apologise to him. But what on earth could she say? It was so hard to articulate what she had gone through at the time and it was so long ago now. But surely Raff deserved an apology at very least?

Sophie stopped herself being sick with huge difficulty. This changed everything. Everything. Why had Coco said what she'd said at the time? Why hadn't Sophie believed Raff?

'My Dad is calling,' Coco said, holding up her phone. 'He must be wondering where we are.'

'Of course,' Sophie nodded. 'Let's get a move on.' She was all over the show after Coco's frank portrayal of the past and she had no idea what to do about it.

'We're on our way, Dad,' Coco said into her phone before dropping it into her pocket.

They moved through the crowds in a comfortable silence. Sophie was deep in thought; she needed to process all of this before she came face to face with Raff again in a second. She felt emotionally and mentally jolted. Even though Eloise had raised this the other week, Sophie now had conclusive proof that she had got Raff wrong and that she had made a gigantic error by walking away from him. She had judged him unfairly without giving him a chance to defend himself.

'You ok?' Raff asked, handing a coffee over with a quizzical grin. 'You've been ages.'

'It was so crowded,' Coco explained quickly. 'Loads of tourists.'

'Yes,' Sophie said, throwing Coco a grateful glance. She hadn't worked out what to say yet so she needed the buffer of time to get her thoughts clear.

'Shall we get out of here?'

Raff threw Sophie a curious stare. She looked startled, as if she had seen or heard something surprising. He had no idea what it was, but he knew it must have come from Coco in some way. Raff inwardly shrugged. He had nothing to hide. He had always been honest with Sophie and anyone that meant something to him, so whatever Coco might have told her, Raff knew he could sleep easy. He wondered if it had something to do with Coco and Estelle. He would quiz Coco about it later.

'I'm totally over this place,' Coco said, sipping her hot chocolate.

'Me too,' Sophie added.

As they walked out, Sophie tried to gather her thoughts. Should she just say sorry? Should she go into the detail or where she was at the time… that she had always felt threatened by Estelle because Raff had told her about his relationship with her, and Sophie had sensed and understood how significant it had been.

They emerged into the sunlight and all felt relieved to be outside again. It had been so busy inside the Louvre. Sophie had her own reasons for feeling as though she needed to get out of there, but still. She took a gulp of fresh air and decided she needed to be brave. Coco walked on ahead; wise beyond her years, she sensed that Sophie and Raff needed some privacy.

'Raff. I'm so very…' Sophie started. She felt so horribly guilty and upset. What on earth could she say? She had ruined their relationship – their lives – by not believing

him. By believing a woman who clearly told lies perpet-
ually. But Coco... it was what Coco had said—

Sophie stopped short as her phone rang, and glancing
at it, her mouth dropped open.

'What's wrong?' Raff asked worriedly. 'Are you ok?'

'It's Mum. Oh my God.'

'What? Mariele? Answer it!' Raff cried.

Sophie answered her phone. 'Mum! Are you ok?
Where are you? What's happening?'

'Hello *chérie*,' Mariele said calmly.

Chapter Thirteen

Sophie almost came undone at the familiarity of her voice. They hadn't spoken in weeks, but it was like coming home.

'Where… where… what…?' Sophie stumbled over her words, not sure which question was more important. Somewhere in the background, she was aware that Raff had taken her hand and was gripping it tightly.

'I'm fine, Sophie,' Mariele said. 'Please try not to worry. I'm sorry I haven't been in touch.'

'But… where are you?' Sophie asked.

'That's not important right now. All I want you to know is that I'm alright and I will come home as soon as I can.'

Sophie gaped. It wasn't important, where she was? How could she say that?!

'What's happening with the business?' Mariele asked.

Sophie frowned. She wasn't sure her mum's voice sounded right. 'Raff's here. I'll put you on speaker.'

'Hey Mariele.' Raff squeezed Sophie's hand.

Sophie gave him a watery smile. She was bewildered; her mum was on the phone and Raff was holding her hand and he hadn't done that in years.

'Don't worry about the business,' Raff said reassuringly. 'It's all under control. Is there anything you need me to do?'

'Raff, *mon chéri*. I'm so glad you're there with Sophie. The business… do whatever you think will boost business,' Mariele replied.

'Really?' Raff laughed. He pulled a quizzical face. 'You know that means I'll probably change the flavours around and all kinds of things.'

'Ok,' Mariele said. 'Maybe the whole thing needs a revamp. The colour scheme, the flavour combinations, the boxes, the look of the shop… everything.'

Raff looked and felt nonplussed. 'Right…' Mariele was usually so cautious when it came to the business. To be honest, he had been surprised when Mariele had called him up wanting to work with him. Even more so when she had disappeared and left him in charge. For her to be suggesting that he could change the flavours and look at colour schemes or anything else was out of character to say the least. Mariele ran a tight ship and liked everything done her way. And she was very much of the '*si ce n'est pas cassé, ne le répare pas*' mindset. If it ain't broke, don't fix it.

'I have to go,' Mariele was saying.

'No, Mum… please,' Sophie started feel desperate. She didn't want her mum to go. She wanting to keep talking to her and she didn't want to lose the connection.

'I'm ok,' Mariele said again. 'I just want you to enjoy Paris, *chérie*. Don't worry about finding me… I'll be home soon. Go to Montmartre, go up the Eiffel Tower. Enjoy Paris.'

'But…'

'*Je t'aime, bébé*,' Mariele said before ending the call.

'Oh God.' Sophie felt like crying. So she did. She felt half elated, half devastated.

'Come here,' Raff pulled her into a hug. 'That must have made you feel better.'

'I don't know how I feel,' Sophie said helplessly. 'Where is she? What's wrong with her? When is she even coming back?'

'I know, I know,' Raff said soothingly. He looked up to see Coco standing nearby. 'Mariele just called.'

'Ah ok.' Coco looked relieved. 'I thought you two had had a fight or something.'

'No, of course not,' Raff said. He tightened his grip on Sophie and she gave him a watery smile.

'Listen,' Raff said, thinking distraction might be the way forward. And part of him couldn't help wondering if that was exactly what Mariele had just attempted over the phone. 'Your mum sounded fine, but she seemed concerned about the business.'

'Yes,' Sophie frowned. 'Which is a bit odd, isn't it? I mean, I'm sure she trusts you to run everything in her absence, but I always thought she liked the macaron shop to be run on her terms.'

Raff nodded. It was true. Mariele liked the shop the way she liked it and she rarely wanted him to make any changes, let alone radical ones, like changing colour schemes and introducing new flavours. He wasn't sure what was going on and why Mariele had changed tack, but at least she had got in touch properly. And Raff had a sense that she wanted him to distract Sophie from worrying about her too much.

'Let's get back,' Raff said, making a decision. He gave Sophie's shoulders another squeeze. 'We have things to do.'

'What things?' Sophie said, wiping her eyes.

'We have a macaron business to revamp.'

'How exciting!' Coco cried, clapping her hands. 'What can I do?'

'Your homework,' Raff told her with a grin.

Coco's face fell. '*Papa*. You're so dull.'

Raff shrugged off the jibe as they started walking. He glanced at Sophie. She seemed deep in thought and he left her to it. But his mind was already whirring with what they could do with the business and how he could get Sophie involved, and if it would, as he suspected Mariele hoped, distract Sophie from worrying about her.

Raff sincerely hoped it would do the trick, and he was willing to do whatever he could to make that happen, but inside he couldn't help feeling anxious and unsettled. What on earth was going on with Mariele that she would stay away for this long and go out of her way to suggest drastic changes to the business?

Chapter Fourteen

'So.' Raff pulled his notepad towards him. 'Where shall we start?'

Sophie considered him. They were sitting in the macaron shop as it seemed the most obvious place to brainstorm. Sun was streaming through the windows, throwing dappled light onto the floor and the tables, and Sophie felt strangely calm for the first time since arriving in Paris. She and Raff had been sitting drinking coffee together and lazily nibbling on fresh croissants which had smelt and tasted delicious but now they needed to crack on. It was Sunday and they were due at Eloise's for lunch later; right now, they were preparing to do as they'd been asked.

Perhaps it was the phone call from her mum – it had been so reassuring to hear her voice – but Sophie felt different today. Essentially, she hadn't had any real answers to the mystery surrounding her mum's disappearance, but hearing her voice had somehow made all the difference in the world. Maybe Raff thought that Sophie had missed her mum's desperate attempt trying to distract her when they had talked on the phone last week. But she hadn't. Sophie was very aware that her mum had done her level best to lead her away from whatever was going wrong with her, because the business was absolutely fine and even if it could benefit from a few changes here and there, they were definitely not essential right at this minute.

However, Sophie had to admit that she half welcomed the distraction, even if she wasn't fooled by it, because it was better than dwelling on what might be going on with her mum. Sophie squashed down the flash of anxiety that shot through her as all the questions and doubt began to rise again, and instead she turned her attention back to Raff.

'Macaron flavours?' she suggested. 'Not my area of expertise at all, but probably the thing you're going to get the most excited about.'

Raff brightened. 'Yes! Perfect. Ok. So here are my thoughts: I don't think we should go too radical on that front because Mariele is such a traditionalist. But I do think I could trial a few new flavours and maybe combine a few. So we're keeping it classical, but just… putting a fresh spin on it.'

'Sounds good,' Sophie nodded. 'So what are you thinking?'

'Well. Mariele loves the champagne macaron so I thought I'd do a gold sparkle version of that.' Raff started scribbling on his notepad. 'And maybe something like… strawberry and lemonade? I love orange blossom as well. And we always have a white chocolate one so I thought I'd add mango to it. Or apricot… I also think we should be more seasonal with the macarons… like gingerbread at Christmas, or a chocolate and orange combination, perhaps. Cinnamon and nutmeg in the Autumn…'

Sophie put her chin in her hands as she watched Raff think aloud and sketch out his ideas. He was becoming more and more animated as he came up with flavour thoughts, rejecting a few and crossing them out. Sophie watched his hair become messier as he raked his hands through it, pausing at one point mid-clutch, before he let it go when he finalised his flavour combo.

He looked… *sexy*, Sophie decided rather reluctantly. God. Raff was an attractive guy; there was no doubt about that. But there was something sexy about how passionate he was about what he did. And he was so *good* at it too. Raff had always been fanatical about food and about being a pastry chef. And about macarons – even though they weren't the most manly of creations in some people's eyes.

What was happening to her, Sophie thought, shocked? She had only just come out of a long-term relationship with Ryan – the man she had thought she might marry, so why on earth was she suddenly thinking about how attractive Raff was? Sophie felt her cheeks flush slightly. She still hadn't said sorry to Raff for leaving all those years ago and for not giving him a chance to explain himself. But Sophie hadn't worked out the right words yet. Were there 'right words' for what she'd done?

'Well, that all sounds great,' she interjected briskly, cutting Raff off even though she wasn't sure why.

Raff looked up and raised his eyebrows. Why was Sophie looking at him like that? She was staring at him with a weird look on her face. Raff was annoyed that he couldn't seem to read her any more. He used to be able to so well; Sophie had been a woman who always wore her heart on her sleeve, and her emotions usually had flitted across her face before she was able to stop them. But she was more guarded now. Maybe it was down to the relationship she'd recently been in, Raff wondered. He really wanted to ask her about that.

'Sorry,' Sophie said abruptly.

'What for?' Raff asked.

'Umm…' Sophie paused. This was the perfect moment to apologise. But she couldn't seem to form the words. Sophie was cross with herself. She wasn't the kind of girl who struggled to say sorry. Not ever. So what was stopping her now? Sophie could only imagine it was because the one required in these circumstances was such a huge apology, such a tremendously poignant sorry, that she struggled to find the right words.

'I'm… sorry I interrupted you,' she offered lamely instead.

Raff smiled, his eyes smiling too. 'Don't be silly, Soph. I know I get carried away when I'm talking about my work. I was going off on a tangent talking about all the flavour combinations and I could literally have carried on for hours.'

Sophie laughed. 'I believe you.'

'Right. So you can leave it with me to trial some of these flavours. I promise I won't go too mad with it and do anything your mum might be horrified by.'

'Great.'

Sophie found herself smiling warmly at him. Wow, she thought, biting her lip. She needed to be careful. She didn't want to start feeling anything other than friendship for Raff now that she knew the truth behind their break up all those years ago. Her life was complicated enough as it was. And… apart from this specific time in her life when it was necessary for her to be here, Sophie lived in England now. And Raff lived in Paris. So… that was that. Even if there was even the remotest possibility that

Raff might have any feelings for her – and Sophie was sure there wasn't – it just wouldn't work.

Raff studied Sophie. She had a lot of thoughts going on in her head; that much was clear. Her thoughts were flashing across her face, but they were disappearing too quickly for him to make any sense out of them.

She also looked absurdly pretty today, Raff decided, running his eyes over her. Not pretty – beautiful, in fact. She was wearing a short dress with a flared skirt that if he'd been more in the know he would have called it a 'skater' dress and it was pale blue. She'd thrown a leather, biker-style jacket over it and teamed it with pink Converse trainers. It was a look she had favoured when she lived in Paris years ago and Raff had always liked it. It personified pretty and edgy and cute… everything that she was. Her long dark hair hung loosely around her shoulders, giving her whole look a relaxed vibe.

Raff was startled to find that he didn't want to tear his eyes away from her. He was jolted by the sudden realisation that she hadn't changed much, and even though there were parts of him that still prickled with fury at how unfair the end of their relationship had been, he was more delighted than he had originally appreciated, by the fact that she was back in his life, albeit probably briefly.

Raff stared at Sophie and Sophie stared right back. What was happening? Sophie felt a bolt of electricity shoot through her. Lust, perhaps? She had always thought Raff was the best-looking guy she'd ever met – even compared to the chiselled features Ryan had boasted. But no, it was more than that… it was… oh god… Sophie felt a sliding feeling in her stomach.

Raff swallowed. He had just seen something in Sophie's eyes. But... surely he was mistaken. It had looked rather like... no, he must have her wrong. The look in her eyes had reminded him of the old days. It made his whole body come alive and feel as if it had been lit up all over. It made him want to kiss her and be with her and throw caution to the wind and just... feel everything he had felt with her when they were together.

Was he smiling like an absolute idiot, Raff wondered? He thought he probably was. And that would never do. Raff was aware that he could easily fall in love with Sophie again. In lust, in love and everything in between. But he was sure she didn't feel the same so he was going to do whatever he could to shoot down any emerging feelings down. Feeling anything for Sophie would be totally point-less.

Raff pulled himself back to the present. They had been tasked with something by Mariele and they owed it to her to follow it through. He cleared his throat and prepared to focus on the matter in hand and adopt a businesslike tone.

'So, what about the colour scheme?'

Sophie swallowed. She felt as though something had just happened: a connection had rippled between them and it had been tangible. She had felt it and she was pretty sure Raff had felt it too, but now it had disappeared Sophie started wondering if she had imagined it. All she knew was that she hadn't felt this way since she and Raff had split up. She hadn't felt this way with Ryan. Not once. It had been real and genuine but different. Sophie had assumed that her relationship with Ryan hadn't been heady and intoxicating and crazy because it wasn't what she wanted.

But here she was feeling all of those things again and there was absolutely nothing she could do about it. She felt that way because it was Raff and that was what they had always had.

Sophie focused herself on Raff's question.

'The colour scheme. Er... well. I rather like the pink if I'm totally honest. I mean, I think Ladurée have it covered with that gorgeous greeny-blue colour. They're the original creators of the macaron and the colour scheme is so distinctive. Obviously they use all the pastel colours on and off... so they have a pink – although not the same shade as ours and they use a lavender sometimes. Pierre Hermé has a modern, classic look with the initials that's cool and stylish.'

'So you don't think we should change it?' Raff leant back in his chair, feeling that a bit of space between might be in order.

'I don't know,' Sophie admitted. 'Maybe I'm being self-indulgent.'

'Self-indulgent? How so?'

Sophie stood up and picked up a box from the counter. 'This really reminds me of my childhood, you know? It's synonymous with my mum and this business and the macarons and with everything that's... her.'

Involuntarily, Raff felt himself soften inside. When Sophie spoke about her mum, she looked vulnerable and young and Raff realised how much she must miss her and how consumed with anxiety about her absence she must be.

'Ok, so let's not do anything to change that,' Raff said. 'If it's synonymous for you, why wouldn't it be for other people? Perhaps we should just leave that as it is.'

Sophie held the box up. 'I just wonder if we could… keep the pink and perhaps add something else? Not gold as that's too Ladurée. Silver? Stripes or spots… no, not spots. I don't know.'

'How about something floral?' Raff suggested. 'A silver flower design all over the box?'

'Yes! That sounds beautiful. And I love that idea. It means we can keep the gorgeous, pastel pink colour and stay true to mum's original thoughts for the macarons.' Sophie felt excited. 'But by adding something like that, it will give the boxes a lovely, fresh look. It should be…' She stared at the box. 'delicate and pretty. I could really see that working.'

Raff nodded. 'Me too.' He liked watching Sophie collate her thoughts. Her cheeks were flushed and her eyes were bright and she looked enthusiastic and… distracted from the bigger issues going on in her life. Which had to be a good thing.

'I'll start working on a design,' Sophie was saying. 'I know the sort of flower I'm thinking of would be absolutely perfect. And I think mum would love it.' Her face fell slightly at her own mention of her mum.

Raff jumped in to change her focus. 'That sounds amazing. So, you work on that and I'll sort the flavour changes. What else? We could… have a mini launch to celebrate the re-brand? Maybe we should go a bit old school and go round some of the famous macaron shops in Paris to see how they do things? Not to copy, but just to…'

'See if it sparks off other ideas,' Sophie finished, placing the box back on the counter. 'No, I totally get that. My boss Pinter often goes to visit other photographic studios because it sets off his own creativity. He's a complete original; he would never steal someone else's work, but he always says it gives him fresh ideas and he comes back all invigorated and fired up.'

'I like the sound of him,' Raff commented. 'The way you describe him, he sounds like a real character.'

'You'd love him,' Sophie admitted. She could see them getting on famously actually. 'He's due over here soon for a wedding, so you'll get to meet him then.'

Raff checked his watch. 'Should we make a move to Eloise's? She said she was doing lunch early I think.'

Sophie nodded. 'I completely forgot about that. Yes, definitely. Let's go.' She helped Raff clear away and they stepped out into the sunshine.

'Do you feel different about Paris?' Raff asked curiously as they strolled towards the nearest *Métro* entrance.

'Different?' Sophie gazed up at him. 'In what way?'

'I always assumed you fell out of love with Paris,' Raff said. 'As well as…' His voice trailed off. *Mon Dieu*. Where was he going with that comment?

'I thought I had too actually,' Sophie admitted honestly. 'But I'm starting to fall in love with… er… it all over again.' She turned her face away, knowing she must be blushing. She had almost fluffed that sentence. She really needed to get a grip of herself. And she still needed to make that apology.

They didn't speak on the *Métro* as it was too loud and busy, and when they emerged at the other end, Sophie still wasn't sure what to say. They walked the scenic route to Eloise's house alongside the Seine, and Sophie stopped to admire it. She wasn't sure how many bridges crossed it, but she guessed it was close to forty. And she knew there were several others outside the city. Her favourite was *Pont Neuf* – which translated as 'New Bridge' – because it looked stunning when the sun set over it and Sophie liked the arches and the stone masks that adorned the sides. From the right angle, it was the perfect setting to highlight the Eiffel Tower in the background. A *Bateau Mouche*, one of the well-known excursion boats that ferried tourists up and down the Seine to see all the sights of the city, sailed past, full of passengers with their cameras and mobile phones out as they captured the beauty of Paris. The Musée d'Orsay, the Notre-Dame, the Eiffel Tower, the Louvre.

'Sorry, let's go,' Sophie said, realising she was slowing them down. 'I can stare at the Seine another time when I'm on my own.'

'I don't mind,' Raff laughed. 'I actually like looking at the sights of Paris with you. I look at them with fresh eyes instead of just rushing to get on with my life without appreciating how stunning it is.'

They carried on walking and within a few minutes, they turned onto the quiet residential street that crossed both the 7th and 6th arrondissements. In a row of houses split into apartments on different levels, Eloise and Georges owned a rather grand house with four good-sized bedrooms with balconies, a large living area, a surprisingly modern kitchen that didn't fit with the traditional feel of the rest of the house and a private courtyard lined with cherry trees and flowery shrubs.

Sophie realised, not the first time, that Georges must have done tremendously well for himself. The house was an enviable gem in the centre of Paris and the pretty, secluded courtyard area was a rare find. She glanced at

Raff. She really should say something about their break up. If she didn't say something now, they would get caught up in Eloise's demands to know every nuance of their mother's voice during the recent phone call while she put together an elaborate dinner that was a fitting testament to the domestic goddess she embodied. Georges would be waxing lyrical about his job and still, no one would be any the wiser about what he did, and Eloise's two boys, Sophie's boisterous nephews, would be dashing about like crazy things and shrieking at the top of their voices as they mimicked dinosaurs or pretended to be astronauts or cowboys while punching the hell out of one another.

'Raff.' Sophie stopped dead in the middle of the street.

'Yes?' Raff turned and looked at her. 'Are you ok?'

'Yes. No. Yes.' Sophie shook her head. 'I just wanted to say something before we go in.'

'About your mum?'

'Er… no. About you. Us. I mean… us before… this. God.' Sophie faltered.

Raff turned round and stood in front of her. His heart was thumping in his chest somewhat, but he said nothing and waited.

Sophie nervously scooped her hair up and dropped it over one shoulder for no other reason than because it gave her time to think. 'I… was talking to Coco at the museum the other day and she started telling me about Estelle.'

Raff raised his eyebrows. Coco rarely spoke about her mum. And the fact that she was talking about her to Sophie showed how much she trusted her. Feeling uncomfortable and unsure about what was coming, Raff thrust his hands into his pockets.

'It's… I didn't realise that you… I assumed and I shouldn't have done… and it's all my fault and now I feel so guilty and horrible and I don't know how you're even speaking to me and I'm so incredibly sorry and I meant to say it the other day at the Louvre and then mum called and…'

Without even stopping to think, Raff stepped forward and took Sophie's hand. 'Wow. Stop.'

Sophie breathlessly stopped talking. She looked down at Raff's hand holding hers and felt herself coming undone. How was he able to do that to her with a mere touch?

'Ok.' Raff took a deep breath. 'You're saying that Coco told you I knew nothing about her until Estelle turned up with her in tow?'

Sophie nodded, feeling agonised. 'I thought you must have known. I couldn't understand why you might have lied to me about something so huge and I was young and stupid and I think I cut my nose off to spite my face and you must have hated me.'

Raff pulled her into his arms and rested his chin on the top of Sophie's head. Her hair smelt lovely but different from how he remembered and it just felt so right to have his arms wrapped around her.

Sophie leant into him. She couldn't help it. It felt too good.

'Look. I was heartbroken when you left,' Raff confessed, staying where he was. He knew that if he looked into her eyes, he probably wouldn't be able to say what he wanted and needed to say now that he and Sophie were finally having this conversation.

'Heartbroken,' Raff repeated, 'and gutted that you wouldn't respond when I tried to get in touch with you so I could explain. But I get that it looked bad. And I can understand why you might have assumed that I already knew about it. But I can promise you, I didn't.'

Sophie wanted to cry but refused to allow herself to. What an idiot she'd been all those years ago. How different her life could have been!

Raff leant back and lifted her chin. 'It's ok, Soph. It's so long ago now. And there's no point in us wondering what if. Maybe it just wasn't meant to be.' As soon as the words came out of his mouth, he regretted them and he felt Sophie stiffen.

Sophie dropped her eyes. She hadn't expected Raff to say something like that. She felt crushed, but she did her best not to show it. Maybe he was right. Everything happened for a reason, after all.

'Good point,' she said, releasing herself from his embrace. She smiled tightly, hoping she looked unfazed.

Raff rushed to cover his gaff. 'I don't even know why I…'

'Raff, it's ok,' Sophie interrupted. 'Let's get to lunch.' She walked quickly to the door, letting out a jerky breath as she felt him join her on the doorstep.

Georges opened the door. 'Sophie! *Je suis content de te voir! Et* Raff. *Bienvenue.*' He kissed both her cheeks and leant across to shake Raff's hand. He always dressed as though he was at the office even when he wasn't at the office, and today he was sporting smart navy trousers, a white and navy pinstriped shirt buttoned up to the neck, and shiny loafers.

'Eloise has prepared chicken in a cream sauce and gratin dauphinois,' Georges said, speaking in French as he always did. He patted his slightly rotund tummy. 'Not good for my waistline, ha ha!'

Sophie smiled at him. Georges wasn't remotely her cup of tea, but he was a good egg as they say in England and he made Eloise happy. Georges led the way into the house, which was tastefully decorated throughout in Georges' favourite colour: white.

'*Tante* Sophie!' Albert and Daniel came rushing to the front door and threw themselves at her.

'Boys!' Sophie bent down and hugged them both. 'I brought you chocolate.' She produced bars from the pockets of her leather jacket. 'Shh! Don't tell *maman*.' They dashed away giggling naughtily, no doubt about to secretly scoff the chocolate before lunch.

'Sophie,' Raff put his hand on Sophie's arm.

'It's honestly alright, Raff,' she lied as smoothly as she could. 'I guess it makes me feel better in some ways.' *And not at all in other ways, Sophie thought painfully.*

'But I didn't actually mean it,' Raff repeated urgently, but stopped as Eloise appeared.

'Hey. Come on in,' she smiled, beckoning them into the living area. 'The boys have trashed the place...' She flung an arm out to encompass the room which was extremely tidy by any normal person's standard, '...but the dining room is actually still quite civilised. Because the boys are *banned* from here.'

Raff and Sophie followed Eloise into the dining room.

'I'll go and grab the food,' Eloise said. 'And then you need to tell me everything mum said on the phone. And what it all means. And where she might be and what's going on. You barely told me anything the other day,' she scolded Sophie as she bustled out of the room.

'*Poulet à la crème*,' Georges announced, looking incongruous in a pair of bright red oven gloves as he juggled a heavy dish that smelt divine. Eloise was an excellent cook.

As Albert and Daniel loudly ran into the room with chocolate-smeared faces, Raff sighed. There was no way he would be able to speak to Sophie about his stupid comment for ages now, and taking stock of her agonised face, he could have absolutely kicked himself.

Chapter Fifteen

'So after Sophie finally apologised to you, you basically told her it was all for the best that she didn't believe you about Estelle – the psycho,' Louis pulled a face at the mention of his least favourite person in the world, '…and then you downplayed the fact that you were devastated for around two years and did nothing but try to play melancholy tunes on your guitar into the early hours of the morning?'

'Yes.'

Raff rubbed his eyes. They were sitting in Louis's favourite bar in Saint-Germain-des-Pres, which was a predictably bohemian musician's establishment with traditional dark wood and an old-worldly air. A young guy was busting out some lively tunes on the piano in the corner and Louis had scored them a couple of bottles of French beer because he devoutly refused to drink anything else. He was wearing another hideous shirt, this time a patterned affair with giant swirls all over it that were making Raff's eyes go funny.

'Idiot,' Louis said, shaking his head.

'Indeed,' Raff agreed flatly. He chinked his bottle against Louis's to ironically toast the absurdity of his comment.

Louis was on a roll.

'So now she thinks you weren't that invested in the relationship anyway and that it was all for the best that she left Paris, even though the truth of it is that you pined after her for years and every girl you ended up with fell by the wayside because they weren't as amazing as Sophie but you didn't want to admit that you never really got over her?'

'Yes.'

Raff sighed. He checked his phone. Unusually for him, it was dead because he'd completely forgotten to charge it. He frowned. He hoped Coco or his father weren't trying to get hold of him. He probably shouldn't stay out too late, just in case.

'Brilliant. So what now?' Louis asked.

Raff had no idea what now. He and Sophie had barely spoken since the lunch at Eloise and Georges, and she had managed to work in the macaron shop with him for two days with minimal contact. She wasn't being stroppy or rude; she just seemed upset. And Raff wanted to make things right. He just didn't know what to do about it.

'Raff!' Louis clicked his fingers in front of Raff's face. 'Luckily for you, I'm the best at sorting these kinds of situations out.'

Raff let out an amused laugh. Louis was the *worst* person at sorting these kinds of situations out! He had a terrible track record. He had once tried to help Raff win back a girl Raff wasn't even that fussed about after Sophie had left, and as a result the girl in question had marched up to Raff in the patisserie he'd been working in, and slapped his face – hard – in front of everyone. That was the last time Raff had ever given Louis access to his phone.

There was a moment's silence while Louis pondered and while Raff waited.

'You'll have to just... tell her how you feel,' Louis grandly announced.

Raff stared at him. 'That's all you've got?'

'It's all you need.'

Raff signalled for two more beers. 'Louis. It's really not as simple as that.'

'Why not?' Louis gave an expressive, very Gallic, shrug. 'And for the record... it is.'

'Because... I don't even know how I feel about her.' Raff matched Louis's shrug.

Louis pulled a face. 'Sure you do.'

'No, I don't.' Raff sipped his fresh beer. 'I knew how I felt about her back then. And seeing her again... well, it's been... amazing. Odd circumstances, for sure, with Mariele disappearing, obviously.' He leant forward. 'But when it comes down to it, my friend, I have no idea how she feels about me. As for me, I feel something, but I don't know what it is.'

That was true enough. Raff wasn't sure if what he felt for Sophie was simply regret at what could have been, or... something else. Was it... lust? Or was he in love with her again? Raff raked his hand through his hair. That was all he needed.

'More to the point, Louis, as soon as Sophie's mum appears again, which I'm sure will be soonish, I should imagine that Sophie will be heading straight back to England. So, regardless of what I feel or what she feels – where does that leave us?'

Raff sat back, deflated by his own words.

'Yes. Yes. But only if you let her.' Louis, on the other hand, looked unperturbed. He checked his phone. 'Anne-Marie might join us. Is that ok? She's out with her friends nearby.'

'Sure. I love Anne-Marie.'

'Me too,' Louis grinning, deftly texting back.

As the jaunty background music lulled, Raff turned and watched the piano player taking a break to neck a quick whisky. There had been a few times after Sophie first left when Raff had been ashamed to admit it to himself but he knew he had been jealous of his best friend. Jealous that Louis was happy. Jealous that he had Anne-Marie in his life. That they seemed to have life sussed out. Because Raff's life had been clear with Sophie in it and then suddenly, it had felt as though none of it made sense any more. And Louis – Louis who had always been the wild messed-up one out of the pair of them – seemed to have landed on his feet and to have his future happily mapped out. Those thoughts had been short-lived and borne out of envy, and Raff had never owned up to feeling them because it wasn't Louis's fault everything had fallen apart for him when Sophie left. Since then, he had been nothing but pleased that Louis seemed to have it made.

'What will Anne-Marie have to drink? Red wine?'

Louis hesitated seeming unsure, so Raff motioned for the waitress to come over and he ordered her a large glass of wine anyway. He was sure Anne-Marie drank red wine; he had no idea why Louis was acting dumb about it.

A few minutes later Anne-Marie arrived. She had a mass of black curls that she always kept tied up in a little bun and she wore black jeans with a slouchy, white jumper and little ankle boots. She carried an unusual tan and white bag with a short chain strap; it had the distinctive 'AM' logo she always put on the corner of her own designs. She was a good foot shorter than Louis which made them look rather strange together, but all told, they worked.

'Raff,' Anne-Marie smiled, leaning over to kiss both of his cheeks. '*Ça va?*'

'*Oui.*' He nodded, pulling her chair out for her. 'Kind of.'

Anne-Marie kissed Louis on the mouth and sat down. 'Oh, is this for me?' She gestured to the red wine and glanced at Louis.

Louis held his hands up. 'I haven't said anything. I've been trying to help Raff with the whole Sophie thing.'

Raff watched them, confused.

'You?' Anne-Marie threw Louis a mock-worried glance. 'Oh dear. Raff, we'll talk about Sophie in a minute. So, Louis. Shall we tell him our news?' She placed Louis's hand on her stomach. 'I'm afraid you might have to drink that red wine for me, Raff…'

Raff's mouth fell open. 'No. You're… you're having a baby?'

Louis nodded, looking absurdly pleased. Anne-Marie clasped his hand around her tummy, looking the picture of glowing delight.

'Oh, Louis.' Raff got up and hugged Anne-Marie, moving round to hug his best friend. 'That's the best news. The absolute best news.'

'Isn't it?' Anne-Marie couldn't stop smiling. 'But that's not all. Go on, Louis.'

Louis pulled back from Raff's hug. 'We'd like you to be the godfather. I don't know what you have to do, but you're the only person I would even want—'

Raff stopped him, overcome. 'What an honour. I'd be delighted. This is amazing…'

There were hugs all round again and Raff ordered more drinks, completely forgetting that Anne-Marie wasn't drinking. After much laughter and congratulations from everyone in the bar including the piano player, they all sat down again.

'Well, a father! Me!' Louis said.

Raff shook his head, grinning widely. Back in the day, he wouldn't have thought Louis to be father material, but now, with Anne-Marie at his side, Raff knew Louis would make the best dad.

'So, Sophie,' Anne-Marie said, tapping Raff's hand. 'What are you going to do about her?'

'Why do I need to do anything about her?' Raff said, bewildered. Why did anyone think it was possible for him and Sophie to rekindle what they had?

Anne-Marie put her head on one side. 'Raff. You were in love with her all those years ago and then she left and broke your heart and now she's back. Are you saying you feel nothing?'

Raff started peeling the label off his beer bottle. 'No. But I don't want to fall in love with her again, Anne-Marie. That's the point. Because she'll just disappear back to England again soon enough.'

'You don't know that,' Anne-Marie scolded him.

'Exactly,' Louis agreed, touching Anne-Marie's stomach again.

157

Raff sighed. Both Louis and Anne-Marie were so caught up in the whole glow of the pregnancy that all they could see was positivity and possibility and love in every corner. But in reality life was rather more complicated than that. And who even knew what was going on in Sophie's head right now?

–

'So what's even going on in your head right now?' Jo asked.

Sophie halted her stroll along the Champs-Élysées and pulled a face at her phone. How was she supposed to answer that? Sophie was all over the place, that was all she knew.

'I don't know,' she admitted. 'I'm so confused.'

'Ok.' Jo said. 'Easy stuff first. Where are you? Somewhere noisy.'

'The Champs-Élysées.'

'Oh wow. I love that place. I bet it looks amazing all lit up at night.'

'Yeah…'

Sophie took a look around. The Champs-Élysées. One of the most famous avenues in Paris, known for its theatres, restaurants, luxury shops and cafes, it ran from the *Place de la Concorde* and the *Place Charles de Gaulle*. Her mum had told her years ago that the name was French for the Elysian Fields, the paradise for dead heroes in Greek mythology, and tonight the colourful sparkly lights from the shops and restaurants lined the avenue, making it look magical.

'It looks gorgeous,' Sophie said.

'Tell me about the shops,' Jo said, sounding envious.

'All the usual high-street ones,' Sophie said, starting to walk again. 'Plus many high end.' She named a few. 'Hang on. I'll Facetime you.' She swapped to Facetime and moved her phone around to show Jo the sights.

'Wow!' Jo's face lit up on the screen. She'd gone platinum blond and it suited her. 'I love it! God, I have to get some time off work and come visit you. I mean, I know it's a really hard time for you, but it just looks...'

Sophie turned the phone back and smiled at Jo. 'That's ok. I'd love you to come over here. Come and hold my hand; someone needs to.'

'Well, I'm your girl.'

'I also want to go to Ladurée tonight,' Sophie told her. 'Just for some ideas. I'm redesigning the boxes for mum's shop.'

'How exciting!' Jo's expression became sober. 'And news about your mum? Anything else after the phone call the other day?'

Sophie shook her head. 'No. I'm just so worried about her, but if I call her, she doesn't answer. The odd text by way of response, but that's it.'

'It's bizarre,' Jo agreed. 'And so hard for you.'

Sophie bit her lip; it was hard. She had no idea what was going on and all she could do was think the worst. The phone call had elated and reassured her, but the comedown from it had sent her spiralling and now all she could do was question and worry and feel confused about her mum's absence.

'Anything from Ryan?' Jo wanted to know.

Sophie rolled her eyes. 'A few texts. I'm kind of ignoring him. I have enough going on.'

'Talk to me,' Jo demanded. 'I want to know everything.'

Sophie took a deep breath and as she carried on strolling down the Champs-Élysées, she filled her best friend in from start to finish. Jo's face changed from a grin to shock, to quizzical.

'Wow,' she said finally.

'Yeah,' Sophie said, by way of agreement.

'Ok.' Jo got straight to the point. 'Here are my thoughts.'

Sophie stopped outside Ladurée, admiring the pretty green, pointy-edged canopies and the swirling, curved, ironwork that gave the cafe/shop a traditional distinctive edge.

'I think Raff said that thing about it being for the best because that's what he told himself at the time,' Jo said, her expression businesslike. 'I think you leaving messed him up badly and he probably struggled to get over you. So he told himself it was for the best, that it meant that you weren't "meant to be" and all of that.'

'Hmm...'

Jo pulled a face. 'You don't believe me. But I honestly think I'm right. It's a male defensive thing. It means he was really into you and he had to explain away the fact that it all fell apart.'

'No, it makes sense,' Sophie admitted. 'It's just that... I felt so awful when I left Paris. I really felt as though I wasn't... good enough for Raff, I suppose. As if... his ex, Estelle, could just turn up and take him away from me. And the fact that they'd had a child together... I just felt...'

'Threatened,' Jo nodded. 'I know. I remember how upset you were when I first met you in that bar all those years ago.'

Sophie laughed at the memory. 'God. Tequila and tears!'

'It's the best way to bond,' Jo grinned. She looked grave again. 'But seriously. I think you ran away from Raff because you felt threatened and insecure. I think it brought both of you to your knees. You probably told yourself it was the best as well, Soph. It's human nature to justify things.'

'Yes, you're absolutely right.' Sophie put her head on one side. 'Why are you so wise? And why are you still in England when I need you here?'

Jo checked her hair in the thumbnail camera shot of herself. 'I'm loving my hair, by the way. Oh I'll come over soon, I promise. Is this wedding Pinter was going on about still happening?'

'I assume so. I'll call him tomorrow. Will you come over for that?'

'Might do,' Jo said. 'I love a good wedding. Anyway. How do you feel about Raff now?'

Sophie sighed. 'Oh man. Kind of… the same as I used to. If I'm being totally honest.'

Jo let out a squeak. 'Do you really? OMG. You're in love with him? Still? Again? Whatever. You're in love with him?'

'Shut up. I don't know how I feel,' Sophie grumbled. 'But I do feel something.'

Jo tutted. 'Oh how annoying. I have a work call coming through, believe it or not. I'm on call, but no one EVER calls. Shit. I have to go, Soph, but keep me posted, ok?'

'Will do.' Saying a hurried goodbye, Sophie tucked her phone away thoughtfully. Maybe Jo was right about Raff. Maybe she was taking it all far too much to heart. And when it came down to it, it was her, Sophie, who had got the wrong idea about Estelle and hadn't given Raff a chance to defend himself. Sophie had run away because that had been easier than facing up to the possible pain to find out that Raff had lied to her and hidden Coco from her, and that having a child with Estelle had created an unbreakable bond between Estelle and Raff that might threaten the amazing love affair that Raff and Sophie had.

Standing outside Ladurée as tourists and Parisians dashed past her, Sophie felt deeply upset and ashamed. And she was also fuming at herself. Furious that she had cut off her nose to spite her face. Leaving Paris and Raff was one thing; not listening to Raff and Eloise and her mum afterwards was entirely another. Also, Sophie *knew* Raff. She knew he wasn't a bad person or a man to shirk his responsibilities as a father. He just wasn't that sort of guy.

Sophie felt tears rushing into her eyes. She knew how desperate she had felt back then and how at the time she'd felt as though she had no choice but to flee Paris because she wasn't equipped to deal with what was going on around her. Sophie had shut down and she hadn't allowed the relationship to continue. She had been so silly back then and she could see that now. She didn't know why Raff wasn't more furious with her, but maybe he just felt disappointed? Let down? Sophie felt herself slumping inside. She felt awful… desolate. So incredibly guilty. What had her relationship with Ryan even been about? She had known that what they had wasn't anything like her relationship with Raff, but at the same time, Ryan had made her feel so safe, just at a time when she had needed to feel that way.

What about all the time they had lost? Five years! Sophie let the tears flow. How could she live with herself after this realisation? How was she supposed to come to terms with it? She was surprised Raff was still even talking to her, let alone being as amazing as he was being?

Was there a way back, Sophie wondered? Could she possibly make up for lost time and make things right with Raff? She didn't even know how he felt about her. She wasn't sure she knew exactly what she felt about him... except for the fact that it was incredibly similar to everything she had felt for him before. It was as though time hadn't passed, as though their feelings had been frozen.

Sophie wiped her eyes and faltered. Well. She could only speak for herself. She didn't know what Raff was truly feeling. She could only know what she felt and what she felt was... that she and Raff had something. Sophie was *sure* they had something. She pulled herself together with an immense effort. She had to think about something else. Macarons. The perfect distraction.

Inside Ladurée, Sophie was assailed by the delicious aroma of the macarons, the familiar almondy sweet scent that always reminded Sophie of her childhood. The cafe was busy and full of tourists, but it had a real sense of style and classic 'French-ness' about it. Weirdly, Sophie knew that macarons were supposed to have originated in Italy, as they created something called a 'maccarone' back in the 15th century and brought it over to France. It was the

French who had the idea to fill the soft, doughy biscuits – or 'crusts', as they were known then – with a creamy ganache.

Ordering herself a serving of the glorious hot chocolate Ladurée had become famous for, Sophie asked for a selection of macarons to go with it, just for research purposes. She asked for a mix of modern and traditional flavours and after a few minutes, found herself a seat at the corner of an already busy table. The hot chocolate arrived in a silver jug, rather like a tea pot. It was made from milk, not cream, but contained so much chocolate, it was rich and sweet and very filling. Moving onto the macarons, Sophie quickly sampled a tiny bite of each one. The classic ones each had distinct, clear flavours: coffee, chocolate, pistachio, rose, vanilla. The more unusual flavours were actually rather delicate: cotton candy, orange blossom, bubble gum and the superbly named 'Marie-Antoinette', which was a subtle blend of black teas from India and China in a gorgeous duck-egg blue colour.

Taking out her phone, Sophie started to jut down her thoughts on it. She jumped when it rang. It was Coco.

Sophie answered it, not sure why Coco would be calling her at this time of the evening. 'Coco. Is everything ok?'

'Not really.' Coco sounded worried. 'It's my granddad. Henri. He's sick… he's not making any sense and I don't know if I should call a doctor.'

'Where's your dad?' Sophie started to get her things together. She was no expert, but Pinter oddly made a point of making them go on First Aid courses periodically, so she could hold her own at a basic level.

'I can't get hold of dad,' Coco explained, sounding tearful. 'Sorry, Sophie. I just didn't know what to do.'

'Please don't apologise. Is Henri breathing? He is? Good.' Sophie briskly asked for her bill and paid. She hurried out of Ladurée and headed for the nearest *Métro*. 'Coco, I'll call when I'm at the other end, but try not to worry, ok?'

Not stopping to think even for a second, Sophie jumped on the next *Métro*. She had no idea where Raff was or why he couldn't be reached, but that didn't matter right now. Once on the other side, Sophie tried Raff twice but to no avail and then she called Coco and talked to her, checking on Henri's symptoms until she reached Raff's house. Sophie was fairly sure she knew what might be going on with Henri, but it could well be more serious than that and she wasn't ruling out having to call an ambulance for him.

'Right, Coco – I'm at the front door now, so you'll have to leave Henri for a moment to let me in.' Sophie waited.

When she opened the door, Coco fell into her arms. 'I'm so worried about grandpapa,' she wailed.

'I know, I know.' Sophie gave Coco a quick squeeze and then grabbed her by the shoulders. 'Ok, so I'm going to go and see Henri. Please could you get me some cold water and a wet flannel. Or a damp tea towel or something. And some ice. Ice would be great.'

Coco stood agog for a moment as if Sophie had spoken in Japanese, and then she suddenly got herself together and dashed off to the kitchen. Sophie dumped her bag and headed upstairs. She found Henri in a chair by the window, pale, mumbling under his breath and breathing rapidly. Sophie was sure she was right. Henri was dehydrated. She mentally went through a checklist in her head. It was hard to tell if the dehydration was mild or more severe without Henri talking to her, which he wasn't yet. But his skin felt dry and cool, his pulse was rapid and his breathing was definitely fast.

There was a glass on the floor that had been knocked over and there was water seeping into the carpet. Obviously Henri had accidentally knocked his glass over, but it also seemed as though he hadn't drunk enough water for the past few days.

'Henri, it's Sophie,' she said loudly and clearly. 'I need to ask you some questions.'

'Eh?' Henri sounded drowsy and confused.

Sophie went through a couple of slightly embarrassing questions about peeing and the colour of it, before moving on to ask about dizziness and thirst.

'So thirsty,' Henri said, his head lolling to one side.

'Water is coming,' Sophie assured him.

Henri opened his eyes and looked at her properly. 'Oh, it's you.'

Sophie smiled.

'So much kinder and lovelier than that other one,' Henri mumbled.

Sophie was startled. Who was Henri talking about?

'Coco's mother,' Henri said, as if reading her mind.

'Oh.' Sophie wasn't sure what to say.

'Prettier too,' Henri said with a slight smile.

Sophie felt herself blushing but it was mostly surprise. Estelle was absolutely stunning, so Henri must be slightly delirious. Coco came in holding a tray with a glass of water on it, a sopping wet tea towel and a bowl of ice cubes.

'Is this ok?' she asked breathlessly.

'Yes, great,' Sophie said briskly, pointing to a nearby table. 'Ok, Henri, I have some water here for you. You're going to take small sips.' She gently helped him sip the water and supported his head. He sank back but his eyes immediately looked brighter. 'Coco, let's get the ice chips. Henri – put one of these in your mouth and suck on it for a bit.'

Henri did so and winced at how cold it was. He popped it into his hand for a second and then put it back in his mouth. Sophie checked his pulse again and it seemed much calmer. She wondered whether Henri had just become agitated because he was so thirsty and perhaps couldn't communicate what he needed to Coco.

'Feeling better,' Henri managed.

'Good,' Sophie said. She made sure his water was next to his hand on a table and put the ice chips nearby. Seeing that Coco was on edge, Sophie took her outside the room for a second.

Coco promptly burst into tears. 'I was so worried,' she sobbed.

Sophie hugged her. God, where the hell was Raff? She heard the front door closing downstairs and let out a jerky breath.

'Coco?' Raff called urgently.

'Hey,' Sophie called back. 'We're up here with Henri.'

'Dad, I've been trying to call you for hours…' Coco was clearly overcome with emotion again.

Raff came tearing up the stairs. '*Mon Dieu*. What's wrong? My phone was dead and I couldn't get away because Louis and Anne-Marie are having a baby and…'

'Are they?' Sophie broke into a grin. 'How lovely. Listen, your dad is fine. He's dehydrated, I think. He hasn't been hydrating himself properly; I would say it's gone on for a week or so. We should probably check with a doctor tonight or tomorrow.'

'God. Coco – I'm so sorry.' Raff rushed into Henri's bedroom and Sophie watched him cradle Henri's head. 'Dad. I'm so sorry. So, so sorry. Are you ok?'

'I'm fine,' Henri assured him. 'Sophie looked after me.'

Raff shot her a grateful glance. He made sure Henri was settled and gently told him he'd be back shortly with more water and ice chips.

'Sophie – I can't thank you enough. Thank goodness Coco got in touch with you.' He put his arm round Coco's shoulder. 'I apologise, *ma petite chérie*. You must have been so worried.'

'I was.' Coco smiled through her tears. 'But Sophie was amazing.'

'It was nothing, honestly,' Sophie shrugged, feeling uncomfortable. She really hadn't done much. 'I just happened to be nearby… well, ish… and I came over and spotted the signs of dehydration. I would still call a doctor if I were you, just in case.' She felt awkward, remembering their last conversation. 'I should go anyway.'

'I will do,' Raff nodded. 'Coco, will you watch grand-papa for me? I'll see Sophie out.' He followed Sophie downstairs.

'Again, thank you,' he said. 'My phone never goes dead, but I've been so busy today.'

'No problem.'

Sophie went to leave but felt Raff's hand on her arm. He turned her round and pulled her into a hug. 'My father means the world to me, the way Mariele does to you. I'm so glad you were here for him. And for Coco.'

'*De rien*,' Sophie said into his shoulder. 'It was nothing, really.'

Raff pulled back. 'That thing I said the other day...'

'Oh no, don't worry...'

'I didn't mean it...'

Sophie stared at him. 'Oh.'

Raff stared back. 'I didn't mean it. It's just something I told myself back then to justify... to justify losing the person I thought was my soulmate. And the love of my life. I couldn't make any sense of it but I had to, and that's what I told myself.' He paused. 'I can't believe I said that to you the other day. It's not how I feel now. And I'm feeling... a lot of things now. About you.'

Sophie caught her breath. 'I-I'm feeling lots of things about you too. And about myself. Mostly hatred for myself right now. Guilt towards you, fury at myself.'

Raff pulled her closer. His heart was hammering in his chest, but it felt right. Sophie had always had the ability to make him melt and nothing had changed over the years. She was still as beautiful to him now as she had been all those years ago.

Sophie was all over the show from being this close to Raff. He had always had this effect on her. She was as weak as anything when he wrapped his arms around her. If he kissed her now...

Raff kissed her. It was a sweet, sensual, probing kiss that slowly but passionately turned into something else and before they knew it, Raff's hands were in her hair and around her face and Sophie's hands were on his waist, pulling him closer and their bodies were pressed hotly up

169

against each other. Sophie was kissing him back and Raff was kissing her harder, and it was as if the years had fallen away and nothing else mattered.

'*Mon Dieu*,' Raff said, stopping and putting his nose to hers. Wow. The way he felt about her... all those feelings that had been simmering just below the surface had rushed up and exploded.

'Yes.' Sophie closed her eyes. She felt exactly the same now as she did back in the days whenever Raff kissed her. Nothing had changed. How could she still feel like this about him? No one had ever made her feel like this – before, or since.

'Ahem.'

A cough halted them in their tracks. It was Coco on the stairs, with a cheeky look on her face. Sophie pulled away from Raff, blushing.

'Oh. Sorry, Coco.' God. What must Coco think of her?

'Don't mind me.' Coco smiled and leant on the banisters.

Raff met Coco's eyes and raised an eyebrow, silently warning her not to put her foot in it.

'I haven't said a word,' Coco said, making a big show of shrugging. 'I just want you to be happy, Dad.' She left them to it and headed back upstairs.

Raff turned back to Sophie. 'I'd better check on...'

'Henri,' Sophie finished. 'Of course.' She turned. 'I'll see you...'

'Tomorrow, at the shop,' Raff said. He smiled. 'We have a lot to do.'

'Yes. I hope Henri is alright. And... Coco.'

Not sure why she seemed totally incapable of speaking, Sophie left. As soon as Raff closed the door, Sophie leant against it. Here she was again.

On the other side of the door, Raff abruptly did the same. History was repeating itself. He just had no idea how it might end this time.

Chapter Sixteen

'Three more coffees please,' Raff called from the other side of the shop.

'Ok,' Sophie called back. 'Coming up. The others are sitting on the side there and the red one is the hot chocolate.'

They were like a well-oiled machine today. Customers were strolling in and either strolling out again clutching coffees and bags of macarons or taking a seat in the cafe. It was a busy day and there had been a non-stop stream of customers, so conversation between them had been limited, but the vibe was relaxed. Raff had spent the first hour stressing about Henri until he'd received a call to say that the nurse he'd temporarily hired to keep an eye on him had arrived. Raff had then visibly relaxed and finally had felt able to get on with his day.

It was a gloriously sunny day outside and Sophie was struck by the upturn in the weather. The sun felt stronger on her skin these days and the wind had completely dropped. It was as though summer had already arrived and Paris was beginning to look astonishingly beautiful, with a sun-kissed rosy glow lighting up the famous monuments and throwing golden light across the pavements.

Sophie was also struck by the fact that she had already been in Paris for a month now. How could the time have passed so quickly? It occurred to Sophie that she was missing work too. She had taken many, many photographs of Paris – not that she'd had a chance to look at them properly yet – but it wasn't the same as working on an actual photography job. Sophie made a mental note to call Pinter later about the wedding; she would love to photograph that. She realised she missed her eccentric boss.

Sophie felt her phone buzz in her pocket and she glanced at it quickly. It was another sweet message from her mum. The texts were coming through in a steady trickle now and they were full of reassuring words and kind thoughts. Sophie was still baffled by her mum's absence, but she must be alright if she was able to send as many texts as she was – especially ones that were so heartfelt and personal. Still, there was a part of Sophie that didn't feel that reassured by the texts. Moved, yes, but not reassured. She was still not sleeping properly because she was so consumed with anxiety and her mum's unexplained absence. She felt fobbed off, albeit it in a very kind, sentimental fashion.

'Was that Mariele?' Raff said as he sailed past her carrying another batch of chocolate macarons. They were fresh from the oven and they smelt exquisitely sweet.

Sophie nodded. 'Yes. She sent a lovely message about the first time she took Eloise and me to the Eiffel Tower. I remember it… every detail – Mum telling us all about the history of it. I love the Eiffel Tower because she made it magical.'

Raff watched Sophie. Every time she talked about her mum, her face changed and she looked wistful and soft. At other times, she seemed more guarded than Raff remembered, and he wondered if their break-up had caused that particular change. It had certainly changed him.

'She is sending lots of messages reminiscing about the past,' he commented, realising he had been staring at Sophie for far too long.

'Yes,' Sophie agreed, biting her lip. 'I'm not sure what that's about.'

'Maybe nothing,' Raff shrugged. However, deep down, he felt that Mariele's messages were slightly strange. They were frequent, which was great, but they often talked about the past, rarely focusing on the present or the future. And that bothered Raff because Mariele was generally a positive person. She might be bohemian, but Raff wasn't sure she'd ever been prone to reminisce over the past quite so much. He knew her fairly well, and once again, he felt as though Mariele might be trying to distract Sophie from whatever was really going on with her. But maybe Raff should leave that well alone; if Mariele was trying to distract Sophie, there had to be good reason for it.

'Nearly closing time,' he noted, nodding at the clock. 'When we've put the CLOSED sign up, I'll bring out some of my new creations for you to try.'

'Ok. And I'll show you my designs for the boxes and bags. And maybe some of my photos,' Sophie added.

They worked together without speaking after that to get the customers served and out of the door so they could clean down and prep for the next day. Once they'd finished, Raff set about bringing his new macarons out and Sophie ducked into the house to grab her sketch pad. Hesitating for a moment, she grabbed the old box of photographs she'd found the first day she'd arrived back in Paris.

'What have you got there?' Raff asked, juggling a tray of macarons.

'Just some photos. I was going to show you my new ones and I suddenly thought maybe I'd show you these old ones I found as well.'

'Great. I love looking at old photos. What are the new ones – all of Paris?'

Sophie shrugged. 'Some of Coco. A couple of you.'

Raff looked up. 'I'd love to see the ones of Coco.'

'I'll get a few nice ones of Henri as well if you like,' Sophie offered.

'That would be amazing.' Raff stopped and gazed at her. 'What a lovely thing to do.'

'Don't be silly.' Sophie avoided his gaze. 'It's nothing.' She couldn't help thinking about the kiss last night and it was hard to concentrate. 'Shall we try the macarons first?'

'Ok.' Raff set them out. 'Right, so I ditched the strawberry and lemonade because it didn't work and came up with raspberry and champagne instead, which I think is much better. Very delicate. We already have an orange blossom so I added more of a bitter edge to it and a Chantilly filling to give it a sweet contrast.'

'Oh my God – so good,' Sophie mumbled as she munched. 'I absolutely love that one. Really love it.'

'Yes?' Raff looked pleased. 'And the final one was the mango and white chocolate. I'm not sure if it's too sweet though. What do you think?'

'It's lovely,' Sophie mused, munching on the soft macaron. 'But I know what you mean.'

Raff crunched on one. 'I'll have another go. I think the balance is wrong. Here. A final one. Not for now, but because I know you love these flavours.'

'Chocolate-orange,' Sophie met his eyes and smiled. 'Aah. You remember.'

One of the things Mariele had always insisted they had at Christmas was a Terry's Chocolate Orange. The English side of the family had always made sure every kid had a chocolate orange at Christmas time and she had continued that tradition every year. Consequently, Sophie loved anything with these flavours… hot chocolate with orange in it, Cointreau over chocolate sorbet.

'That… is divine,' she sighed. 'You should include that one. Regardless of whether or not it's Christmas. I'll eat them, even if no one else does.'

'Is the balance right? Not too strong on the orange?'

'It's perfect. Absolutely perfect.'

Raff felt pleased. Sophie had always talked about the chocolate orange tradition and he was glad he'd managed to capture the flavour combination accurately.

'So that's me with the new flavours. Do you think Mariele will approve when she's back?'

'Definitely. She'll love the chocolate orange for sure. And the others. That raspberry and champagne one is delicious too, and none of them is too crazy or too out there.'

Raff pulled the box of photographs towards him. 'So what's in here then?'

'Old photos. I didn't even know mum had kept them.' Sophie held up a folder. 'And these are the new ones I've taken since I've been here.'

Raff started rifling through the faded photographs. 'Wow. Look at your grandmother in that fur. That's probably real.'

'It *is* real! It looks and smells disgusting, aside from the cruelty aspect which I definitely don't agree with.'

Raff wrinkled his nose. 'A very French thing back in the day and I doubt she wears it much now. I love Fifi anyway – she's such an amazing lady.' He looked up. 'I assume she doesn't know about Mariele? She'd be here, surely?'

Sophie shook her head. 'She messaged me a few weeks ago, but I didn't even let her know I was here. I was going to tell her everything once mum was back, but I was assuming mum would be back by now, you know?'

Raff put his hand on Sophie's. 'Yes. I thought she would be too. Hopefully she'll get back soon, although…' He stopped, thinking better of it. He'd been on the point of mentioning that he was worried about what would happen when Mariele came back, only because selfishly he couldn't help wondering if it meant that Sophie might head back to England.

Sophie bit her lip. She knew what Raff was alluding to, even if he hadn't uttered the sentence out loud. Because she had been thinking the same thing herself. Sophie couldn't wait for her mum to come home so she could find out what had been going on with her and reassure herself that Mariele was ok. But she also knew… she would have to return to England after that. And where did that leave her and Raff?

Sophie internally shook her head. Her and Raff? What were they anyway? They had shared one kiss; that hardly made them a couple again. It might just be a little bit of unfinished business. Sophie frowned. Ryan had not stopped messaging her over the past week or so and he had called her four times. She had taken the stance of ignoring him, especially since she and Raff had become closer, but oddly, Ryan appeared to be becoming more and more persistent. Sophie hoped to God he wasn't planning to turn up or anything. She didn't know how she'd feel about that. Sophie was fairly certain she was well and truly over Ryan, but she wasn't sure she wanted to come face to face with him any time soon. Sophie continued to feel calmness as far as Ryan was concerned though; he had always been that strong, stabilising influence.

'There are quite a few of me here,' Raff commented. He couldn't help feeling rather pleased about that. He had thought Sophie might have binned any photos she'd taken of him. When they were together, he would often turn to find a camera aimed in his direction and at first, it had unnerved him, but he had slowly got used to it, to the point where he barely noticed the lens on him. It was strange seeing these photos of himself. They took him right back to all those special moments with Sophie. God, but they had been happy together. Raff felt his heart ping slightly at the rush of feeling he got from the recollection.

Sophie wasn't sure what to say. She could see the smile on Raff's face and she felt guilty for leaving the photographs behind. And yet… she was so glad she hadn't thrown them away. If she'd taken them with her, they would have been too painful to look at anyway, so at least her mum had held on to them here in Paris.

'Who's this?' Raff held up a black and white photo-graph. It was a photo of the handsome man Sophie had a vague recollection of, the one that her mum had photographed several times at some stage.

'I have no idea. I kind of recognise him, but I'm not sure why. I assume my mum knew him.'

Raff tapped the photograph. 'I mean… is it worth trying to get in touch with any of these people? Some of these people from years ago? Mariele said something in that written message about finding her heart or whatever. Maybe she's trying to track down an old lover. Someone who meant something to her.'

'God, maybe. It's definitely a route we haven't gone down yet.' Sophie felt a rush of expectation. 'Is there anything on the back on the photo?'

Raff checked. 'No. But let's check all of them.'

Feeling a buzz of excitement, Sophie picked up a stash of photographs. Why hadn't she thought of this? Her mum wasn't the most meticulous person when it came to details, but she did hoard things, so there might be something…

Sophie and Raff went through the photographs together, pulling batches out and flipping them over to see if there were any clues. At the end, they had a sparse pile. There was a group one with a date and some names, but only first names. There were dates on a few others, but no names. And one of the handsome man simply had a 'T' on the back.

'Well, that's another dead end,' Sophie said, disappointed. 'I really thought we might be onto something there.'

'Are there any other photographs around? A diary? Anything else we can check?'

'I'm not sure.' Sophie felt crestfallen.

'Ok, listen.' Raff gathered the photographs up. 'It was just a thought. Your mum is constantly in touch so she must be ok. She's just taking some time out for a while. So let's make her happy by working on the business, as she asked. Yes?'

'Yes.' Sophie let out a jerky breath. This was one of the best things about Raff. He was both practical and positive and he always seemed to make things better.

'Show me your new photos and then we'll have a look at your design stuff.'

Sophie handed him the folder and grabbed her sketch book.

'Wow. These are stunning, Soph.' Raff shuffled through the photographs. 'You have such a good eye. Paris looks totally different through your lens and I really mean that.'

'Thank you.' Sophie couldn't help feeling delighted that Raff loved her photos. She was pretty sure he wouldn't say such a thing if he didn't mean it.

'I love this one of the macaron shop,' Raff said, narrowing his eyes as he held it away from him. 'It looks really pretty with all the flowers hanging over the doorway and around the main window. It's old-fashioned, but so charming.'

Sophie raised her eyebrows. She hadn't taken much notice of the photo after she'd taken it; it was just one of the shopfront and she thought her mum might like to see it when she came home.

'*Mon Dieu.*' Raff stared at one of the photos. 'This one of Coco. It's… stunning.' His heart was in his mouth. He rarely took photographs of Coco – and seeing this, he really wished he had taken more – and of course, he was used to seeing her. But looking at her like this, frozen in time for a moment, Raff was taken aback by how beautiful his daughter was. She looked innocent and young and fresh, and Raff felt inordinately proud of her.

It was a colour photograph of Coco outside the Louvre as Sophie had approached them, but it was quite a close-up shot. Sophie had used her most powerful, long distance lens and it was a head shot. Coco had been turning towards Sophie so it was a very natural shot, with her hair blowing in the wind and her lips parted expectantly.

Sophie leant over. 'Oh yes. That's a beautiful one. But she's easy to photograph, Raff. She's a lovely-looking girl. So naturally pretty.'

'I am so blown away by that,' Raff said, not sure why he felt as though he had a lump in his throat. 'It's just that… I don't often take photographs of Coco. And I really regret that because I've probably missed lots of stages of her life.' He met her eyes. 'Well. Not just the ones where I've been around her. All the other times too.'

Sophie's brow furrowed. Of course. Raff had missed out on so much of Coco's life. From birth to the age of ten, to be exact. Perhaps Estelle had photos of Coco as a baby and toddler, but since none of them were in touch with her, the issue of photographs was a dead end.

'Never mind,' she said reassuringly. 'I'll take as many photographs of her as I can before I… before I…'

Raff met her eyes. 'Leave?' he finished.

'Erm…' Sophie couldn't tear her eyes away. 'I… I…'

'Let's not talk about that,' Raff said briskly. 'Let's focus on the business and on getting your mum back here. Your designs?'

Sophie was shocked to find herself blinking tears away. Was the thought of heading back to England so terrible? Her whole life was there! Jo, Pinter, work. Although her work was obviously portable. And actually, her entire family lived in Paris. She was all over the show at the moment: right now Sophie had no idea where her head or her heart were.

'So... anyway, this was my first attempt.' Sophie showed Raff a silver, swirly pattern that could be a repeater pattern across the boxes and bags.

'Lovely. It's classy and timeless. I really like it.'

'These are some other versions of it.' Sophie turned the pages. 'And some other ideas I came up with and rejected.'

They discussed all of them, and Raff agreed that the rejected ones had been rejected with good reason. Sophie had also changed the style of the logo and name of the shop to match the new, swirly pattern.

'I wonder whether it needs to be more personal though,' Raff considered.

'More personal?'

Raff shuffled through the photographs. 'How about using the design as the background and use this photograph of the shop on the boxes? Or just the bags?'

'Do you think so?' Sophie was unsure. She wasn't convinced the photograph would look that great as part of the design. Maybe a glossy version? 'It's something to play around with.'

'Definitely. I just think Mariele might like it. But we can always ask her when she's back.'

'Ok.' Sophie collected up her photos and her folders. 'I'm going to call Pinter tomorrow; I think he wants me to check out the hotel before the wedding. Did you want to come with me?'

'Of course.' Raff grabbed her hand. 'Hey.' He pulled her towards him. And kissed her again. 'That wasn't a one-off last night,' he said close to her ear.

'Good,' she whispered back. Giving him a smile, Sophie pulled away. She didn't want it to go any further. Yet. She needed to stay focused on getting her mum back and doing whatever was needed with the business.

'See you tomorrow then,' Raff said, lazily smiling at her. 'I need to get back to check on Henri and Coco.'

'Ok. I'll take those pictures of Henri soon too. And some more of Coco.'

Raff watched her walking away, feeling absurdly happy. After making sure everything was in order for the following day in the macaron shop, he made his way outside and locked up. Strolling away from it, his phone rang and he answered it without looking at it.

'*Allo?*'

'Raff.'

Raff stopped dead. Estelle.

'*Ça va?*'

Raff felt a flicker of annoyance rising up. He hadn't seen or spoken to Estelle in what? Ten months? And neither had Coco, and now Estelle was casually phoning up out of the blue and asking how he was?

'Is Coco with you?'

'No, she's not,' Raff replied sharply. 'Why?'

'Just asking,' Estelle said airily. 'She's not answering her phone.'

'We haven't heard from you in a while.'

Raff felt intensely irritated. Estelle always did this. Popped up out of nowhere and expected them all to drop everything because she'd decided she wanted to get in touch and come and see Coco.

'I've been ridiculously busy,' Estelle informed him breezily.

Raff started walking again. He was sure Estelle had been busy. She always was, even though he wasn't exactly sure what she was doing most of the time. She still seemed to be doing a bit of modelling here and there, and she also wrote a tongue-in-cheek blog about it. She travelled around France and other countries in Europe, sometimes further afield, always documenting her travels and using social media to the max.

Not that Raff ever paid much attention to it. He had a feeling Coco had stopped looking long ago too, even though at her age, she was a social media aficionado. Estelle was still talking, mostly about herself. Raff waited for her to ask how Coco was, how Henri was. Predictably, she didn't.

'Anyway, I'll be in Paris again soon,' Estelle finished.

Raff stopped walking again. What?

'How soon?'

'Oh, in the next week or so I should imagine.'

Raff's heart sank. This was all he needed. Wherever Estelle went, drama followed. She was just one of those people who attracted drama and trouble – Raff was fairly sure Estelle courted it in fact. There was a commotion every time Estelle came back, usually for Coco. Raff felt a rush of trepidation. He worried so much about Coco when Estelle was around; it was as though Coco suffered from extreme silent anxiety, perhaps from feeling completely incapable of vocalising what was going on in her head.

Raff also couldn't imagine Sophie feeling over the moon about Estelle turning up. And how would Estelle react to Sophie? She had always been horribly jealous of her. Louis and some of Raff's other friends were certain that was why Estelle had turned up with Coco in the first place five years ago – because she had heard via friends that Raff was serious about someone, that he was settling down and talking about marriage and children. Raff had no idea if that was true or not and he wasn't arrogant enough to automatically believe such a thing. All he knew was that whenever Estelle came to Paris, Coco became rebellious and badly behaved, and trouble ensued.

That said, Estelle had often said she would be arriving at a certain time and then wouldn't. More than once, when she was younger, Coco had got her hopes up, only to be desperately let down when Estelle hadn't appeared. These days, Coco kept herself in balance until Estelle physically arrived, but the change in her behaviour and attitude always angered and saddened Raff.

'Right. Well, maybe call nearer the time to confirm,' Raff said firmly.

'Oh of course, of course,' Estelle agreed. 'I'll be in touch soon. *Des bisous*, Raphael.' And with that, she was gone.

Kisses? Raff was fuming. Estelle had signed off her phone call with 'Kisses'. That was typical of Estelle; she always assumed she and Raff would pick up where they had left off whenever she sailed through Paris on a whim. Which had only happened twice in the whole time since Sophie had left – and alcohol had been involved both times. But Raff was still livid with himself for falling for Estelle's sycophantic, temptress act, even if he had been stupidly lonely at the time.

Raff tucked his phone away and hoped to God Estelle was talking rubbish as usual and that she wouldn't rock up in a few weeks' time. Especially not now that Sophie was finally back into his life. Because one thing he knew for sure: whether Sophie was staying or leaving him again, as far as his feelings were concerned it was already too late; despite doing his very best not to, Raff had fallen head over heels for Sophie all over again.

Chapter Seventeen

'You've *kissed*?'

Sophie rolled her eyes. Pinter was like a small child at times. Especially when it came to relationships. He used to wind her up about Ryan until he met him properly and felt a bit meh about the whole thing.

'Sophie. You've gone quiet. You've just told me that you and Raff have kissed and now you're not talking. Don't do this to me.'

'Pinter, pack it in. What else do you want to know?'

Pinter sighed dramatically down the phone. 'Everything, Sophie. I want to know *everything*.'

'There's nothing else to know,' Sophie said, laughing. 'Not yet, anyway.'

'"Not yet." Ooooh!' Pinter was clearly fizzing over with anticipation.

'Oh, shut up. I don't even know what any of it means.'

Sophie stopped laughing. That was true. She really didn't. She was only supposed to be in Paris for a short time until her mum came home. And despite the regular, heartfelt texts, Sophie still had no idea when her mum might make an appearance and much less about what was going on behind the scenes. But either way, Sophie's stint in Paris was supposed to be just that: a stint. Not a complete life change or a move from one country to another.

'Well, I don't think you should focus too much on what any of it means,' Pointer said reasonably. 'I think you should focus on getting your mum back – in whichever way you can – and on doing what she's asked you to do: sort out the shop in her absence.'

'Oh, I am,' Sophie assured him. 'What did you think of those designs I sent over?

'Loved them,' Pinter said immediately. 'I agree with Raff. I think the silvery swirl pattern is perfect – classy, classic and timeless – but I do love the photo of the shop. It's beautiful. I'd go with a rich, colour version rather than black and white, so it looks modern and lush. Not too much tampering with it, but maybe just deepen the colours a little? And I'd only put the image on one thing. Either the bags or the boxes.' He paused and then carried on. 'The bags, maybe? Then everyone will see them as they're carried around Paris.'

'I love that idea,' Sophie said, visualising it in her head. 'I think Mum will love it too.'

'Great!' Pinter sounded pleased. 'So, have you had a chance to check out the wedding venue yet?'

'Not yet, but I'm planning to head over there later. I promised I'd take a few photos of Raff's father; he's quite old and I think Raff wants to make sure he has some lovely images of him. Coco, also.'

'That's very nice of you. Very.'

'Oh, shut up, Pinter,' Sophie said again, knowing he was being sarcastic and making a point. 'We get it. You think I'm in love with Raff and doing whatever I can to make him happy.'

'I didn't say that!'

Pinter was protesting, but Sophie could hear the laughter and mock-innocence in his voice.

'Listen.' Pinter sounded serious again for a moment. 'I'm happy that you're happy. You've been so worried about your mum and it's been a really stressful time for you. And you and Raff… from what you've told me, it was the biggest love affair of your life when you were together. And if there is any chance, even the slightest chance, that you might be falling in love again, the pair of you… then I couldn't be happier. Even if it means me losing you to Paris.'

Sophie swallowed and clutched her phone to her ear. Pinter had never spoken to her like this before. Not about anything. Definitely not about Ryan. Actually, he was never this serious with her.

'I don't think you'll lose me to Paris,' Sophie managed, not sure what else to say. She didn't know what was happening between her and Raff. It was making her heart race and her cheeks flush and every part of her body tingle, but Sophie would be hard pushed to put a label on it because she didn't have a clue where it was going to go, how it would ever work or what was unfolding between them at the moment. And with her mum and the shop and everything else, she already had way too much to think about.

'Well, we shall see,' Pinter said, as if sensing that she was spiralling internally. 'Anything from boring Ryan?'

'He's not boring,' Sophie said automatically. 'But yes, he sends me texts every so often.'

'Do you think he wants to get back together?' Pinter asked. 'And I apologise for being nosy. But I am nosy and I care about you.'

Sophie laughed again. 'I know. On both fronts. I have no idea if Ryan wants to get back together. He does text a lot but I have no idea what he's thinking because I don't respond, so we don't ever chat properly.'

'Ok.' Pinter sounded relieved. 'Listen, I'll let you go, darling and I'll be in touch soon about the wedding. Let me know what you think of the venue and we can discuss the photographs beforehand.'

'Fab. Speak soon, Pinter. Love to Esther.'

Sophie rang off and immediately headed for Raff's house. He was at the macaron shop, and as he had hired the daughter of a family friend to work there for a few hours each day, Sophie didn't feel guilty about focusing on other things for a while. When she arrived at Raff's house, she was greeted by a flustered Coco and the pungent aroma of burnt onions.

'Sorry, sorry,' Coco wailed, letting Sophie in. 'I've had a bit of a disaster in the kitchen. I was trying to cook dinner for Papa and Grandpapa and I burnt everything and it smells disgusting and I'm so…'

'Calm down, Coco!' Sophie waved her arms in the air to get rid of the dense smoke billowing out of the kitchen. 'Wow. Let's open this window for starters.' She pushed the kitchen window open, and the back doors of the lounge too for good measure. It was warm and sunny enough outside, but it was more to get rid of the smoke.

'Where is Henri?' Sophie asked.

'He's upstairs asleep,' Coco answered, looking distressed. 'He comes downstairs occasionally to sit with us in the living room, but he doesn't go outside.'

Poor Henri, Sophie thought to herself. He was practically house-bound these days. She felt so sorry for him, but she wasn't sure how to help him; she had limited knowledge or experience of agoraphobia. Or grief, she thought, remembering what Raff had said about his mum dying and Henri going rapidly downhill afterwards. Well, she had experienced a kind of grief after leaving Raff and Paris, but she was sure it wasn't remotely the same as what Henri was going through.

'What were you trying to cook?' she asked Coco, peering through the smoke at the frying pan on the hob.

'*Boeuf bourguignon*,' Coco said, wringing her hands. She was wearing a short, white, off the shoulder dress and it was covered in cooking splashes. 'It's dad's favourite. Well, that and…'

'*Moules mariniére*,' Sophie finished without thinking.

'Oh.' Coco smiled. 'Of course you would know that.'

Sophie met Coco's eyes and found herself smiling back. 'Do you want me to help you with this? I was going to take some photographs of you and Henri, but I can do those later?'

'Yes please.' Coco nodded gratefully. 'I was trying to help dad out, not burn the house down.'

'Ok. So let's start again. My mum used to cook *Boeuf bourguignon* a lot, so I know how to do this.'

Coco looked delighted. 'Let me just check on Grand-papa and then I'll come and help.' She disappeared upstairs for a few minutes and Sophie stood thinking about the recipe, working out what they needed to do. When Coco returned, Sophie handed her the burnt pan with a rueful smile and got started, chopping up some more onions and getting some button mushrooms out.

'We should have really left the steak in some red wine and fresh herbs overnight, but no matter, we can get started this way instead. We need to start frying these chunks of meat in batches.'

Sophie got started with cooking the beef in a fresh pan and it was soon sizzling away. Coco soaked the other pan and started chopping up the other ingredients.

'Ok, so let's cook the onions now. Slowly... on a low heat,' Sophie grinned.

Coco looked embarrassed but she laughed. They continued cooking together in a companionable silence, with Sophie giving instructions and Coco a willing student. Finally, Sophie carefully slid a well-worn, almond-coloured Le Creuset dish into the oven and made sure the heat was turned down.

'Done,' she said, wiping her hands on a tea towel. 'That will start smelling delicious very soon.'

'Thank you,' Coco said. 'I really appreciate all your help.'

'*De rien*,' Sophie said. 'It was nothing, really.' She studied Coco. She looked lovely as she always did, but today, she looked rather more naturally beautiful than normal. She was wearing less make up, although the heavy black eyeliner was present and correct as always, and she had pulled her long dark hair up into a ponytail. Maybe it was the fact that she was wearing slouchy jeans and a t-shirt tied up at the waist, but Coco looked her age for once. Young and fresh-faced and rather vulnerable.

'So… what's happening with you and Dad?' Coco asked.

Sophie glanced at her. The question sounded almost shy rather than nosy.

'I'm not… entirely sure,' Sophie admitted. 'But I'm not a person who… plays with anyone's feelings and I wouldn't be doing this unless I… felt something, unless this was… genuine. This thing between Raff and me is… it's…' She faltered, not sure how to articulate what she felt.

'Real?' Coco suggested.

'Yes,' Sophie agreed. 'Yes. Real. That's it.' For some reason Sophie felt taken aback admitting that out loud.

'I get that.' Coco frowned. 'Well, I haven't experienced any of this love stuff myself, but I think I know what you mean.'

'It's all very hard to explain,' Sophie mused. And it was. She wasn't a writer or a musician; she didn't have the words to describe love. If that's what it was between her and Raff. All she knew was, her heart leapt when he was around her.

God. Who was she kidding? Sophie had fallen hook, line and sinker for Raff again. Nothing had changed. Sophie was now beginning to think she had stayed in love with Raff after she had left for Paris; she had simply buried the feelings in the deepest place possible. Which made Sophie feel horribly guilty about Ryan and made her doubt that entire relationship. How could she have carried on with him the way she had when she had probably still been in love with Raff?

At the same time, however, Sophie hadn't ever anticipated seeing Paris – or Raff again. She had put both of them firmly in the past and made them part of her history, and she had focused on the present. Ryan had been that present; he had lifted her up and pulled her out of the terrible place she had been in. And she had had feelings for Ryan – she had. It just hadn't been the magic of her and Raff, the magnetic passion and the intense love. It had been different and at the time, it had been exactly what she needed. Not a substitute for Raff, because nobody could be. Sophie hadn't wanted to replace Raff; she had wanted to obliterate his memory from her mind and she had wanted to start over.

Sophie let out a long breath. Where had all that insight and wisdom come from?

Coco took her phone out of her jeans pocket. 'It's my friend Aimee. She has some coursework I need for school.' She bit her lip. 'I should go and collect it, but Dad wants me to keep an eye on Grandpapa.'

Sophie checked her watch. 'Go. I'll stay here and watch over Henri. Your Dad is due back here shortly as we need to go and look at this wedding venue together.'

Coco's eyes widened and she almost dropped her phone.

'Oh.' Sophie shook her head vehemently. 'Not for us! For my friend. His sister is getting married here in a few weeks' time.'

'Aah ok.' Coco smiled, revealing the gap in her teeth that so reminded Sophie of Raff. 'Thought that might be a bit fast.'

A bit fast? A wedding for her and Raff? Sophie looked away, feeling her cheeks burning. God. Coco really was getting ahead of herself! Sophie had barely worked out what she was feeling for Raff and how it could ever work… let alone thinking further ahead than that.

'I'll go to my friend's then if you're sure it's ok?' Coco was saying.

Sophie pulled herself together. 'Yes, of course. I'll go and check on Henri and then I'll just… chill until your Dad gets here, and I'll make sure dinner doesn't burn.'

'I'll be half an hour at most,' Coco said, grabbing her jacket from the back of the door. 'And there is fresh parsley in the garden if you'd like it for the *Bourguignon.*'

Sophie heard the door slam and she went upstairs to check on Henri. He was dozing in the chair by the window, but he looked peaceful enough. He wore smart shirt and trousers, which suggested he was perhaps more together than he was, but that had always been Henri's daily uniform.

Heading back downstairs, Sophie decided to grab the fresh parsley Coco had mentioned grew in the garden. She stepped outside and took stock of how out of control the garden was beyond the main decking area. It hadn't always looked this way – but Raff's mum had always been the one to take care of it. Sophie doubted it had been touched since Camille had died and that was apparent in the tangle of weeds and all the admittedly pretty wild flowers that were woven in between the shrubs and flowers that had been carefully planted originally.

Stepping off of the decking, Sophie carefully made her way through the wild flowers and weeds. If memory served her correctly, Camille's herb garden had been on the right-hand side, near a bench that Sophie and Raff used to curl up on to look at the stars. They had seen a shooting star there once and Sophie remembered thinking it was the most magical thing she had ever seen and she had felt ridiculously happy that she had seen it with Raff. It felt like a silly memory now, but at the time it had felt amazing.

'*Merde!*'

Sophie yelped as she suddenly felt herself falling backwards and her ankle twisted awkwardly. She landed with a thump and banged her head on something. Shocked, she lay sprawled in the long grass and wild flowers, winded and a tad humiliated. What had just happened?! There must have been a pot hole or something and she had fallen backwards into it and her ankle had gone one way and she had gone the other. She had cracked her elbow at the same time and she was all tangled up in the weeds now. Sophie couldn't move without something hurting.

Wow. Her ankle in particular, was throbbing like mad. Literally throbbing and pulsing and feeling as though it was badly bruised and probably swelling up. Sophie tried to get up, but realised she couldn't. Oh man. This was bad. She had at least half an hour of this while Coco was out and Raff wasn't due in for a while.

Henri. Sophie lifted her head towards the upstairs window. Henri's room faced out onto the garden. Could he see her? Craning her neck, Sophie could see him slumped in his chair. He was clearly still asleep. Damn! She called out to him, but her voice sounded weedy and weak. Sophie tried yelling instead. Nothing. She flopped back down again, feeling defeated. What on earth was she going to do?

She winced as she tried to move again. Maybe she could… roll over and pull herself out of the hole. Sophie put all her effort into it and did her best to yank her body over. Nothing happened. One side of her body felt as though it had shut down; it simply wasn't playing ball. Sophie felt like crying, but she knew that wasn't going to help one bit.

She reached around for her phone, but realised she'd left it on the kitchen table. Brilliant. She heard a noise coming from somewhere and looking up, she saw Henri's face pressed up against the window and he was knocking on it to get her attention. Feeling foolish, Sophie waved her arms and pointed at her foot, hoping Henri would realise that she was incapacitated and couldn't move. He stood starting at her from the window, but didn't seem to understand what she was trying to say, nor did he move from his position at the window.

Sophie flopped down again. What was the point? Henri was housebound. He didn't even venture outside; Coco had told her that earlier. She was just going to have to wait it out.

At least it was sunny, Sophie thought to herself in vague amusement. Her ankle felt horrific; the pain was so intense, she was sure it must be sprained at the very least. She felt sorry for Henri too. He must know she was in a pickle, but his anxiety was preventing him from helping her out. It wasn't his fault and Sophie wasn't cross with him. It was her own stupid fault she was lying in a pothole right now. She hadn't even found the parsley for heaven's sake.

'*Que s'est il passe?*' What have you done?

Sophie looked up. 'Henri! What… how…'

Henri looked terrified at being outside. He was visibly shaking. 'You've fallen down the old well,' he said, still speaking in French.

197

Yes, of course! Sophie suddenly realised she was lying next to the spot that used to be a well years ago. It had been filled in, but the grass and mud always seemed to sink into itself on this spot.

'You're outside,' Sophie stated stupidly.

'Yes,' Henri said. He didn't look at all happy about it, but he was here and Sophie could have kissed him. 'Is it your ankle?' He pointed at it.

'Yes. It's so painful, I can't get up. The whole of my side feels bruised.'

Henri leant over and grasped her arm. He was obviously weak himself, but he managed to pull Sophie up onto her feet. She let out a scream as her ankle came loose and leant more heavily on Henri than she meant to. He wobbled and she had to steady both of them.

'Sorry, Henri,' she said, clutching him.

Henri shook his head and together they slowly hobbled back to the house, leaning on one another. Sophie couldn't put her foot down and she could see that, encased in the Converse, it was already bulging and starting to turn purple. When they were together, Raff used to joke that she bruised like a summer fruit.

Once inside the house, Henri gently let Sophie slump down on the sofa and then he shuffled into the kitchen emerging with a frozen pack for her foot. He gently put it around her ankle and then sat heavily in a nearby armchair.

'Thank God you came to get me,' Sophie said, glad for the cold. 'I'm so grateful, Henri. I know how hard it must have been for you.'

Henri clasped his hands together to stop them shaking and Sophie felt tears pricking at her eyelids. Poor Henri. What an ordeal that must have been for him.

'Camille loved that garden,' Henri mumbled.

Sophie struggled to sit up. 'She did, didn't she? I was trying to find her herbs.'

'She just loved gardening.' Henri stared out of the window. 'She made it look so beautiful. The herbs and the flowers.' He pointed. 'Raff wanted to pull all the weeds up, but I wouldn't let him.'

'Why not?' Sophie asked gently.

'I don't want anyone to touch it,' Henri said sadly. 'It was hers. She made it beautiful. I don't want someone else doing what she used to do. I miss her,' he added, his voice breaking slightly.

Sophie swallowed. 'I know you do. It must be so hard without her.' She could only imagine how hideous it was for Henri. All she could compare it to was walking away from Raff and that had broken her heart. Someone dying and being gone forever was more final, a different kind of grief.

'It is.' Henri nodded, his mouth downturned. 'I feel so lost without her. Nothing seems as fun.'

Sophie winced as she shifted position, realising that Henri had just highlighted yet another contrast between Raff and Ryan. Why hadn't she felt like that when Ryan had left? She had been thinking about marrying the guy and she'd been gutted when he'd left for Dubai, but it wasn't as though she had thought life wasn't going to ever be fun again. Whereas, when Sophie had left Paris, it had felt as though the lights had gone out. For a very long time.

'Raff talks about you,' Henri said, out of the blue.

Sophie was startled.

'You're the one who broke his heart all those years ago.'

'Oh.' Sophie felt crestfallen. Was she ever going to stop regretting leaving Raff and not giving him a chance to explain himself?

'Everyone makes mistakes,' Henri said reasonably. 'And Raff is happy again. Happy that you're back.'

'I'm happy too,' Sophie said, meaning it.

'Are you leaving again?' Henri fixed her with a piercing gaze.

Sophie wanted to drop her gaze, but she bravely held it. 'I don't know,' she answered honestly. 'When mum is back, I'll know more.'

As soon as the words came out of her mouth, Sophie stopped and thought. Was it about her mum coming back? What difference did it make? She wanted her mum back because she wanted her back. But did that have any bearing on what she was feeling for Raff? No. It didn't. It was just that with her mum still missing and having no idea why, there was too much confusion in her head. Once the mystery of her mum's disappearance was solved, Sophie knew her head would gain much-needed clarity.

Henri shrugged, but it was obvious he didn't want Raff hurt again. Sophie could understand that. She didn't want to hurt Raff either, or herself.

'Did Coco cook?' Henri sniffed the air. '*Boeuf bourguignon?* It smells good. Better than it did earlier.'

'We cooked together,' Sophie smiled. She wasn't going to mention Coco's burnt onions.

The front door opened and Raff came in. His face registered shock at seeing Sophie sprawled across the sofa and Henri downstairs.

'Dad! Sophie. What's… oh my God, are you hurt? Dad, are you ok?'

Sophie and Henri looked at one another and nodded.

'We're both shaken up and we're both ok,' Sophie said. 'I'll explain later.'

'Where's Coco?' Raff frowned. 'I left her in charge and she's not here.'

'She's popped out and she'll be back shortly,' Sophie said smoothly. 'I told her I'd keep an eye on Henri, but actually, he kept an eye on me. He was incredibly brave and rescued me from the garden.'

Raff's eyes widened and he stared at Henri. 'What? You've been outside?'

Henri nodded. 'She fell down the well hole.'

Raff dragged his hand through his hair. 'That well hole. I should have had that filled in again.'

'I haven't let you sort the garden out,' Henri said gruffly. He looked mournful again. 'It looks terrible and it's clearly a death trap. Maybe you should get it cleared, Raff.'

Raff put his hand on Henri's shoulder and squeezed it. He met Sophie's eyes, on the edge of tears. His father hadn't wanted that garden to be touched in a year.

'I think mum would really love that,' Raff said, choked up.

Henri rubbed his eyes and struggled to his feet. 'I'll be down for dinner.'

Raff gaped. His father hadn't had dinner downstairs in months.

'Thank you so much, Henri,' Sophie said, wishing she could get up and give him a hug. 'I'd still be lying in the garden now if it wasn't for you.'

Henri gave her a smile. '*De rien.*' He shuffled away and went upstairs, climbing them slowly but with slightly more spring in his step.

'Well.' Raff sat down on the sofa. 'I didn't think I'd be coming home to this, that's for sure. I thought Coco would be here burning dinner and dad would be upstairs asleep.'

Sophie smiled inwardly at the irony as that had been the reality an hour or so before. She lifted the ice pack from her foot and grimaced at the sight of it.

'*Putain de merde!*' Raff swore uncharacteristically and looked at it in more detail. 'That looks terrible. We need to get you to the doctors.'

'No, no. I just need to rest it, I think. I think I've twisted it. It's happened before when I was five and it was as right as rain the following day.'

Raff looked unconvinced. 'Hmmm. Then I'll wait on you here and serve you dinner. We'll move our plans to tomorrow. It's probably a bit late to check out that wedding venue now anyway.'

'Fair enough.'

Coco burst through the door, clearly flustered that Raff had arrived home before her.

'I just popped to Aimee's house to get my homework and Sophie said it was alright and I'm...'

Raff waved a hand. 'Yes, yes, Coco. Calm down. I'm not about to shout at you.'

'*Mon Dieu!* What has happened?' Coco rushed to Sophie's side.

'Twisted ankle,' Sophie said, mentally crossing her fingers. She hoped to God it wasn't broken; she didn't need that. 'Henri rescued me from the garden.'

'And he's coming downstairs to have dinner with us,' Raff interjected.

Coco looked stunned. 'I only went out for half an hour...'

Sophie laughed then stopped as she moved her ankle and a bolt of pain shot through her. God. Maybe not just a twist after all.

Raff watched them, feeling contented. Why did this all feel so right?

'I'm thinking Sophie could stay in your room overnight and you can have the sofa?' he said.

Sophie protested and Coco shushed her. Coco nipped out into the garden, skipping round the side path and returned with the parsley.

'The least I can do,' she said, pulling a face.

Sophie sighed. The bloody parsley.

Raff's phone buzzed and he glanced at it.

> *Don't be silly, Raff! Can't wait to see you all, will be there soon. Estelle X*

Raff's heart sank deeply. He had messaged Estelle two days ago advising her that it was a bad time to visit, but she was clearly ignoring him. He was doing his best to protect Coco from the pain her mother's visits usually caused. Raff wanted to protect Sophie too. He wasn't sure what from exactly, but Estelle was always, without fail, bad news. Raff just hoped to God this was one of the times Estelle was a no-show.

Chapter Eighteen

'Wow,' Raff said in awe.

'Wow,' Sophie echoed.

Having gone through the cast iron gates that framed the hotel outside, Sophie and Raff were now standing in the foyer of the Shangri-La Hotel, the venue for Esther's sister's wedding. Inside, Raff and Sophie took in their surroundings. Opulent, elegant and quite simply breathtaking, the façade of the hotel was reminiscent of the former home of Napoleon Bonaparte's grand-nephew, Prince Roland Bonaparte, and was located in the very heart of Paris, overlooking the Seine and the Eiffel Tower. Inside there was a grand staircase, which was so commanding, it was hard to tear one's eyes away from it. Sophie knew there was an incredible restaurant in the hotel called La Bauhinia, which took its name from the iconic orchid flower gracing the flag of Hong Kong and it had a magnificent 1930's, Eiffel-inspired steel and glass cupola, as well as a Murano glass chandelier.

'I can't believe I've never been here before,' Raff said.

'Me neither. It's gorgeous.'

'The wedding is going to be stunning,' Raff said, shaking his head. 'But I can't even begin to imagine what it must cost them.'

Sophie did a mock-shudder. 'It even *smells* expensive in here.'

'How's the foot?' Raff asked.

Sophie tested it on the beautiful floor of the Shangri-La foyer. 'It's ok. Definitely not sprained or broken. I'm lucky it turned out to just be a twist. I seem to get over those quickly.'

She'd spent the night in Coco's room, which had been slightly odd, but she had had a surprisingly good night's sleep. The evening had been lovely; her boeuf bourguignon had gone down very well and the best thing had been that Henri had kept his word and joined them downstairs for dinner. Raff had beamed all night, which was a relief as Sophie had detected an edge to his behaviour earlier on, but she'd no idea what was on his mind. He'd been on the phone early in the morning to arrange cover at the macaron shop, so perhaps it'd been that, Sophie wasn't sure, but after they'd checked in at the shop and she had had a shower and changed, Raff seemed to relax.

'So. How are we doing this?' Raff wanted to know.

Sophie tugged her camera out of her bag. 'Well, I spoke to the manager this morning before we came here and I need to check in at reception. Someone is going to show us around so I can get an idea of the kind of photos I can take on the day.'

Raff lead the way and Sophie spoke a young lady called Agathe in a smart uniform and a tight chignon who started to efficiently show them around.

'The hotel has 101 rooms and the bride has booked out a number of those for some of her guests who are coming from outside Paris,' she said, talking and walking.

Raff raised his eyebrows at Sophie as they minced after her, struggling to keep up with Agathe, especially with Sophie's weak ankle. She took them upstairs in the lift.

'The rooms are a fusion of European empire with Asian aesthetics,' Agathe continued.

'I don't even know what that is,' Sophie whispered to Raff.

'Sounds impressive,' he shrugged.

'This is the salon Roland Bonaparte,' Agathe said, throwing an arm out grandly. 'But your friend is not holding their reception in this one.'

'It's amazing,' Sophie said, blown away by the frescos and the chandeliers. The tables were all set for a function, with immaculate cloths, shining cutlery and pink and white flowers in the centre of each one, plus an extravagant arrangement at the end of the room with trailing blooms.

'Looks just like my living room,' Raff joked as they strolled through it.

'This might seem odd but we're now going back downstairs for the room you need to see; I just didn't want you to miss seeing this one.' Agathe led them back to the lift and downstairs again.

'This is the room your friend has booked,' she announced.

'No way,' Sophie breathed as they stepped into it.

'This is one of the largest banquet rooms in the hotel and I think, the most superb,' Agathe commented. 'It is steeped in history and it has been restored to its former Louis-XIV décor.' She gestured to the large white-marble fireplace embellished with gold bronze. Glass trumeaus and original chandeliers enriched the room which was cream and gold in its colour scheme, apart from the stunning, heavy drapes in a gold and blue hue.

'This holds 180 guests in total for a reception-style wedding breakfast,' Agathe added.

'I'm not sure how many people Savannah has at the wedding...' Sophie asked, almost rendered speechless by the lavish beauty of the space.

Agathe consulted her leather-bound folder. '180,' she confirmed.

Raff let out a low whistle. 'I hope you have plenty of film in your camera. Or gigs on your memory stick or whatever it is.'

Sophie wandered around the room, finally remembering to take some photos. Wow. What a venue. The place was absolutely stunning. Sophie could visualise it set up with gorgeous flowers and all the personal touches a bride would no doubt add. She took her time taking photographs from different angles, focusing on where the top table would be so she could get the best shots of the bride and groom. It wasn't going to be hard to make the photographs look show-stopping in these surroundings.

'Wait until you see the terrace,' Agathe said gleefully, leading them out of the salon and back through the hotel. 'We have a few terraces and several rooms with views of the tower, but this main terrace has the best perspective. Your friend would be mad not to get some photographs from here. It's called *La Terrace Eiffel.*'

Sophie and Raff stepped out and looked at one another wordlessly. The terrace was vast, with glass panels surrounding it, to make the most of the view. It was decorated with huge white candles in glass globes and ornate rattan-style tables and chairs but all of that was completely irrelevant because seemingly rising majestically out of the earth, was the Eiffel Tower, the picturesque Seine at its base.

'I literally have no words,' Raff said. 'This is a view I've not seen before, not in all the years I have lived in Paris.'

Sophie couldn't help breaking into a smile. How incredibly romantic this was! How beautiful this wedding was going to be! She started to take photographs, but she knew she didn't need to worry too much. The view spoke for itself and the backdrop to the bride and groom, when they were in residence, could not be more extravagant, nor more exquisite.

'God, I love the Eiffel Tower,' Sophie breathed.

Raff nodded. 'I never tire of looking at it, even if I occasionally feel blasé about living in this city.'

Even the stoic-looking Agathe seemed impressed by the view. 'You can have drinks on this terrace while you enjoy this wonderful view. I think it's a fairy-tale end to a wedding, personally.'

'It really is,' Sophie said.

'Can I help you with anything else? Would you like to see the room the bride will be getting ready in?'

Sophie shook her head. 'No, that's ok, thank you. I can figure out my angles on the day, I think. As long as it has good lighting in it, I think we'll be fine.'

'*Trés bien*. The lighting is superb. I'll show you out.'

They followed Agathe back through to the foyer and headed outside into the sunshine.

'Well, that was more fun than I thought it would be,' Raff admitted.

'Definitely. This is going to be a fantastic wedding to photograph. Hey, isn't there a Pierre Hermé shop near here?'

'Yes, you're right. I'll grab us a taxi so you don't have to walk on that foot.' Raff signalled for a taxi and they were on their way. They embarked on Avenue Paul-Doumer, admiring the front of the shop, which was suave and modern with MACARONS & CHOCOLATS emblazoned above the Pierre Hermé name. They went inside, admiring the clean lines of the shop with its smooth chocolate-brown hues and the brightly coloured blocks of relief around the upper curve.

Like the contemporary feel of the shop, the macarons followed suit. Colour-wise, there were mostly pastels with the odd rich shade dotted in, but flavour-wise, the macarons featured sophisticated flavour combinations: vanilla, violet and blackcurrant; olive oil with mandarin orange and red berries; lemon and candied grapefruit. Some were dusted with sugar or cocoa but they all looked sublime and they had names such as Eden for the peach, apricot and saffron combination, Mosaic for the pistachio, Ceylon cinnamon and Morello cherries, Plenitude for the chocolate and caramel and Pomposa for the delectable-looking chestnut and rose macaron.

As well as the rows of pretty macarons, there were individual, miniature cakes and larger versions of them. The signature Pierre Hermé was the 'Ispahan' which was made up of a rose macaron biscuit of the same name, rose petal cream, whole raspberries and lychees.

'I love the way the flavours are layered,' Raff said. 'Like this one.' He pointed at the glass cabinet. 'Rose and rose petal. Not just rose. Jasmine flower and jasmine tea. Citrus fruits with honey. Sharp, with sweet.'

'They look so delicious.' Sophie ordered a selection so they could taste them later. 'But I think they're maybe a little too modern for mum on the flavour front. This one has foie gras in it... and this one, balsamic vinegar. I think mum would keel over at the mere thought of such ingredients in a macaron.'

Raff laughed. 'Agreed. But I think there's much to be learned from the way they do things here. And I still think we could be a tiny bit more daring with our flavours, using essential oils or candied elements for instance. But perhaps they could be in a separate section, not part of the main macaron selection. What do you think? Like... a limited-edition section. A specialist corner.'

'I think that could work. As long as we keep all the traditional flavours as well, because that's what Mariele's Macarons is known for. But I love the idea of three flavour combinations... that might be a way to bring something fresh to the macarons.'

Walking out of the shop, they talked non-stop about macarons and possible flavour blends before Sophie's ankle started aching again.

'Let's find somewhere to eat,' Raff suggested. 'Then you can rest your foot.' He signalled for a taxi to take them to a restaurant he knew on the other side of the Seine near the Eiffel Tower.

'Now we can still enjoy the view,' he said, helping her out of the taxi, 'and eat *moules* if you're in the mood.'

'Perfect,' Sophie said happily. What could be better? They ordered some mussels and relaxed with a glass of Muscadet each.

Raff watched Sophie discreetly. She looked gorgeous today, with her dark hair loose, her shades holding it back from her face. She was simply dressed in jeans, a white t-shirt, a navy suit-style jacket and Converse. It felt so natural being here in Paris with her. Which Raff couldn't understand, because it had been five years since Sophie had been in Paris. Five years since they had sat and eaten mussels and drank white wine together.

Raff watched her happily, but his stomach lurched. He couldn't stop panicking about Estelle turning up. It would be the worst possible timing, and Raff had a gut instinct that it might all go horribly wrong again between him and Sophie. Things were amazing but rather fragile right now. Estelle arriving would be like throwing a hand grenade into the mix and Raff couldn't help feeling huge apprehension about her possible arrival.

'Shall we go to Montmartre later?' he blurted out impulsively. They used to love hanging out in Montmartre, strolling around the artists quarters, sitting in cafes.

Sophie finished her wine. 'I would absolutely love to.'

Again, what could be better?

'Would it be ridiculous to order champagne?' Raff suggested. 'It feels like the right thing to do today after that hotel and all the wedding talk.'

'No, it wouldn't be ridiculous,' Sophie answered with a smile. 'When have I ever said no to champagne?'

Raff grinned. 'Very true.' He called a waiter over.

As they sat and chatted over the *Moules mariniére*, enjoying the crisp chilled champagne that shot bubbles up their nose and the delicious white wine, cream and shallot sauce the plump mussels sat in. They shared *frites* and dipped French bread in the rich sauce, and Sophie suddenly realised that her life back in England seemed like a lifetime ago. Jo was due to visit shortly, so Sophie was sure she would feel much closer to England then, but right now, it was almost as though she hadn't ever left Paris.

'Let's go,' Raff said, paying the bill. He took her hand and it felt like the most natural thing in the world.

Sophie found that she couldn't stop smiling. Taking yet another cab because of her achey ankle, they got out as far up as the taxi would take them. Sophie used to enjoy getting to Montmartre by approaching the Sacre-Coeur by going first up all the steps, and then walking round, but today wasn't the day for that. It was gloriously sunny and full of tourists, which was how Sophie had always remembered it whenever she had allowed herself to think about Paris.

'Your ankle is going to feel awful on all the cobbles,' Raff realised.

'I didn't even think of that,' Sophie said, clutching her head. 'I'll probably go over on it again.'

'Let's just see how we go. And maybe duck into a cafe.'

They went for a careful wander, choosing the streets with the flatter pavements where they could. The bright white façade of the Sacre-Coeur rose up in the background and the air was full of bohemia with artists selling their work, musicians playing music in the streets and restaurants churning out good food and wine. Slightly further out, they enjoyed the charm of the side streets, the houses heavy with greenery and floral blossoms draped over the doorways. They saw *La Maison Rose*, the famous cafe-bistro in the heart of Montmartre, with its pink exterior and green shutters. They avoided steps where they could, which was slightly tricky, but Sophie resigned herself to having to test her ankle at some point.

Raff loved Montmartre at night and there was also a very pretty 'secret' vineyard nearby he would love to visit with Sophie, but they were running out of time and Raff wanted to get back and check on the macaron shop.

'Let's get you down these steps,' he said, wondering if he should give Sophie a piggy back or a fireman's lift over his shoulder.

'Don't you dare,' Sophie said, as if she could read his mind. 'I'll walk down and I'll be fine.'

'Ha. You know me so well. Ok, but hold my arm and don't be all brave and silly about it.'

Sophie climbed down the steps, leaning heavily on Raff's arm, and they grabbed another taxi at the bottom, which felt stupidly extravagant, but Sophie couldn't help it; her ankle was throbbing badly again now.

In the taxi, Sophie's phone pinged. Thinking it was Pinter checking in after the visit at the wedding venue, she was surprised to find that it was a text from her mum.

> *Sorry if I've worried you, ma chérie, but I'll be home in two weeks' time. Can't wait to see you. Am sending this message to Eloise as well. Hope the shop is doing well. I love you xx.*

Sophie felt a rush of shock. Home in two weeks' time? Where had that come from?

'Are you ok?' Raff asked, concerned. 'That's the news you've been waiting for all along, but I guess it's a bit unexpected.'

Sophie mouth curled. She was overjoyed and taken aback and anxious all at the same time: overjoyed because it was the best news; taken aback because Sophie felt as though she had been in limbo for the past two months; anxious because she still had no idea where her mum had been or what any of it meant, but also because… she had no idea what it might mean for her and Raff.

'Don't worry about us,' Raff told her, sensing her apprehension from afar. He took her hand. 'And I mean that, Sophie. Just get your mum back and we'll just take it from there. Ok?'

'Ok,' she nodded. She was reminded of her conversation with Henri the night before. What difference did it make to her and Raff that her mum was coming back? She supposed it negated the reason for her being in Paris; after all she had only come back to find Mariele. So once she had been found or returned, Sophie had no reason to stay in Paris any longer. Did she?

At the same time, England seemed alien to her now, and that wasn't what she thought was going to happen. She had thought that she wouldn't have been able to wait to go back to England and for her life to get back to normal – whatever that was. But maybe that normal no longer existed because Ryan was no longer there, and her friends… she was speaking to them almost every other day so they didn't feel that distant. And her job was portable…

Sophie hadn't ever imagined settling down in Paris once more. But she had such strong feelings for Raff again… God, it was all so confusing!

'Why is the light on in the house?' she said, noticing it as they pulled up.

'No idea.' Raff helped her out. 'Perhaps Eloise has come over for some reason. No one else has a key, do they?'

Sophie shook her head and pushed the front door open. 'No. Apart from... *Grand-mère!*'

'Sophie!'

Fifi. Raff leant against the door frame and watched Sophie and her grandmother embrace.

'What are you doing here?' Fifi asked, kissing Sophie's cheeks repeatedly. 'I had no idea you were in Paris. Why didn't you tell me? I would have come here sooner.'

Sophie wasn't sure what to say.

'I'm so happy to see you,' Fifi said, pulling Sophie into a hug again. 'What's happening with that boy you were seeing?'

'Nothing,' Sophie said, avoiding Raff's eyes. 'He's... out of the picture.'

'Aah well.' Fifi raised her heavily painted in eyebrows. 'Your mother said he was a bit girly. I'm sure you can do far better.'

Sophie stifled a giggle. Girly? God, poor Ryan. He was actually built like a tank, so Sophie had no idea where they got the 'girly' idea from.

Fifi removed herself from Sophie's arms and fixed her beady eyes on Raff. 'Raphael. Come here, you delicious specimen of manhood.'

Raff laughed and hugged her. Fifi was an absolute minx. A flamboyant colourful character, French to the core, with dark hair cut in a sharp bob and held in place by a lot of hair lacquer. Dressed in a genuine pink Chanel suit, with a scarf knotted around her throat and decorated with an oversized brooch – also Chanel – Fifi wore higher heels than most women her age and her tan handbag clashed with her suit, but it was quality and in her eyes that was all that mattered. Painfully thin, she owed her slender frame to the complete avoidance of butter and a heavy reliance on nicotine; she smoked wherever she pleased, despite the new laws in place in most cafes and restaurants. Fifi was old school and felt that the new rules simply didn't apply to her.

'Now.' Fifi pulled off the signature leather gloves she always wore regardless of the weather. 'Where is your mother, Sophie? I haven't heard from her in ages apart from a few silly texts and I want to know what's going on.'

Sophie and Raff exchanged a glance.

'Well, that's the problem, *Grand-mère*,' Sophie said, shrugging. 'None of us know what's going on.'

'What?' Fifi looked astonished. 'How can that be? Someone must know.'

'No. No one knows. I've spoken to her once on the phone, but that's it.'

Fifi looked perplexed, but determined. 'Well, that won't do. We're going to have to figure out where she is and what's going on.'

'We've tried everything we can think of,' Raff informed her. 'Photos, childhood places, hints in Mariele's messages. And we've hit a dead end every time.'

Sophie showed Fifi the text she had just received. 'Look, she's due home in two weeks' time. We might just have to wait it out.'

Fifi snorted. 'How ridiculous! What is she playing at? I'm not happy about this at all.'

'I'll take your luggage upstairs,' Raff said, throwing Sophie an amused glance.

'Thank you, *mon chéri*,' Fifi said distractedly. She sat down in a nearby armchair and took out her cigarette case.

'You're going to have to tell me everything, Sophie, and I'm going to need a very strong brandy.'

'I'll get you one,' Sophie said.

'Good. And then, *mon bébé*,' Fifi said, snapping her cigarette lighter shut with a smart click, 'then, we are going to call the police.'

Chapter Nineteen

'So you managed to deter Fifi from calling the gendarmes?'

Sophie rolled her eyes. 'Yes, just about.' She carefully placed one of Raff's latest, rather daring creations – an almond praline shot with lime – into a new pink and silver swirl boxes. The bags weren't ready yet, but the boxes were receiving lots of comments and compliments.

'*Merci beaucoup,*' she said cheerily to the customer. '*Au revoir.*'

Raff laughed as he carried in a tray of fresh macarons. 'Listen, it's understandable that Fifi wants to take some sort of action. I have wondered at times if we should report this whole thing to the police, but I assumed they would probably just dismiss it out of hand because we keep receiving texts from her. She's not exactly a missing person if she's staying in touch, is she?'

'I guess not,' Sophie sighed. She just wished she understood what was going on. It was so frustrating not knowing what had prompted her mum to leave. Sophie could recall word for word the cryptic message her mum had left and she still couldn't make any sense of it. Her heart wasn't happy – whatever that meant.

'Where is Fifi now?' Raff asked.

Sophie started refilling the macaron trays. 'She's rifling through all the drawers in the house to try and find some sort of clue as to where mum is. I've told her that I've already done all of that, but she wants to do it herself and I can't stop her anyway.'

'No one could stop her,' Raff commented wryly. 'She's a force to be reckoned with, your grandmother.'

'Indeed.' Sophie stopped what she was doing and regarded Raff seriously. 'But I honestly don't know if I can deal with her while we waiting for mum to return. She's going to be an absolute nightmare. I can only hold her back from calling the gendarmes for so long.'

Raff started up the coffee machine even though the shop was momentarily empty. 'Cappuccino? Ok, so maybe Fifi needs a project to distract her for a couple of weeks. What can we task her with? Something in here?'

Sophie looked around the shop. 'I mean… she's fairly artistic and creative. She might have some thoughts about the colour scheme or about changing a few things around. It's worth a try, I suppose.'

'Well, let's go with that for now. Or… I could intro-duce her to my dad and see if they hit it off?' Raff looked mischievous. 'You never know…'

Sophie looked horrified. 'Imagine! Well, actually, I guess it isn't that weird…'

'Yes!' Raff corrected her. 'It definitely *is* that weird. But they might get on as they're both… old.'

'Who is?'

Fifi appeared behind Raff. She'd clearly come in from the house using the other door, but she'd been extremely quiet, even in her red court shoes. Despite being desper-ately anxious about her daughter, Fifi was in full make-up, her hair coiffed, and she was wearing a stark but very well-cut black dress that Raff was sure must have an old but well-respected designer label.

'Oh.' Raff turned around and hoped to God he wasn't bright red in the face. 'Not you, obviously.'

'Obviously,' Fifi said, catching his eye with a smirk. 'Well, I've been through all of Mariele's things and aside from finding a few… unsavoury things I'd rather not have seen' – she raised an eyebrow, but didn't elaborate – 'I haven't found any clues as to where she might be. Which is very frustrating.'

'What are those?' Sophie said, pointing to whatever Fifi was clutching in her hands.

'Just some photos,' Fifi shrugged. 'I don't know if they mean anything.' She gave a Gallic shrug. 'I'm just trying to find something… anything… which might tell us where she is.' She looked downcast.

Raff put his arm around her tiny shoulders. 'I know how distressing this is. Sophie's been really upset – and Eloise too. But try not to worry. If she's coming home in a few weeks' time, it should all be ok.'

Fifi nodded.

'We wondered if you might have some ideas about how to revamp the shop, *Grand-mère*,' Sophie said hesitantly.

'Why?' Fifi frowned. 'The shop is beautiful and Mariele likes it this way.'

Raff and Sophie exchanged a glance.

'Very true,' Raff said. 'But Mariele asked us to revise some of the macaron flavours and look at the packaging in her absence. We think she's happy for us to review and assess everything. You have such flair that we thought you might come up with some ideas with regard to the décor.'

Fifi eyed him beadily as though she knew exactly what Raff was playing at, but she inclined her head. 'I'll give it some thought,' she conceded.

'*Bon.*' Raff poured her a black coffee. 'And we thought you might want to meet my dad, Henri, too.'

'What, so we can be… old… together?' Fifi sniffed her coffee appreciatively and broke into a smile. 'That smells good.'

'Not so you can be old together. No… just so…'

Fifi waved a hand. 'Stop, Raphael. I understand. You think we might have things in common because we're… old. Is he coming here?'

'Actually no.' Raff sipped his own coffee, knowing his thoughts must show on his face. 'He's… rather reclusive these days. My mum died a year ago and he's not been the same since. He… never leaves the house.'

Fifi tutted. '*Quel dommage!* What a shame. Poor man. Mariele did mention that your mother had died, Raphael. I'm so sorry for your loss.'

Raff smiled. 'Thank you. But anyway, we'll have to take you to the house so you can meet him.'

'I will be very happy to do so,' Fifi said, taking a seat. 'Where are all the customers?'

Sophie checked her watch. 'Next batch expected any second now. They come in waves.'

The door opened and they all looked up expectantly.

'*Grand-mère!*' Eloise burst through the door. 'I'm so happy to see you.'

'*Chérie!*' Fifi put her coffee down and held her arms open. They hugged tightly. 'How are you, *mon enfant*?'

'So worried about mum,' Eloise responded.

'Me too, me too.' Fifi patted her shoulder. 'But hopefully she is home soon, yes?' She cupped her hands around Eloise's face. 'We must be strong, *ma petite*.'

'Yes.' Eloise straightened up and turned to Sophie. 'So, how are all the new plans going with the shop?'

Sophie talked her through the new designs and Raff's macarons, and Fifi joined in, telling them to move a few items and remove a few things. She thought they should *désencombrer* – de-clutter, essentially – and make it classier. Sophie did actually agree and felt that the shop looked fresher and brighter.

'I also suggest a fresh coat of paint on that woodwork,' Fifi said, pointing to a shabby area. 'And I think… perhaps a change of colour on this wall here. Maybe to match your silver swirl pattern. What do you think? I have a contact, someone who could come in and do it. No paint… a high-quality resin to make the shop feel more modern.'

'Sounds great.' Raff looked pleased.

'I would also commission for a new sign above the door,' Fifi finished. 'Again, I'm thinking something modern with silver to replicate the traditional look of the *magasin*.'

Sophie felt concerned. Were they changing too much? 'Are you sure mum will like that?' she wondered out loud.

'I don't know, but if she were here, she could say so,' Fifi replied briskly. 'If she doesn't like it when she's back, I'll have it removed and put everything back to how it is now.'

Sophie shrugged. That was fair enough.

The door opened and Raff's friend Louis came in. '*Salut*,' he said. 'How are you all? And who is this young lady?' he asked, noticing Fifi.

'*Tsk*,' Fifi said, coquettishly pretending to be offended by the 'young lady' comment by holding her hand out to be kissed.

'*Enchanté*,' Louis said, bending over her hand and kissing it loudly.

'And you are…?' Fifi enquired, giving him the once over.

'I'm Raff's best friend,' Louis said with a charming smile.

'And he's taken,' Raff added with a twinkle.

'*Zut!*' Fifi said. 'Damn it. All the good ones are.'

Louis grinned and Raff punched his arm.

The door opened again and they all looked up expectantly. Sophie's mouth fell open.

'Jo!'

Jo whooped and threw herself into Sophie's arms. 'I decided to come a day early! Is that ok?'

'Of course it is!' Sophie hugged her best friend. 'It's so good to see you.' She pulled away to get a better look at her. Jo's blond quiff was in full force again and she was dressed in bright red jeans and a black t-shirt. She looked stylish and rather French.

'I love the shop,' Jo commented looking around. 'It's gorgeous.' Catching sight of Raff and Louis, her eyes went back to Raff; she obviously recognised him from the photo Sophie had sent over.

'Raff. So pleased to meet you,' she said.

'And I'm Louis,' Louis said, bending over Jo's hand and giving it a plump kiss, the way he had with Fifi's.

'Soon to be a dad,' Raff said, nudging him. 'Not that you'd know from all the flirting today.' He held his hand out to Jo, then kissed her on both cheeks. 'I'm very pleased to meet you too. Sophie has been really looking forward to you coming.'

Jo beamed at him.

Sophie introduced Fifi, and Eloise said hi having met Jo a few times before during visits to England, and then Sophie quickly made a coffee for Jo. A stream of customers suddenly turned up and Raff was soon back behind the counter serving, with Louis hindering him at every turn.

'*Emmenez* Jo *faire les courses*,' Raff called to Sophie. 'Go shopping, you two.'

'Shall we?' Sophie said to Jo. 'I could take you to *Galeries Lafayette* and a few other places.'

'Lovely!' Jo dumped her bags inside the house and they left via the main door as customers were lining up outside the shop. 'Wow, it's so busy.'

'I think it's Raff's new macarons,' Sophie said, pleased at all the new business.

'He's gorgeous by the way,' Jo said, giving her a mischievous sideways glance.

Sophie's mouth twitched, but she said nothing.

'You're going to have to tell me absolutely everything,' Jo said reasonably, linking her arm through Sophie's. 'With shopping goes gossiping. And I… need to know *everything*. Your mum, Raff, Ryan… your scary-looking grandmother… the lot.'

'Ok, ok.' Sophie felt so much better for having Jo here; she was like a piece of home.

They made their way to *Galeries Lafayette* on Boulevard Hausmann. Jo didn't seem blown away by the exterior, but as soon as they went inside, she couldn't stop gasping at the art–nouveau beauty of the interieur.

'Wow,' she kept saying. 'Wow…'

Sophie didn't blame her. The upmarket department store was one of her favourites and as with most of her favourite places in Paris, it reminded her of her mum. Sophie wasn't sure who had opened the store in the first place, but she knew it had been a tiny fashion shop to begin with and that the company had bought more and more of the adjacent buildings until they had owned the entire block. It now housed everything from fashion to furniture, from beauty to bed linen.

Sophie especially loved the beautiful glass dome that sat over the grand hall – the main part of the store – with the golden light streaming through the stained-glass windows and flooding the hall especially on a sunny day. The magnificent staircase inspired by the Paris opera and the curved balconies that were like loops of piped icing all lent the store an opulent, luxurious feel.

After Jo had treated herself to a few beauty items that Sophie assured her she could have found cheaper back at home, and after they had perused every floor – lingering endlessly in the vast shoe department where Jo had fallen in love with the array of trainers on offer – they finally made it outside. They checked out some of the other shops along Boulevard Hausmann, then paused.

'Where to now?' Jo asked.

'I want to take you to the *Palais Garnier*,' Sophie said, turning Jo the other way.

'What's that?'

Sophie pulled a mock-shocked face. 'The Paris Opera house, Jo. I cannot believe you haven't heard of it. This place inspired the setting for the famous musical, "Phantom of the Opera".'

Jo shrugged. Paris had always been on her to do list, but she had never got around to it, even though Sophie had always raved about how gorgeous it was.

After purchasing tickets and struggling through the crowds, they arrived in the *Grand Foyer*, with its sumptuous main staircase – the *Grand Escalier*. The style of the building was described as 'Napoleon lll with some baroque thrown in' and it was designed by Charles Garnier in the late 19th century.

The grand staircase was made of white marble with a balustrade of red and green marble and it split into two staircases that lead to the *Grand Foyer*. The pedestals at the bottom of the staircase were decorated with female *torchéres*, and the ceiling above the staircase, which was apparently too dark originally and had to be re-painted, had only been finished the day before the opening of the opera house.

The *Grand Foyer*, Sophie read, was designed to act as a drawing room for Paris society and its ceiling was painted to represent various moments in the history of music. The foyer opened up onto an outside conservatory-style area with octagonal salons flanking the sides. The paintings and lighting were exquisite and breathtaking, and Jo seemed momentarily lost for words. They made their way through the Member's Rotunda and finally to the main auditorium, which was gloriously lavish and sumptuous with a huge swathe of burgundy curtain stretched across the imposing stage.

It was the part that always gave Sophie goosebumps, and the time she had been lucky enough to see *The Nutcracker* there as a child, she remembered gaping in awe at her surroundings. She had never forgotten the experience and her skin prickled as she recalled her tiny hand inside her mother's, with Eloise on the other side. As it sometimes happened in these moments, Sophie was struck by the magical things her mother had managed to achieve as a single parent.

'It's stunning,' Jo breathed. 'It has such a lovely feel about it. I'm not really into opera, but even I want to come and see... *Carmen* or something here.'

Sophie nodded. 'Amazing isn't it. Ok. So... how about *Fauchon* for some chocolates and then a lunch stop?'

'Sounds good to me.'

Maison Fauchon, the modern, kitsch delicatessen and chocolate shop in *Place de la Madeleine* was a revelation to Jo, who immediately fell in love with the hot pink décor, the glossy floors and the funky vibe. After guiltily purchasing some foie gras, because she adored it but didn't agree with the production process, and half of her body weight in chocolate and pastries for her parents and older brother whilst loyally avoiding even looking at the brightly coloured macarons, Jo needed a break.

'I'm treating you to lunch and I want some-where outrageously expensive and self-indulgent,' she announced.

'Have you had a pay rise?' Sophie asked in amusement.

'No. I earn enough as it is, thank you very much,' Jo returned smartly. 'My job as estate agent is paying so well, my poor boyfriend is feeling all emasculated, the big wally. Come on. I'm hungry and I want something very, very FRENCH.'

Choosing *La Maison de la Truffe Madeleine* nearby as it seemed to fit the bill, they ducked inside and were soon shown to a table. The décor was grey and white, with much emphasis on the truffle, with arty shots of every kind of truffle known to man adorning the walls as though they were beautiful rather than nobbly and rather potato-like. The décor was art deco in places and very elegant.

'Wow, I might be able to have foie gras here,' Jo giggled, checking the menu, 'and not feel naughty.'

'You can eat foie gras anywhere in Paris and not worry about it,' Sophie told her. 'It's *de rigueur* here.'

'Thank God,' Jo sighed in relief. 'My brother is practically a vegan these days. He introduces himself as a "Brand New Vegan" before he says "Hello, my name is Jeff."'

Sophie mock-shuddered. 'Oh dear.'

After Jo had gleefully ordered a steak with foie gras – and truffles – and Sophie had ordered the truffle pizza which came highly recommended, they relaxed with glasses of wine.

'So. What's your news?' Jo asked. 'How come your grandmother has turned up like that? Did you call her?'

'No… she didn't even know I was here…' Sophie filled Jo in with the Fifi gossip.

'She's fabulous, but quite intimidating,' Jo commented. 'I wouldn't want to get on the wrong side of her.'

'She's just very forthright,' Sophie explained, 'and rather bossy. But she's lovely too. I always used to think she was the most glamorous lady I knew, after my mum. Always wafting in reeking of Chanel and wearing pearls and heels to breakfast.'

'I noticed the heels.' Jo wrinkled her nose. She wore low heels at work, but was far more at home in trainers. 'Impressive at her age.'

'Don't ever say that to her face!' Sophie laughed. 'Fifi likes to think she hasn't aged in years.'

Jo shuddered. 'I don't have a death wish, Soph!'

'Anyway, on a serious note, we're all still worried about mum.' Sophie fingered the stem of her wine glass. 'She's staying in touch loads… in fact, more than she probably does normally. And the messages are… sentimental and lovely and full of heart. It's like she's somewhere reliving our childhood, and it's reminding *me* of what a great childhood me and Eloise had, despite not having our dad around, whoever he is.'

Jo sipped her wine. 'Hmm. Worrying, but I guess with her being in touch that much, she must be ok. Surely?'

'I don't know. I mean I hope so, but oddly, they haven't made me feel that reassured.'

'Are the messages… weird then? Not the sort of thing she'd usually send?'

'Maybe.' Sophie frowned. She thought about what Jo had said. There was something… 'I suppose the problem is that mum is always very chilled as you know, but she's not necessarily prone to sentimentality.'

'Interesting. If baffling.' Jo shrugged. 'I don't know what that means, if I'm honest. Ok. So. Ryan.'

'Messaging constantly, actually.' Sophie held up her phone for Jo to see.

Jo flipped through the myriad of messages. 'Gosh. He's obviously missing you. How does that make you feel?'

'I'm not sure,' Sophie said honestly. 'Flattered rather than affected, I think. But I was with him for such a long time. And I did love him. Not in the same way as Raff, obviously, but still. It was a good-enough relationship.'

'A good enough relationship,' Jo repeated. 'Did you hear what you just said?'

Sophie nodded. 'Yes, I know. But… I can't help thinking that Raff is still the scary option, you know?'

'What, and Ryan is the safe one?'

'Maybe.' Sophie felt uncomfortable saying that, but in essence, it was what she was getting at.

'So, you want to go back to feeling safe and… sensible… and boring again?' Jo drained her glass of wine. She looked cross. 'Well, I'm going to need much more of that if you carry on talking that way.' She ordered more wine.

'Don't get all bossy with me,' Sophie protested. 'I'm not saying I want to be with Ryan. I just mean that Raff is… complicated. And Ryan isn't.'

'Because he's a bit boring,' Jo interrupted. 'Nice enough, but not that exciting. And he really hurt you,' Jo reminded her. She inhaled in delight as her foie gras arrived. 'Oh that smells good. Ok, enough about Ryan – you know my thoughts. What about Raff?'

'Good subject change,' Sophie said approvingly. 'But as a last note on Ryan, I didn't for one second say I wanted to get back together with him. I just said it was flattering, by which, I probably should have said "gratifying" or "satisfying". And it feels as though there is unfinished business. No closure. Do you get what I mean? It's not so much about him being safe… it's just that he's always been there. Almost from the point I split up with Raff and came back to England. Even though we were just friends, Ryan was there for me.'

'Well, he's not now,' Jo pointed out reasonably. 'And all he's doing is sending a few texts here and there. It's quite passive, isn't it? He's not exactly sweeping you off your feet. And texting like that is something anyone can do because it's easy and really, these texts… they don't amount to anything.' She stopped, thinking about what she had just said. 'No disrespect to your mum there, by the way.'

'None taken,' Sophie was amused, but her head was slightly all over the place again for some reason.

'Anyhoo. No matter.' Jo had become rather more docile – clearly in heaven eating her favourite forbidden food. Or perhaps it was all the wine. 'I'm more interested in gorgeous Raff. I mean… he's delicious, Soph. You've not really mentioned that about him.'

'Haven't I? Ah well.' Sophie's truffle pizza was sublime.

'You're going to stay here, aren't you?' Jo asked out of the blue.

'What?'

'You're going to stay in Paris,' Jo said again. Her expression was upbeat, but her eyes were slightly sad. 'You look so at home here. You and Raff have fallen for one another; it's plain for everyone to see. And when your mum comes back, surely you won't want to leave her?'

Sophie put her knife and fork down slowly. 'Wow. When you put it like that, it seems so cut and dried. But it really isn't, Jo.'

'Why not?'

'Because… I have no idea of Raff's long terms plans or what he really feels about me.' Sophie gazed at Jo earnestly. 'I don't want to presume anything and actually, I'm amazed he's found it in himself to forgive me for leaving without giving him a chance to explain, because it broke both of us.' She cast her eyes down. 'I still feel awful about it.'

'Everyone makes mistakes,' Jo countered cheerfully. 'It was ages ago and you thought he'd lied or been a neglectful father. Is that the only fly in the ointment?'

Sophie shook her head ruefully. 'No, it isn't! There are loads of things. It's Raff and it's work and Pinter and it's England versus Paris and it's… lots of things.' Her phone buzzed. It was Raff checking they were having a good time. 'And now, seeing you again, I'm reminded of all the stuff I love about home. And London. And my work and you and all of it.'

'Well, let's hope it resolves itself quickly,' Jo said, sitting back, replete. 'I am a happy, happy girl. I might move here too. And I'll get horribly fat and end up alone with cats because Rich hates chubby girls. Anyway, isn't Pinter due to visit soon?'

'Pinter, Esther and their whole entourage. Imagine. Paris won't know what's hit it.'

'I'll grab the check and then we need to walk this off,' Jo stated pushing her tummy out.

'The *Musée d'Orsay*?' Sophie suggested.

'Get me there, woman.' Jo took out her purse to pay.

–

The *Musée d'Orsay* was busy, but not unbearably so. On the left bank of the Seine, it was one of the largest art houses in history and it was housed in the former *Gare d'Orsay*, the railway station. Holding mainly French art, the museum was full of paintings, sculptures, furniture and, Sophie's favourite part, photography. It held the largest collection of Impressionist and post-Impressionist masterpieces, including work by Monet, Renoir, Degas, Seurat, Van Gogh and Manet.

They wandered around for a few hours, taking in the famous pieces and checking out some unusual artefacts and photographs.

'Ok, I'm shattered now,' Jo moaned. 'And I haven't seen the Eiffel Tower properly yet.'

'Tomorrow,' Sophie promised. 'Ok, old lady, let's get you home. To your Paris home, I mean. Let's be lazy and get a taxi.'

They found one outside and got in it, pleased to be resting their aching feet.

'We've done so many lazy, naughty things today, I couldn't be happier,' Jo sighed as they wove their way through Paris. 'I'm definitely moving here.'

'No, you're not,' Sophie said, helping her out of the taxi. 'You can't stand the pace.'

Inside, Sophie went around turning on some lights, calling out to her grandmother while Jo threw herself into an armchair and eased her feet out of her trainers.

'What are these?' Jo picked a pile of photographs up from the table.

'Not sure. I think they might be the ones *Grand-mère* found earlier. Have a look, see if there's anything interesting there.' Sophie found a note. 'Ah. She's gone out to dinner with some friends.'

'Who's this?' Jo held up a photo. 'He's pretty hot.'

Sophie narrowed her eyes. 'I don't know, but there are a few photos of that guy.'

Jo turned it over. 'It says "Theo M, 1985, Surrey."'

'What?' Sophie grabbed it. 'None of the others had anything on the back. Theo…' She turned it over again and stared at the handsome face. Who was this guy?

An old flame from England, perhaps? Or someone more significant?

'Mean anything?'

'I really don't know. God, I wish I knew what mum was up to. I'm beginning to think she might have a whole other life I don't know about.'

Jo looked at her watch. 'Well. I'd better Facetime Paddy so he doesn't think I've gone off with some sexy Frenchie and then I might have a bath, if that's ok?'

'Yes, of course. I'll run it for you now.' Sophie went upstairs and got the bath running, absent-mindedly squeezing far too much of her mum's *Anaïs Anaïs* bubble bath into it.

Sophie sat on the edge of the bath staring at the photograph. Who was he and why did she feel he might be important somehow?

Raff called and Sophie was pleased to hear from him. 'Good day?'

'Lovely. Tiring, but really lovely.' Sophie told him about the photograph.

Raff was intrigued. 'I wonder who he is. It might be a red herring though, Sophie. Just someone your mum used to know.'

'Yes, maybe.' Sophie felt a bit deflated. She felt sure the man was significant, but Raff was probably right; he could be anyone and not relevant to her mum's disappearance.

'I… missed you today,' Raff said suddenly.

'Yes. I know what you mean.' Sophie felt herself smiling. 'Which is silly, isn't it? I haven't been here long enough for you to miss me.'

There was a pause.

'I missed you every day when you left last time, Sophie,' Raff said quietly. 'So yes. You have been back long enough for me to miss you when you're not around.'

Sophie fell silent.

'I just wanted to say that…' Raff started to speak then seemed to dry up. 'It's… I think I've fallen—'

Sophie cut in. 'I think I've fallen too, actually. So, that's ok I think.'

'It's more than ok.' She could hear the broad grin in Raff's voice. 'Let's leave it there for tonight though. I'll see you tomorrow, yes?'

'Yes.'

Sophie ended the call. Where on earth was all this headed?

Chapter Twenty

Raff checked the food for the dinner he'd prepared for everyone. He'd made individual cheese souffles, which he suspected might be a little rich for Fifi, so he had prepared her a light salad with asparagus and he would add small slices of a very good, over-ripe goat's cheese if she would like it. Raff had also made a summery *Bouillabaisse* with a basil rouille as it was so warm outside, and for dessert, an almond frangipane tart with honeyed pistachios. He had kept the menu very French to please Fifi, who Raff knew had very exacting and traditional tastes, but also for Sophie's friend, Jo, so she could enjoy a real, French, home-cooked meal.

'What time are they getting here?' Coco asking, bounding into the kitchen, wearing dungarees and a bright red t-shirt.

'Soon,' Raff said. He stole a glance at her. He wondered why it didn't remotely bother him that sometimes Coco looked so much like Estelle, with her dark hair swinging around her shoulders and her long legs on show. But it didn't, probably because she had many of his characteristics and mannerisms too. He simply thought that Coco was a beautiful girl and that he was lucky to have her, and that he would need to keep a much closer eye on her as she grew older. The thought of boys taking her out made Raff feel sick, and he and Louis had already decided Raff had to be one of those threatening, menacing fathers who would make a boy feel extremely uncomfortable and think twice before daring to lay a finger on Raff's wonderful girl. He wasn't sure that was really his vibe, but Louis said as long as Raff put a gun out on display at all times when young men knocked on the door or wielded a knife a lot, that would probably be enough. Raff wasn't convinced, but he knew he was something he'd have to think about soon. He'd seen a few messages flash up on Coco's phone from her girlfriends mentioning 'sexy boys' at school. Raff shuddered at the thought of his little girl growing up. All he wanted to do was protect her.

'Mm, that smells good. Does everyone like fish?'

Raff batted her hand away. 'I don't know. But I have some leftover Coq au Vin I can warm up if not.'

'What are we having with it… some bread?' Coco tore off a piece and munched on it.

'Yes, if there is any left, you annoying child. And some new potatoes, buttered with fresh herbs. And a good salad.'

Coco leant against the worktop. 'So what's Sophie's grandmother like?'

'Terrifying,' Raff grinned. 'She'll probably even scare you.'

'Never,' Coco said daringly. 'Who else is coming? There is loads of food here.'

'Sophie's friend, Jo… she arrived a day early. And I think Sophie's boss, Pinter and his wife might come over if they get here early enough.'

'Ah for the fancy wedding.' Coco stole another chunk of bread. 'And… how is Sophie?'

'Sophie is fine, thank you and stop it,' Raff warned, shaking his head.

'I'm just happy for you, *papa*. I really like Sophie. You go so well together… you must be so glad she's back.'

Yes, but for how long, Raff thought to himself? He knew his feelings were already out of control and he was pretty sure Sophie felt something too, especially from their last conversation. They had admitted they had fallen for one another and that was a huge thing. But Sophie's trip here was intended to be a temporary one, so everything was up in the air for now. Raff wondered if the ex-boyfriend was in touch and trying to get her back as well, although he wasn't sure that was even the issue. At the end of the day, Sophie now lived in England and Raff just wasn't sure if she would want to uproot her life and move back to Paris. Yet, whenever he was with her, it felt as though it was how life should be.

'I think they might be here,' Coco said, striding out of the kitchen. 'Shall I open the door?'

'Yes.' Raff took a bottle of chilled Chablis out of the fridge.

Sophie, Jo and Fifi came in. Sophie and Jo looked freshly showered after another day of sightseeing, wearing summer dresses and Converse, and Fifi was resplendent in a pair of tailored, white trousers with a hot pink, silk shirt with flat, shiny, brown brogues rather than her usual heels because 'her arches were aching' by all accounts. She wore plenty of heavy costume jewellery around her wrists and throat and a tan scarf around her shoulders, which oddly went well.

'Hey.' Sophie came up to Raff with a bottle of white wine in her hands. 'I wasn't sure what we were eating. Oh, you have a Chablis…'

'I'm sure we'll need another.' Raff leant in to kiss her cheek and felt her turn her face. He kissed her on the lips, taking her face in his hands.

'I didn't realise it was that kind of dinner!' Jo joked behind them.

'*Pardon*,' Raff apologised, stopping. 'How rude of us.'

'That's ok,' Jo said, kissing his cheeks. 'I understand completely. She's fab, isn't she?'

'She is,' Raff said. 'Fifi, can I get you a glass of wine?'

'Just a small one,' she conceded, putting her bag down on a nearby table. 'And who are you?' she asked Coco.

'C-Coco,' Coco stammered. 'I'm Raff's daughter.'

'Of course, of course.' Fifi accepted her wine glass graciously. 'You are a beautiful young lady. You must be very proud of her, Raff.'

'I am. If a little concerned about her dating boys soon.'

'Papa!' Coco wailed. 'Stop.'

Raff ignored her, turning to Jo. 'Where have you been today?'

'Everywhere,' Jo sighed, taking a seat. 'The Centre Georges Pompidou, Notre-Dame, the Pantheon, the Eiffel Tower, the *Champs-Élysées* and oh, the Arc de Triomphe. And we had such a busy day yesterday too…'

'That's a lot of walking,' Coco said, standing near Sophie.

'I adore the Eiffel Tower,' Fifi said agreeably. 'So majestic, *oui*?'

'*Oui, oui*,' Jo nodded rapidly, while Sophie hid a smile. She hadn't witnessed an intimidated Jo before.

'I do not care much for the Centre Georges Pompidou,' Fifi informed Jo disdainfully. 'So modern, so grotesque. Do you care for it?'

'No, I definitely do not care for it,' Jo replied vehemently, even though she seemed to find it quite fun and funky when she was there.

Sophie couldn't help laughing, shaking her head when her *grand-mère* looked at her, perplexed. 'Where is Henri?' she asked Coco in a low voice.

'He's in his room,' Coco told her. 'But he promised he'd be down for dinner.'

'That's a shame. I thought after his stint in the garden, he might be spending more time down here.'

Coco nodded. 'Me too. He's better, though. So much better. But it's going to take him some time. He still misses Grandma and just doesn't have any purpose in life.'

'That will never do,' Fifi said, shamelessly eavesdropping. 'Shall we ask him to join us now?'

'I'll go,' Coco said. She disappeared upstairs and returned with Henri in tow.

'What did you say?' Sophie whispered to Coco as Henri shyly introduced himself to Jo.

'I told her there was a scary lady downstairs who didn't believe he had the balls to say hello to her.'

Sophie watched Henri walk over to Fifi.

'It is very nice to meet you,' Henri said formally, proffering a hand.

'It is very nice to meet you too,' Fifi said, shaking it. 'What a lovely house.'

'Isn't it?' Henri agreed.

Fifi turned to Raff. 'Are we eating outside?'

'Er...' Raff met his dad's eyes. 'I wasn't planning to, no...'

Henri lifted his chin. 'It's fine, Raff. I think that would be nice.'

'Ok...' Raff looked doubtful, but he asked Coco to grab all the cutlery.

Soon, it was all hands on deck and they had cleaned and laid the outside table. Coco found some navy linen napkins in the cupboard and she put one next to each set of cutlery.

'We should put some flowers on the table,' Fifi said, her hands on her hips. 'What are your favourites, Henri?'

Henri hesitated. He glanced at Raff, then turned back to Fifi. 'I-I like roses. They were my wife's favourite. Yellow.'

'I'm so sorry for your loss,' Fifi said, placing her hand on his arm, squeezing it briefly then removing it. She somehow managed to convey deep sympathy with the brief, brisk gesture. 'Shall we... go and pick some from the garden?'

Henri let out a jerky breath. 'Yes. Yes, we can do that.'

'You're lucky I have my flat shoes on,' Fifi said as she led the way outside. 'Do you have secateurs?'

Henri disappeared into a nearby shed and handed a pair of secateurs over.

Raff followed them out, placing wine glasses on the table.

'God, she's so bossy,' Sophie asked worriedly, coming up behind him.

'Persuasive,' Raff corrected. 'She's... persuasive.'

'This garden needs tackling,' Fifi was saying. 'It is wild and messy. But I think it must have looked beautiful once.'

Henri nodded. 'It was,' he agreed. 'My wife used to look after it.'

'I see.' Fifi pointed to a tangle of yellow roses. 'These are lovely.' She started snipping at some roses, then passed the secateurs to Henri.

'Flowers are so pleasing,' Fifi said approvingly. 'If you'd like to get the garden back to how it was, I have some friends I could introduce you to... Victor and Ruben. And also Margaux. They could come over and help you.'

Henri started to smile. 'That's... that's very thoughtful of you.'

Raff felt a lump in his throat as he watched them. He wasn't sure his dad could handle being outside so much, but maybe it was the perfect thing for him.

'That's so sweet,' Sophie said. 'I have honestly never seen my grandmother being so... tender with anyone.'

'She's very kind.' Raff couldn't even describe how seeing his father outside having a conversation with someone else besides him and Coco was making him feel, let alone anything else his father might now achieve. 'I'd better get the food on the table.'

'I'll help,' said Sophie. Together, they got the cheese souffles cooked and on the table.

'Oh, that looks lovely, but rather rich,' Fifi began, smoothing a hand along her tiny waistline.

Raff placed the asparagus salad in front of her. 'I made you this, just in case.'

'What a good boy,' Fifi said, giving him a dazzling smile. 'I do like a man who knows that a woman's appetite can be delicate.'

Jo paused with an enormous spoonful of Raff's delectable cheese souffle halfway to her mouth. 'Oh. I mean… my appetite is—'

'Not delicate at all,' Sophie grinned. 'And neither is mine.' She tucked in with gusto. 'This is fantastic, Raff.'

'Thanks.' He stood up. 'Enjoy and I'll get the Bouillabaisse finished.'

The doorbell rang at that point and Raff answered the door. A man with sleek, silver hair and a sharp suit stood there with a magnum of champagne, next to a stunning woman with a mass of wavy blond hair, a deep tan and legs up to her armpits. She was wearing the most fabulous orange leather trench coat that made her long legs look even browner with gold gladiator sandals that were laced up her calves.

'Pinter?' Raff guessed.

'Raff, I assume?' Not bothering to attempt speaking French in any form, Pinter held his arms out. 'I am so happy to meet you.' He hugged Raff tightly before releasing him and pressing the champagne into his hands. He turned to the woman. 'This is Esther, my wife. I know, I know. I'm punching, but for some reason, she adores me.'

'Punching?' Raff was baffled. 'I'm very happy to meet you.' He kissed both her cheeks and stood aside to let them both in. 'We're in the garden and you're just in time for *Bouillabaisse.*'

'Oooh I love that. Fish stew, right?' Esther shrugged her arms out of her leather coat and hung it carefully over a chair. She was wearing a flimsy, black smock dress that hung off one shoulder. 'What a gorgeous place, Raff! Really, it's lovely. We've just checked into the Shangri-La

Hotel.' She let out a mock-gasp, 'which is off the charts, but Pinter, we really should get a house in Paris.'

Pinter rolled his eyes. 'Oh dear. Here she goes. This woman bankrupts me daily, Raff. I can't even tell you. If she had her way, we'd have places in Morocco, L.A., New York, Singapore…'

'Not Morocco, darling,' Esther said, flashing a set of perfect white teeth. 'It wasn't really my bag.'

'Sophie!' Pinter held his arms out again. 'I've missed you, my little apprentice.' He squeezed her.

'Oh, I've missed you too.' Sophie caught sight of Esther. 'Look at you! Where on earth did you get that tan… you look amazing.' They air-kissed.

'Fiji,' Esther said airily. 'Bikini shoot. Terribly long flight. And the food made my IBS flare up and I had a dodgy bum.'

'Sounds dreadful,' Sophie said, giggling as she caught Raff's eye.

'I'm definitely going to help you with dinner,' Pinter told Raff firmly,' because I am the *best* cook.'

He's not, Sophie mouthed at Raff.

'As soon as I have said hello to these delightful people in the garden,' Pinter continued, suavely moving outside. Esther followed him. 'Hello, hello! Sorry to barge in. Jo, Henri, very nice to meet you. *Enchanté*, yes? And who is this *fantastic* woman? Fifi, I can't tell you how happy I am to meet you. What fabulous shoes! Esther, come and look at this stunning example of French chic.'

'I'm right behind you, Pinter, you idiot,' Esther told him, swatting him on the arm.

Sophie nudged Raff as even Fifi started simpering in the face of Pinter's smooth feel-good charm and together they got the *Bouillabaisse* on the table.

'Wonderful,' Pinter said, diving into his bowl with some French bread. 'You must give me the recipe.'

'Don't bother,' Esther said, smiling broadly. 'He can't cook and he doesn't actually know where the kitchen is.'

Pinter shrugged good-naturedly. 'It's true, it's true. But Esther barely eats anyway and I only have to *look* at a cake to put on weight.' He regarded Fifi seriously. 'Honestly, inside this powerhouse of a perfect body, I am actually a fat little schoolboy.'

Fifi looked amused and confused at the same time.

'That's also true,' Esther laughed, giving him a kiss. 'Maybe we shouldn't get a place in Paris, Pints. You'd devour all the butter known to man.'

Pinter pulled a shocked face, then started laughing because he couldn't pretend for that long. 'Guilty,' he said, holding his hands in the air.

'You won't want a slice of almond frangipane with honeyed pistachios then,' Raff asked innocently.

'I will want *all* the slices,' Pinter said, meaning it. He guffawed and turned to Sophie as Raff disappeared indoor. 'Oh, I like him, Sophie. He's really great. He's a good guy but he looks like a bad guy. Handsome. But he's one of the best, I think.'

Sophie nodded. 'I know.'

'Is he the reason you left in the first place?' Pinter asked astutely.

'Yes,' Sophie replied, not seeing any point in lying about it now.

'Ok.' Pinter squeezed her shoulder. 'You need to tell me about this another time please.'

Sophie nodded.

'Because that man is very much in love with you. And you look just as besotted.'

Sophie bit her lip.

'But anyway, your mum is due home soon and that's amazing news,' Pinter said loudly as Raff returned with the frangipane tart.

Pinter gasped. 'Look at that. I'm in serious trouble now...'

As Raff started to cut into the tart, the doorbell rang again. He frowned.

'I'll go,' Coco offered, getting up. She opened the door and there was a pause.

'*Maman*,' she said quietly.

Raff's head snapped up. Estelle. No way.

Henri looked up, his expression distasteful.

'Raff!' Estelle wafted in wearing tight black jeans, an emerald-green shirt knotted at her waist and some spike-heeled black sandals. 'Oh, I'm sorry. I didn't mean to interrupt anything...'

Sophie swallowed. Estelle. Raff's ex. The woman who had turned up out of the blue all those years ago. With Coco in tow. The woman who had turned Sophie's life upside down, making her doubt everything and convinced her that she had to flee Paris, leaving Raff behind. The woman who had told her lies about Raff and made Sophie believe he was something he wasn't.

Sophie felt panicked. She wanted to run. She didn't want to overreact, but this was Estelle. Back again, in Raff's house.

'Sophie Marchant.' Estelle paused at the table. 'I didn't know you were back in Paris.'

'Just… just for a while,' Sophie managed. She felt a bit short of breath. Was she overreacting? She felt so threatened by this woman.

Raff shot a glance at her.

Seeing Sophie's distress, Pinter jumped to his feet. 'My name is Pinter,' he announced. 'I'm Sophie's friend and sort of her boss. And you are…?'

'I'm Estelle,' Estelle said, flicking her long, dark hair over her shoulder. 'I'm Coco's mother.'

Coco wrapped her arms around her body, suddenly looking vulnerable and childlike.

'A text would have been helpful,' Raff said.

'We've been texting a lot, as you know,' Estelle said, touching his arm. 'Just not today…'

Sophie looked at Raff, feeling her stomach tighten. Why hadn't he mentioned Estelle getting in touch? She felt nauseous suddenly, as though her *Bouillabaisse* might make a reappearance. It felt as though history was repeating itself somehow. But Sophie didn't want that to happen.

Raff looked at Sophie anxiously. Why hadn't he told her about Estelle getting in touch? And possibly turning up? Now he looked like a liar and he looked shady and he could see that Sophie looked upset. Rightly so.

God, what an idiot he'd been! He had been so desperate to put Estelle off of her visit and to protect Coco and Sophie from it, he'd made it worse. He stared at Estelle. Why had she announced to everyone that they had been texting? She must have done it on purpose. Raff fumed inwardly. Like he said, everywhere Estelle went, drama followed. It was the main reason Raff couldn't be around her long term. It was just too exhausting. And he hadn't helped himself by not mentioning to Sophie that Estelle might turn up... that she had been texting.

Fifi was fixing Estelle with a chilly stare and Sophie was surprised Estelle hadn't turned to ice on the spot.

Raff felt compelled to defend himself on the texting front, even though he knew it was potentially too late. 'Actually, you've been texting me a lot and I texted you back twice telling you it wasn't a good time for a visit,' he said tightly.

Estelle shrugged and helped herself to a glass of wine. 'I think you've sent a few more texts than that, Raff!' She let out a throaty chuckle.

Fifi made a disapproving noise and pursed her lips primly. Jo was gaping like a goldfish and she pulled a 'what a bitch!' face at Sophie.

Frustrated, Raff looked away from Estelle deliberately and turned back to Sophie. He genuinely didn't care what Estelle did anymore. He only cared about Sophie. He shook his head at her to try and make her understand that this wasn't what it seemed.

'Well, isn't this lovely,' Pinter said, sitting down and putting his arm firmly around Sophie's shoulders. Esther gave her a supportive smile from the opposite side of the table too.

Sophie felt immensely grateful for Pinter's overt loyalty. She also felt like slapping Raff. Why was it always so complicated with him?

'I think it's time we left,' Fifi said in an imperious voice.

Sophie got up. 'Yes.' She squeezed Pinter's arm to thank him for his support.

'Don't leave on my account,' Estelle said innocently, throwing herself into an empty chair.

Sophie gave her as lovely a smile as she could muster in the circumstances. 'I'm not. It's just late and I need to get my friend and grandmother home.'

'Well, it's lovely to see you again, Sophie.' Estelle smiled and sipped her wine languorously.

Jo and Fifi got to their feet and started to gather their things. Esther sighed and valiantly started to engage Estelle in 'model' chat, throwing Pinter a meaningful glance as if to say that he owed her for taking one for the team. He inclined his head and followed Sophie out into the hallway.

'Thank you for dinner,' Sophie was saying to Raff formally. God. Perhaps she should shake his hand as well. She turned to Coco and hugged her.

'Are you ok?' she whispered.

'I don't know,' Coco whispered back. 'Are you?'

'I don't know,' Sophie whispered back. She let go of Coco who gave her a watery smile and hesitated before reluctantly heading back towards the garden.

Sophie felt a warm hand on her arm.

It was Raff. 'Sophie, it's not… I'm so…'

Sophie shook her head, not remotely in the mood to discuss anything. 'I'll see you tomorrow at the shop.'

'Ok.' Raff felt totally deflated, but he understood. He hugged Jo goodbye and politely kissed Fifi's powdered cheeks. As he closed the door behind them, Raff heard Pinter behind him and turned with a rueful expression.

'*Merde*,' he said.

'*Merde* indeed,' Pinter agreed heartily, giving him a sympathetic smile.

'She hates me.'

'She thinks she has reason to.'

Raff raked a hand through his hair. 'I'm an idiot.'

'You are. But only for not mentioning the texts. Men – we're so stupid with things like that. However, I don't think you're a bad guy.' Pinter considered him. 'And I don't think you're remotely interested in that trouble-making minx sitting in your garden.'

Raff wasn't sure what a 'minx' was, but he got Pinter's drift. 'I couldn't be any less interested in her. She's just Coco's mum and she's a nightmare every time she turns up. Coco goes off the rails a bit… I wanted to protect Sophie too.' He rubbed his chin worriedly. 'It was her arriving out of the blue with Coco all those years ago that sent Sophie spiralling last time. We were just getting things back on track…'

Pinter nodded gravely. 'Yes, I can see that. I know her very well because I've worked with her for years and we're good friends. I've never seen Sophie like this before. Never. I think she loves you very much.'

'You do?' Raff lifted his eyes hopefully. 'I don't know… this ex of hers…'

'Ryan?' Pinter scoffed. 'You don't need to worry about him! He's an absolute woopsie.' He saw Raff's puzzled expression and followed up. 'Oh, I see. Right. He's a… wet blanket. Oh God. He's… look, just don't worry about him. He's not right for her. I think he makes her feel safe and all of that, but at the end of the day, he still let her down. I can't see her ever going back with him.'

Raff sighed. 'Ok. I trust you. I don't know why, but I do.'

'You should.' Pinter grinned then his expression became sober. 'Because I think you're right for her.'

'How? Why?' Raff cringed. *Sacré bleu.* He was asking for reassurance from a man he had only just met.

'She left Paris because of how deeply she felt about you,' Pinter pointed out reasonably, unruffled by Raff's obvious need for validation. 'She stayed away from Paris because of how she felt about you. And she came back to find her mum, but in the meantime, she found you again. And I think you've both been lost since you... lost each other. Am I making any sense?'

'More than you know,' Raff told him.

'So.' Pinter clasped his hands together. 'The issue we have now is this. Well, we have two issues.' He counted them on his fingers. 'One, we need to get Mariele back and find out what's been going on there. And two... two... we need to get you two back together.'

'I really, *really* like you,' Raff said, breaking into a smile.

'Everyone likes me,' Pinter said affably, slinging his arm around Raff's shoulders. 'It's a thing. And I really like you too. Now. Let's go and rescue my darling wife from the claws of that messed up *femme fatale* out there and as for Sophie... well, you're just going to have to leave her to me.'

Raff sighed. 'I think you're probably the best chance I have.'

Pinter patted his shoulder. 'That's right, young Raphael. I'm your guardian fricking angel and you're just going to have to let me do my thing.'

Raff didn't think he had much choice, but he felt strangely comforted. Both by Pinter's firm grip on his shoulder and by his endearing overconfidence. Because right now, it was all Raff had.

Chapter Twenty-One

'Are you sure you're ok?' Jo said for the sixth time.

'Yes,' Sophie said firmly. For the sixth time. They were sitting in the kitchen at the house, nibbling on croissants. 'What else can I say to convince you?'

'I don't know.' Jo looked unsettled. She put her croissant down. 'God, those almond ones are just divine. I mean that… it's just so annoying because we had such a lovely weekend together – it was literally perfect – and then Estelle turned up and it all feels really… weird.'

Sophie sipped her coffee. Jo wasn't wrong. That wonderful feeling she'd had about Raff seemed oddly tainted now. It had felt pure and as though it was just the two of them falling again and now Sophie realised that Estelle had been lurking in the background the whole time, and she felt like such a strong… damaging presence.

'I detest women like that,' Fifi said, joining them at the table. She was wearing the same, stark black dress she had been wearing the other day, but with smart, patent beige pumps and a beige and red scarf knotted at her neck. 'The Estelles of this world just want to cause trouble. She probably doesn't even want Raff back.'

Sophie frowned. She wasn't so sure about that. Estelle had come back for a reason. She didn't know what it was, but she didn't think it was a coincidence that Estelle had turned up at such a crucial time. And for what other reason could she be here unless it was to do with Raff? She poured her grandmother a coffee.

'Thank you.' Fifi didn't sip it yet; she preferred her coffee tepid. 'Mark my words, Sophie. Estelle wants drama. Do not give it to her.'

'She's right,' Jo agreed. 'We all know women like that, Soph. Don't let her ruin things.'

'Exactly,' Fifi said, attempting to drink her coffee then thinking better of it.

Jo preened herself at being on the same page as the woman she was terrified of.

'It's just him not saying anything about those texts,' Sophie mused. 'It just looks shady, doesn't it? Even if it isn't.'

'There could be any number of reasons for that,' Fifi dismissed. 'Speak to Raff and see what he has to say for himself. Men can be so silly, *ma chérie*. Silliness doesn't make him a liar. I suspect he was hoping she wouldn't turn up at all. Perhaps she promises to come and doesn't.'

Sophie nodded. That made sense.

'And he may not have wanted to – how do you say it? – "Rock the boat", when things were going so well between you two. Because they are going well, *oui*?'

'*Oui*.' Sophie shrugged. She wasn't sure what was going on now. Raff had sent a few texts last night apologising, but Sophie just felt as though she didn't trust him at the moment.

'Right.' Jo stood up. 'I have to go, otherwise I'll miss my flight. I'm all packed and ready; my bags are by the door.'

'I'm going to miss you so much. You're leaving at such a bad time,' Sophie said, pulling a sad face. 'I think that's your taxi outside.'

'I know. But I'm needed in the office tomorrow... three big properties coming up for sale.' Jo also pulled a sad face. 'I hate leaving my bestie at a time like this.'

'Goodbye,' Fifi said, getting up and placing her hands upon Jo's shoulders. She kissed both of her cheeks. 'It was lovely to meet you. Stop being so scared of things.'

'Erm... I'm not scared of "things",' Jo admitted. 'Just... you.'

Fifi beamed. 'Oh I love it when people are scared of me. I'm just a pussycat underneath, I can assure you.'

'She's really not,' Sophie said under her breath as she showed Jo to the door.

'I know,' Jo said fervently. She hugged Sophie. 'Listen. I don't think Raff meant anything by not telling you about Estelle. I think he was trying to protect you. Don't lose this all over again over something so silly.'

'I don't know.' Sophie shrugged. 'It just feels crap and I need to be able to trust him, you know?'

'I think you can. Don't lose him again, Soph.' Jo grabbed her bags. 'He's too gorgeous. Inside and out. Stay in touch – I want an hour by hour account.'

Sophie saw Jo into her taxi and waved her off. She was due to work in the shop now, but she felt really awkward towards Raff after last night. Wandering back through the house, she found Fifi tidying the sitting room.

'Are you alright, *ma chérie*?'

'I'm ok.' Sophie threw herself onto a sofa. 'I just want mum to come home. I want to know where she's been and if she's ok.'

'Me too,' Fifi said, efficiently plumping the cushions around her. 'She has given us a date and we are going to get the shop ready for her arrival.' She straightened up. 'How about we have a little reopening to unveil all the changes?'

Sophie nodded. 'Sounds good.'

'Let's go and speak to Raff about it.' Fifi held her hand out and pulled Sophie up. 'And then we can clear the air between you two.'

'You can't just fix everything, Grand-*mère*,' Sophie grumbled. 'Just because you managed to get Henri outside, it doesn't mean you can fix everything.'

Fifi put her chin in the air. 'I don't see why not. But thank you for reminding me. I'll get in touch with Ruben and he and I can go over there and tackle that garden. I mean, not me personally, you understand, but still.'

'Of course not you personally, *Grand-mère*. Not unless Chanel do gardening gloves.'

'I've never looked,' Fifi said with a mischievous smile, 'but I like the idea. Henri is a lovely man. I know it's a way off yet, but my friend Margaux is single and I think she could be perfect for Henri...'

'*Grand-mère!* You can't interfere in people's lives like that.'

Fifi looked hurt. 'I'm not interfering. I'm *matchmaking*. It's different.' She led the way into the macaron shop. It was extremely busy, but Raff had the girl who covered for them working with him as well.

'Raff. A moment?' Fifi smiled brightly.

Raff looked up and caught Sophie's eye. He put down what he was doing and came over.

'Hey.'

'Hey,' she said back. He looked tired, as though he hadn't slept all night and she felt bad for him. And then she wondered if he had been up all night with Estelle and felt furious and not remotely compassionate.

Sophie caught herself. She wasn't sure if she was losing the plot about Estelle or not.

Fifi cut in quickly. 'I was thinking… how about we have a little launch for the shop?'

'A launch?' Raff frowned.

'Yes. The shop is closing tomorrow for a few days so that all the paintwork and internal changes can take place,' Fifi pointed out, 'and to get the new sign up. We could put covers over the shop and heavily advertise the reopening. A party to celebrate the new and improved "Mariele's Macarons". My treat, of course.'

Raff shrugged. 'That sounds like a lovely idea. Can we get it organised in time?'

'I can,' Fifi said confidently. 'I'll treat it as a little project and I've got excellent contacts.'

'What do you think, Sophie?' Raff turned to Sophie.

'Same as you,' she said non-committally, avoiding his eyes. 'It sounds like a lovely idea. I'm not sure what's needed and I'm going to be tied up with the wedding tomorrow, but I'm happy to help aside from that.'

Fifi watched both of them beadily. 'Good. That's decided then. We'll have a relaunch on Saturday. We'll text Mariele and let her know, and maybe she can time her arrival with that.'

Sophie caught her breath. She wasn't convinced her mum was going to be back at the weekend. She didn't know why, but it didn't seem to ring true for some reason. Yesterday she had tried to find the photo of the man with the inscription on the back and couldn't, so had decided that maybe it was just someone her mum used to know, but that he was nothing to do with her disappearance. But the likelihood of her turning up for the reopening of the shop? It was a dream Sophie couldn't allow herself to focus upon. She didn't dare.

Her phone beeped and she checked it. It was Pinter asking to meet her.

'I'd better go,' she said. 'Pinter wants to see me about wedding stuff.'

Raff suddenly looked upbeat for some reason. 'Ok. I'll take care of things here. The new bags have arrived, but I can show you another time.'

'Right.'

Fifi let out an audible sigh. 'You two…' she said. 'Ok, *bon*. Sophie, you go and do the wedding stuff; Raff, you run the shop. I'll arrange for caterers and balloons and make sure all the work is done here. And I'll get my friend Ruben over to your house to help Henri with the garden.'

'I'll text mum about the opening. And Eloise,' Sophie added.

'Wonderful.' Fifi clapped her hands. 'Let's go!'

Raff stared at Sophie and Sophie stared at Raff. And then they went their separate ways.

–

'So. How are you feeling?' Pinter asked.

Sophie raised an eyebrow. 'How do you think?'

'I would imagine… not great.' Pinter poured out two glasses of a crisp Sancerre. 'And I wish you could teach me to do that one eyebrow thing.'

'It's a gift.'

Pinter rolled his eyes.

They were sitting in a picturesque bar in one of the famous cobbled streets of Montmartre. They were on a slight slope and the cafe was drenched in sunshine. The magnificent Sacre-Coeur sat to the side of them, looking even brighter in the brilliant sunshine. It was a phenomenal view and tourists bustled past them, chattering and taking photos. Even though Montmartre was set on a hill and away from the heart of Paris, it still felt as though they were right in the thick of things.

'Where's Esther?'

'Primping herself in earnest of course,' Pinter said. 'Anyone would think it was Esther who was getting married, honestly. Do you remember our wedding, Soph?'

'I do. It was stunning. Magazine-worthy.'

'Well, I put my foot down about that. And I don't think Esther has ever forgiven me.' Pinter ordered another bottle of wine. 'But anyway. Today is about hair, nails, massages and lashes. And probably some other lady things I'm not privy too.'

Sophie smiled. She loved Pinter and Esther's relationship. It made her heart feel rather heavy today, but she aspired to their happiness. 'I feel as though I need to book myself into a salon now. Even though I'm there to photograph, not as a guest.'

'You're both,' Pinter protested. 'Esther's sister, Savannah, loves you.'

'I'll be working,' Sophie said firmly. 'I won't sit down and eat or anything. I think they want a few photos on the dancefloor in the evening, don't they?'

'God, probably,' Pinter sighed. 'Savannah is even more high-maintenance than Esther.'

'That's fine. It's her wedding day. She can do what she likes… be a diva, whatever.'

Pinter guffawed. 'Savannah is *always* a diva. No, seriously, it should be a great day tomorrow. I'm looking forward to it.'

'Me too.' Sophie sipped her wine. She didn't want a hangover tomorrow, but at the same time, she really needed a drink today.

Pinter took the liberty of ordering some pâté and French bread. 'Oooh I fancy some *escargots* too. Do you eat snails, Soph? You do? Esther freaks out if I order them.' He did so gleefully and rubbed his hands together. 'How exciting!'

'I love how easily pleased you are,' Sophie commented with a grin. 'A plate of snails and anyone would think you've won the lottery. They're not my favourite thing; but I'll share a plate with you. By the way look at this message from my mum about the launch.'

Pinter read it.

> *Chérie, that sounds wonderful. I hope I can be there. I can't tell you how proud I am that you have done all of this without me and that you have grown into such a confident, intelligent woman. I hope Raff has helped with all the work and that Fifi isn't being too bossy. I love you very much and can't wait to see you. Xxx.*

'Lovely. Those messages are very eloquent.'

'Yes.' Sophie frowned at it. All of the messages were eloquent. Beautifully worded and spoken from the heart.

Very open, too. Which was how her mum was. Kind of. But also not. Hmmm…

'Show me your photos of Paris,' Pinter said.

Sophie produced them and sat drinking her wine while Pinter leafed through them.

'Exquisite,' he ruminated. 'Really. I love both the colour, and the black and white ones. And you've found some interesting new angles, which is hard to do when anything has been photographed as much as these monuments have.'

'Thank you.'

'And the other thing that really shows is how much you love this place.'

Sophie picked up a photograph of Notre-Dame. 'How so?'

'You won't be able to spot it,' Pinter said. 'It's just something I always notice with photographs. It's like… someone putting love into cooking. Do you know what I mean? Someone can be a good technical cook, but put nothing of themselves into the food.'

'Y-es…'

'Whereas someone else can flood that recipe with everything they have. Put their heart and soul into it, so much care and attention that you can taste it.'

Sophie propped her sunglasses on the top of her head. 'That's all very flowery, Pinter. And I kind of get where you're coming from. But I don't see how my photos show how much I love Paris.'

'Then you'll have to take my word for it, Sophie. Because I can always tell when you love something you photograph. It leaps out of the image – like an expression on someone's face. It's plain for me to see, at any rate.'

He carefully laid a black and white photograph of Raff concentrating on making a batch of macarons on the top of the pile.

Sophie blushed and said nothing.

'So what else is new?' Pinter asked with an innocent expression.

Sophie raised her eyebrow again, partly to make him jealous. 'Stop it, Pint. You know what's new. And if you have something to say about it, I'd rather you just said it.'

Pinter tore up a piece of fresh French bread that had just arrived. 'Still warm. Divine. Fair enough. Ok, well. I wanted to speak to you about Raff.'

'What about him?' Sophie took a gulp of wine. She needed it.

'I know you're cross with him about that whole Estelle thing, but…'

'Only because he didn't mention it,' she interrupted. 'Because now it looks shady. And I hate anything shady.'

Pinter swallowed a chunk of bread. 'Who doesn't? But you must know that Estelle is a troublemaker. She has it written all over her. I think Raff was doing his best to deter her from coming and hoped she wouldn't.'

'He still should have mentioned it' – Sophie shrugged – 'in the interests of honesty.'

'Yes, indeed. But I think he was hoping she would stay away,' Pinter explained earnestly, 'which is stupid, but it's what we men do: bury our heads in the sand a tad. He did say that Coco goes off the rails when her mum turns up. Ravishing girl, isn't she?'

'She's lovely,' Sophie agreed, feeling a spark of interest. 'What did he mean about Coco going off the rails?'

'I'm not sure. This pâté looks good. Try some.' Pinter smeared a dollop onto a hunk of French bread. 'Get your chops around that. She changed though, didn't she, when Estelle turned up. Even I noticed that and I'm a mere man.'

Sophie munched on the pâté. 'God, that is good. I suppose she did, yes, thinking about it. She seemed… more vulnerable, somehow.'

'Exactly that. She suddenly looked younger and anxious.' Pinter patted his stomach. 'I don't know how I stay so trim. I'll have to find space for the snails as well. And fit into my suit tomorrow.'

'You stay trim because you work out quite a bit,' Sophie told him distractedly. Pinter was right. Coco had changed when Estelle turned up. And she had no idea what that meant exactly, but it meant that Estelle's presence definitely caused drama or, at the very least, change.

Sophie supposed that Raff's worry over Coco could have caused him to try and deter Estelle's visit, but she still didn't understand why he hadn't mentioned it to her. He must know that the whole subject of Estelle was touchy because of last time.

'Will you tell me what happened when you left Paris last time?' Pinter asked gently. 'No judgement.'

'Ok.' Sophie took a deep breath. She hadn't really talked about leaving Paris to anyone much before. Her mum briefly, Eloise a little. Jo had been a shoulder to cry on. She started hesitantly and then got more into her stride. She was brutally honest with Pinter about everything. Every single detail. How she had felt about Raff, what they had, how she'd seen their future. And finally what had happened after Estelle had turned up.

'Do you understand?' Sophie asked Pinter solemnly. 'I was so in love with him. And I mean, totally and utterly, head over heels, besotted, blindly and desperately. Estelle turned up with Coco, out of the blue. And it knocked me for six.'

'Of course,' Pinter said, struggling to pluck a snail from its shell. 'But why didn't you trust Raff when he said he knew nothing about Coco? Why were you so quick to doubt him?'

Sophie looked away. 'Because Estelle told me Raff knew. She told me he knew all about Coco and that he'd shirked his responsibilities.'

Pinter shook his head. 'She's not a nice girl. Very messed up. Oh, the garlic butter in these! But still. I don't understand and I apologise, but you know Raff. You *knew* him. You must have known he wasn't that kind of man. He's decent and good; he's not the kind to run away from something like that.'

Sophie stared at him. 'It wasn't just Estelle who said that Raff knew. Coco said the same thing.'

'Coco?' Pinter paused with a snail halfway to his mouth. 'What did she say?'

'What her mum said. That daddy knew about her and didn't want her.'

Pinter recoiled. 'Oh that's bad. That's really, really bad. And super-manipulative.'

Sophie nodded tiredly. 'This is the thing. It was either… accuse a little girl of lying or just get out of there, Pinter. I had no idea what was going on between Raff and Estelle, but I didn't want any part of the drama. Either Estelle was brainwashing Coco into believing that her dad

264

rejected her – or maybe Coco genuinely believed it – or Raff was lying.'

'So you pulled out of it and left them all to it.'

'Yes.' Sophie took a gulp of wine. 'Rightly or wrongly, I didn't want to get into a massive row over a child's word. I didn't want to put her on the spot and accuse her of lying. But equally, I suppose I had doubts about Raff as well. Not because of who he is as such, but because of his involvement with someone like Estelle, who would have always continued to pop up in our lives because of Coco.'

'So you didn't know that Estelle had left Coco with Raff?' Pinter asked. 'That she had absconded shortly after that, dumping her own daughter on him?'

Sophie shook her head. 'He tried to get in touch with me, but I wouldn't speak to him.' Tears sprang into her eyes. 'I feel awful about it, but I just couldn't get my head around it. Maybe I was just jealous, Pinter. *I* wanted to have a baby with Raff. Further down the line, obviously, but that's what I wanted. I felt devastated that he'd shared that with anyone else and I know that must sound really pathetic, but it's honestly how I felt at the time.'

Pinter topped up their wine. 'No, I get that. I'd feel like that about Esther. I don't even know if we'll have children because it suits us not to right now, but I'd hate it if she'd done that with someone else. It's… too intimate a bond, isn't it? It's sharing something that no one else can be a part of.'

'That's it, Pinter! That's exactly it. Throw into the mix Estelle being utterly gorgeous and telling me Raff was a bad father, letting her down when she needed him the most… and a little girl giving me the big eyes and saying her daddy knew about her and didn't want her…'

'It was too much.' Pinter put his hand over hers kindly. 'Don't beat yourself up, darling. That's a horrible situation. Does Raff know all the details?'

Sophie shook her head and wiped her eyes. 'Not exactly. I've said a few things, but not everything.'

'And what about Coco? Have you mentioned what she said to you?'

'No. She told me recently Raff didn't know anything about her until they turned up that time and I expected her to say something about it to Raff then. And when she didn't, I just left it. I didn't want to start accusing her or anything when we were getting on so well.'

'Odd though. Ah well, I'm sure it will all become clear soon enough.'

Sophie sipped her wine. 'I don't know where I stand with Raff. I don't know what any of it means, Pinter. My whole life is so confusing right now. Mum, Raff, Estelle, Coco. Ryan, even...'

'You two need to talk,' Pinter said decisively. 'You and Raff. You need to be honest and talk about all of this stuff. He would understand that, I'm sure.' He leant forward. 'I think you love this man very much, Sophie, and I will be very upset if you two can't sort this out. Because he loves you and would do anything not to lose you.'

'How do you know that?' Sophie felt like crying all over again.

'Because I bloody well do, alright? Because his eyes say so rather than his words... because of the way he is around you. Because we both know that Estelle is behind all that awful stuff all those years ago and that she must have convinced Coco that Raff deserted them and that's why Coco was probably primed to say those things.'

Pinter moved the snails out of the way. 'Sophie, this is worth saving. Do not let it get away from you again.'

Sophie put her face in her hands. 'I don't want to let it go again; I promise you. But I'm so scared. Scared of trusting him again and it all going wrong. Scared that Estelle might have been telling the truth, even though deep down I do know that she wasn't. Scared that she has some sort of weird hold over Raff and that he might think he should be with her and not me.'

'Well, that last one is madness,' Pinter said dismissively. 'Raff doesn't have any feelings whatsoever for Estelle; I can assure you of that. That's one thing I can say with good authority because I'm a man and I can spot the signs and we are all very stupid creatures, but I know my own species.'

Sophie couldn't help smiling.

'You're smiling and crying at the same time… does that mean a rainbow appears? Or a unicorn trots up?' Pinter laughed. 'Listen. The only bond those two people have is Coco. And Coco lives with her father and loves him very much. And I think she couldn't be happier that you two have fallen in love all over again.'

Sophie breathed out slowly. 'God. You make it all sound so simple.' Her phone beeped and she frowned at it.

'Raff?'

'Ryan. Voice message.'

'Play it,' Pinter insisted. 'Let's see what that silly sod has to say for himself.'

Sophie obliged.

Hey, Sophie. How are you? Listen, I've been thinking about everything since I've been in Dubai

and although it's great here, something is missing.
It's you.

Pinter pulled a dramatic 'I'm going to be sick' face. Sophie ignored him.

I'm missing you too much. It was a mistake coming
here. I think we should talk. And I think we need
to talk about our future. About the plans we had.

There was a pause.

I still have the engagement ring, Soph. And I'm
willing to come to Paris with it and make it official.
If I don't hear back from you by tomorrow night,
I'll assume you want me to come and see you.
With the ring.

The message ended.

'*Mon Dieu*,' Pinter said flatly.

'I was thinking more "bloody hell",' Sophie said.

'That's a curveball. Or is it?'

'I really don't know.'

Sophie downed her glass of wine. What the hell was she supposed to do with that?

Chapter Twenty-Two

Sophie juggled her camera and a smoked salmon and horseradish cream canapé, almost dropping both. She hadn't eaten all day and she had to snack on something.

'How's it going?' Esther asked, looking glorious in a bright yellow midi dress, black sandals and a black fascinator pinned to the side of her head.

'Very well, I think,' Sophie said. She popped the canapé in her mouth whole and flicked through some photos on her camera for Esther to see.

'Oooh, they're gorgeous!' Esther looked delighted. 'Oh, Sophie, Savannah will be so pleased. Those ones of her getting ready are beautiful.'

'The dress is breathtaking,' Sophie commented. 'It was easy to get beautiful shots.'

'If rather inappropriate.' Esther pulled a face. 'Savannah doesn't observe the boobs or legs rule, does she?'

Sophie grinned. She didn't, but she looked fabulous, so who cared? Her dress plunged at the front, making the most of her cleavage and it was cut short at the front, showing off her knees and just above. But she had the most fantastic figure and she looked incredible, so Sophie was fairly sure everyone would forgive her for having lots of tanned flesh on display.

'If you've got it flaunt it, I say.'

Esther hurried over to Savannah to update her about her photographs.

Sophie was pleased with her photographs from the day so far. And it was an extremely good distraction from Raff. And Ryan. Sophie's stomach flipped over at the thought of Ryan's message the day before. What on earth had he been thinking? Why had he suddenly changed his mind and what had made him think she wanted him to hotfoot it over to Paris with the engagement ring he had refused to give her all those months ago? It would be laughable if it wasn't so ridiculous. Sophie had put it out of her mind and focused on the wedding.

She had got up at the crack of dawn to get half ready and then she had got herself over to the Shangri-La Hotel. She had been present while Savannah and her six brides-maids got ready, taking some candid shots of them with their hair in rollers and while the make-up artist worked on them. She had managed to get some cute shots of all of their shoes and their bouquets, and some black and white ones of the youngest bridesmaid who was very photogenic and loved posing in her frothy peach-coloured dress. Savannah was as beautiful as Esther, also a model and well versed in posing and offering her best angles. In short, she had been a joy to photograph and she made Sophie's job feel easy.

Sophie had then taken some photos of Mason, Savannah's handsome husband-to-be with his best man and ushers, although they had been rather more inter-ested in getting down to the bar than posing for wedding photos. Mason had handed out some money clips to his ushers and Sophie had then left them to it so she could quickly get ready in Savannah's room. Throwing on a one-shouldered silk dress in a vivid shade of purple, she had teamed it with nude sandals, and a nude clutch that she had left with Esther somewhere.

The ceremony had been short but emotional, with some beautiful vows from both sides. Savannah and Mason had sat upon chairs in a pagoda covered in white roses and adorned with huge white candles in glass jars. Savannah had cried but not enough to smudge her make-up, and Mason had endearingly looked rather choked up as well. Sophie had taken even more photographs of the happy couple, and now canapés and champagne were doing the rounds and she was giving them some space without a camera shoved in their faces for a while.

'Have you messaged Ryan yet telling him not to come?' Pinter said in her ear.

She swatted him away. 'No, not yet. But not because I don't want to, but because I haven't got time.'

Pinter looked unimpressed. 'I would have sent a text last night personally. Do you want him turning up like a wet weekend brandishing a diamond in your face?'

'Of course not. And he's not a wet weekend.'

'Ok then. He's a plonker.'

Sophie nudged him. 'We get it. You're team Raff all the way and you want to put Ryan on the subs bench.'

'I don't even want him on the subs bench if I'm honest,' Pinter said directly. 'But I'm worried you do.'

'What? Don't be daft.'

'So text him.'

'I will. Where's my phone?'

'Esther has it.' Pinter looked around vaguely. 'But I don't know where she is or where your bag is. But I'll hunt it down for you. The last thing you want is Ryan turning up when you're trying to sort things out with Raff. He's coming here later by the way.'

'Of course he is. You're head of the Raphael fan club.'

'Does he have one?' Pinter said, playing along. 'If so, I'll become a fully paid-up member. Don't be jealous darling; I love you more.'

Sophie let out a breath of frustration. She didn't want to deal with any of it: Ryan, Raff, Estelle.

'Lovely dress, by the way,' Pinter commented. 'Super hot.'

'Thanks. Good suit. Glad you got into it after all those snails and French bread.'

'Naughty, naughty, darling.' Pinter kissed her cheek. 'I think it's time for food. I'll find your phone as soon as I can.'

Sophie ignored him and prepped her camera.

–

A few hours later, the guests were being entertained by a jazz trio as the day turned into night and Sophie was having a much-needed sit down with a glass of champagne in a quiet corner of the *Grand Salon*. The guests had dined already and Sophie had taken lots of photographs; she had then used up an entire memory card to capture the bride and groom on *La Terrace Eiffel*, because it was such a beautiful sunny day and there was just so much to photograph. The views were gorgeous, the couple were gorgeous and Sophie's job had been incredibly easy and fun. She would pop out onto the terrace again shortly as the lights came on in the heart of Paris and she wanted to capture the Eiffel Tower at night as well as during the day.

Sophie tucked into a four-course meal prepared by the Michelin-starred chef at the hotel, amazed at the quality of the food. An exquisite smoked duck starter followed by sea bass with scallops, prawns and a wonderful sauce Sophie suspected had taken days to create. Some tender pink lamb with a light redcurrant sauce and tiny garlicky balls of fondant-style potato that looked as though they had been individually crafted by hand, accompanied by fresh vegetables, each with its own delicate, unique flavours.

Savannah had chosen the *Nutcracker* as her dessert, which was a mouth-watering shortbread chocolate biscuit with praline, mousse and chocolate icing, as well as a majestic orange-blossom-flavoured Croquembouche as the wedding cake.

Sophie sipped her champagne. It had been a beautiful wedding and one that Sophie would have been happy to attend simply as a guest as well. The photography had been straightforward due to both the bride and groom being very easy on the eye —which made more of a difference than people might think in terms of getting fewer shots but all of them being worthy of choice — but also because the surroundings were so stunning. Sophie hadn't had to work hard to find good angles or the best lighting; every angle was fantastic and all of the lighting was flattering. And the whole wedding had been wonderfully distracting. Sophie was aware that she needed to check her phone soon and get back to Ryan, but for now she was still focused on work.

Finishing her food, Sophie switched to a different lens and went outside to get some more shots as the lights were coming on in the city. Guests gasped as the Eiffel

Tower suddenly lit up with dazzling yellow-hued lights, and Sophie got busy with her camera. There was the cutting of the cake – not that they actually cut the gigantic Croquembouche, just posed with it – and the first dance, all of which Sophie captured. As a hip young DJ took over from the jaunty jazz trio, guests started to hit the dance-floor, especially the ones who had drunk more champagne from others. Sophie discreetly moved around the dance floor taking some candid shots. She made sure she had plenty of Savannah and Mason dancing together and with their bridesmaids and ushers respectively.

'Do you have everything?' Pinter asked as she threw herself into a chair.

'I hope so,' Sophie said, letting out a breath. 'I'm shattered!'

'I'm not surprised. You worked really hard today. I finally found your bag. It had somehow ended up in our room upstairs.'

Sophie rested her camera on a nearby table then thought better of it and put it in her camera bag. Handing it to a member of staff, she turned back to Pinter. 'Thanks. I wouldn't have been able to check it until now anyway.' She pulled her phone out and frowned.

'What's up?' Pinter grabbed two glasses of champagne from a passing waiter and led Sophie outside onto a quiet corner of the terrace.

'I have a few missed calls from Coco. I hope she's ok.'

Pinter looked apprehensive. 'Do you think she's… gone off the rails, or however Raff described it?'

'I don't know,' Sophie said, already dialling her. 'No answer. God. I'll try again.'

'Leave a message,' Pinter urged. 'Has Raff called?'

Sophie shook her head. There was no answer again so she left a short message saying she was worried, asking Coco to call her as soon as possible.

'Maybe it's nothing to be concerned about,' Pinter said, not sounding as though he believed a word he was saying. 'Oh look, Raff is here.'

'With Estelle,' Sophie said, her heart sinking. Estelle looked stunning in an emerald-green dress that made the most of her colouring and put Savannah's cleavage and leg faux pas to shame. Sophie stared at her. Despite Pinter doing a very good job of convincing her that Raff wasn't interested in Estelle, Sophie still struggled to believe it. Seeing Estelle again made her want to panic and run, just like she had the last time.

How many more times would Estelle be coming back to visit? Surely this wouldn't be the only time? Sophie wasn't sure she was staying in Paris yet, but the thought of Estelle being a constant visitor filled her with dread.

'Yes, that's weird that they've arrived together,' Pinter said, his brow furrowed.

'I just don't think she will ever go away, Pinter,' Sophie said glumly. 'And I'm not giving up or giving in or running away. But it doesn't feel good, is all I'm saying.'

'I get it,' Pinter nodded. 'But don't you let her ruin everything, Sophie,' he warned. 'Because it's happened once before and you can't let it happen again. Trust Raff. Trust him.'

Sophie gritted her teeth. She knew that Pinter was right. But Estelle had this ability to unnerve her. It might be the negative association she brought with her: five years ago, Estelle's presence had destroyed Sophie's world. Or had Sophie allowed Estelle to do that, now that she thought about it? Was it not about Sophie's reaction to Estelle as much as about Estelle's herself? Sophie suddenly felt stronger.

Raff spotted them and made a beeline in their direction. 'Hey.' He looked somewhat put out, but his face softened when he was next to Sophie. 'How did it go today? You look amazing. And you, Pinter. Very smart.'

'Have you heard from Coco?' Sophie and Pinter said in unison.

'No. Why?' Raff immediately looked panicked and took out his phone.

'What's going on?' Estelle said.

'We're worried about Coco,' Sophie said shortly. 'It might be nothing, but she's left a few messages for me and she's not answering her phone now.'

'I'm supposed to be meeting her for dinner,' Estelle said, pouting.

'That's why Estelle is here with me,' Raff explained swiftly. 'We haven't come here together; she's waiting for Coco.' He called Coco. 'No answer.'

'Can you think of anywhere she might be?' Pinter asked, going into practical mode. 'She might not be missing as such – just with friends or something.'

'Why wouldn't she answer her phone?' Raff turned to Estelle. 'She did this last time you were here.'

Estelle looked petulant. 'I don't know why you're blaming me.'

Raff looked furious. 'I don't want Coco's life disrupted. She's happy, Estelle. We have a good life here in Paris. She's the model kid. And the only time she does stuff like this is when you turn up. I don't know why, but it happens every time.'

Pinter exchanged a glance with Sophie. Sophie felt her heart thumping in her chest. For some reason, this felt like a significant moment.

'I'm her mother,' Estelle said angrily.

'You're her biological mother,' Raff snapped. 'And that's about it. You left her with your mum until your mum said she couldn't look after her any more and then you realised you had no other choice but to let me know for the first time since Coco was born that I was her dad so you could leave her with me all those years ago.'

'I-I...'

'That's exactly how it happened,' Raff said firmly. 'You know it and I know it. You've never wanted to be a mother to Coco. You turn up when you please and upset her. She's the most balanced, most amazing kid you could ever meet. Until you get here.'

Pinter slipped his arm around Sophie's shoulder and squeezed it, knowing she would be devastated to hear what she was hearing. Sophie felt a stab of fury at hearing proof that Estelle had deliberately lied to her.

Estelle met her eyes warily.

'You told me Raff knew about Coco,' Sophie blurted out before she could stop herself. 'You told me he was a bad father and that he didn't want to know his own daughter.'

Raff gaped. 'What? *What?* You said that to her?' He clutched his hair. 'Oh Sophie. No wonder you left. No wonder you thought I was a waste of space. Why didn't you tell me? We could have sorted this out so quickly. It all makes sense now.' He turned back to Estelle. 'Can you see what you've done? What you've caused?'

'I didn't exactly say that—' Estelle started.

Pinter let go of Sophie's shoulder and cut in. 'I think it's time you stopped telling lies and put Coco first.' He turned to Raff. 'Let's leave all of this for another time and focus on Coco. Why don't you go and wait in the restaurant for her?' he said to Estelle, his expression telling her exactly what he thought of her. 'Raff, Sophie, go look for her. Leave me Coco's number and I'll keep calling.'

Raff was galvanised into action. 'Ok. Estelle, do as Pinter says. Sophie, let's go.'

Looking furious, Estelle turned on her heels. Raff grabbed Sophie's hand and they walked quickly through the beautiful lobby and straight outside.

'Where might she be?' Raff said despairingly. 'I can't lose her, Sophie. I just can't.'

'You won't lose her,' Sophie reassured him firmly. She thought for a moment. 'Let's call Henri and put him on alert in case she turns up at home. He might find a clue in her room as to where she is.'

Raff was already dialling. 'Dad? Is Coco there?' His face fell. 'No, it's ok. It's just that she's not answering her phone. Yes, I do think it's because her mother is here. You'll call yes? Check her room? Good.'

'Not there.'

'Right.' Sophie wished she'd brought her jacket with her; it was chilly.

Raff took his off and put it round her shoulders. 'What about that friend of hers, Aimee, is it? The one she does her homework with.'

'Worth a try. But you won't have her number, surely?'

'Not hers, but I have her mum's number. They used to have sleepovers when they were younger.' Raff called Aimee's mum and rapidly explained. '*Allo*. It's Raff,

Coco's dad.' He spoke quickly. 'Aimee spoke to her? And she sounded upset. Ok, thanks for telling me. Yes, if you could please.'

He came off the phone and wrung his hands. '*Mon Dieu*. This is awful. She's done this a few times before.'

'Ok.' Sophie squeezed his hand hard to stop him shaking. 'And where did she go?'

'Different places,' Raff said, racking his brains to remember. 'Another friend's house one of the times. My place of work another time because she thought I was working late.'

He met Sophie's eye.

'Could she be at the macaron shop?' Sophie said, already dialling Fifi.

'It's worth a try,' Raff said. He raced to the front of the hotel and hailed a taxi. Giving the address in clipped tones, he glanced at Sophie who was talking to Fifi.

'Ok, if you could check please. Call me back?' She shook her head. 'She doesn't think she's there, but it's all closed up because of the renovations. She's going to have a proper look for us now though.'

Raff put his head in his heads. 'I could actually be sick.'

'I know,' Sophie rubbed his back. 'I feel horribly worried myself and she's not my child.'

'You're very close,' Raff said, lifting his head. 'I've never seen her bond with anyone the way she has with you.'

'I don't even want to ask about previous girlfriends,' Sophie smiled.

Raff shook his head. 'Not that many to comment on and that's the truth. And no one Coco was ever fond of. Not the way she is of you. It's... almost like you're a second mum to her, but a friend at the same time.'

Sophie's phone rang; it was Fifi.

'She's there? Oh thank God. She's there, Raff.'

Raff took the phone out of Sophie's hands. 'Fifi, please don't let her move an inch. Not one inch. We'll be there in… ten minutes, maybe five.' He ended the call. 'I'm going to kill her.'

'You're not. You're going to hug her and tell her how much you love her and you're not going to let go of her.'

Raff sat back in his seat, relief flooding through every pore. 'Yes. You're right.' He grabbed Sophie's hand again. 'I can't believe Estelle said those things to you all those years ago. Hang on.' He sent a curt text to Estelle telling her Coco was safe and advised her to go back to her hotel.

Sophie bit her lip. 'I can't believe I left all those years ago without giving you a chance to explain, Raff. I feel so terrible about it still.'

Raff kissed her. 'Don't. Estelle can be so convincing. I've believed her in the past about lots of different things. But she's a liar and she says whatever she needs to get her way.'

'I can see that now. At the time, I just thought you had this child with someone else, that you'd maybe rejected, and I was jealous and I'm really ashamed of that.'

'Jealous?' Raff looked confused.

'It was something I wanted with you,' Sophie confessed, feeling emotional. 'And you'd shared it with someone else and it hurt me. I know that sounds stupid.'

Raff turned to face her properly. 'No, it doesn't. Not at all. I understand that. And it's what I wanted with you. Want with you, if I can say that.'

Sophie felt a rush of excitement at the thought of them having a baby one day in the future. She had no idea how any of this would come about or even if it could, but just for a moment, she was going to be thrilled at the thought of it.

Raff was speaking again. 'But you have to know: I had no part in the whole thing apart from... you know, the obvious bit. Sorry, but you know what I mean.'

'Yep.' Sophie dismissed that image from her mind. But she knew what Raff meant.

'But I had nothing to do with the pregnancy or when Coco was a baby. I honestly had no knowledge of her until she turned up that day with Estelle. It was the most shocking thing I'd gone through. And then you left. All I wish is that you'd told me what Estelle said to you. I honestly believe we could have sorted this out and avoided losing all this time together.'

'Don't.' Sophie kissed him and he kissed her back, urgently. 'I can't bear the thought of it. All that wasted time and the misunderstandings and... why didn't I speak to you?'

'Stop.' Raff put a hand up. 'I should have known Estelle had something to do with it... that she had interfered. I know her and you don't; I don't blame you for doubting me, Sophie. It was all so shocking at the time. But it's done and it's in the past. I wish you'd believed in me, but I know what Estelle can be like. If only I could have explained... anyway, we're here.'

Raff paid the driver and they jumped out of the taxi. Inside the house, they found Coco curled up on the sofa with a soft cashmere blanket wrapped around her. She was cradling a cup of something and she looked about ten. Her eyes were wide and she was make-up free.

'Hot milk with honey,' Fifi said, coming in. 'She was in the cafe, trying to make herself a drink and she needed some space. But it's cold in there tonight so we're warming her up. I've put a fresh pot of coffee on for us.'

'Coco.' Raff stopped in front of his daughter and dropped to his knees.

'Dad.' Coco started crying and Fifi took the hot milk out of her hands. 'I'm so sorry...'

'You can't keep doing this to me,' Raff said, gathering her up in his arms. 'You're my baby. My heart can't take it.'

Coco put her head on his shoulder. 'Sorry, Dad. It's just that when mum gets here, I can't cope... and I don't even know why. I think I want her to be a mum and she doesn't want that and it hurts, and I want to run away and get away from her.'

'Ok, but you have to talk about it, Coco.' Raff lifted her chin. 'You have to talk to me about these things. Not just disappear.'

'I'm sorry,' Coco said, crying again. 'It's just that this time, it was even worse.'

'What, with your mum coming back? Why?' Raff hadn't a clue what Coco was getting at.

Coco looked at Sophie but couldn't meet her eyes properly. Sophie suddenly guessed what might be bothering her and she shook her head rapidly, urging Coco to stay quiet. But to no avail.

'No, I want to say it,' Coco said bravely. 'Dad, when Mum first turned up with me, she made me do something. I'd buried it so far down that when Sophie mentioned the incident to me, I honestly didn't even remember it at first. But then when mum came back, it all came flooding back to me and that's why I ran away. I just feel so guilty…' She started crying.

Raff clenched his jaw.

'Coco, no…' Sophie tried to stop her.

'She made me tell Sophie that you knew about me.' Coco was weeping loudly now. 'That you were a bad father and you just didn't want to know me. She made me say it and I didn't know it was wrong. Not until I got older. And then Sophie turned up and I didn't want to say anything.'

'Is this true?' Raff was livid.

'I'm afraid so,' Sophie admitted. 'But it wasn't Coco's fault and I don't blame her. Not one bit. She was a child and she didn't know she was doing anything wrong.'

'It's my fault you left Paris,' Coco wailed.

'No, it isn't,' Sophie told her resolutely. 'It's my fault. I should have had more faith in your dad. I should have stayed and listened. Instead, I ran away. So you must know that that's never the answer.'

Coco nodded, her bottom lip trembling.

'I'm the one who's wasted all this time we could have had together,' Sophie stammered. 'It's my fault, not yours. Coco.'

Raff looked shell-shocked. He hadn't realised how truly manipulative Estelle was. He didn't want her anywhere near any of them, not now. Not ever.

'Right.' Fifi stepped in. 'Enough. Let's just say that everyone had a part in this. Apart from Raff. I think you've had a really bad time with all of this.'

Raff sighed. 'It's in the past. You're back, Sophie, and that's all that matters. For however long you're going to be here for,' he added quickly.

'Listen,' Fifi said calmly. 'We have the launch in a few days' time. Why don't we all get a good night's sleep and we can review things in the morning.'

Raff and Sophie both nodded.

'Sleep here,' Fifi said. 'We have plenty of rooms with fresh bedding. I can send my friend over to Henri to keep him company tonight.'

'Maybe I should get back,' Raff said worriedly.

'It's up to you, but I think he's feeling much better now,' Fifi said. 'I spoke to him earlier.'

Raff looked pleased and he phoned Henri again. 'You're sure? You don't want anyone to check on you. No, I know you're not a child, Dad. Fair enough.' He came off the phone. 'Well, that told me.'

Fifi smiled. 'He sounds more independent already. Come on, Coco. Let's get you into bed. You can have the room next to the one I'm using. It's probably not as 'cool' as your room at home, but it's very pretty.'

Coco kissed Raff goodnight and hugged Sophie.

'Sorry,' she whispered. She went upstairs willingly with Fifi, looking utterly exhausted.

'*Zut.*' Raff sank down onto the sofa. 'What a day! I never want to go through that again.'

Sophie joined him. 'Me neither.'

'I can't believe Estelle made Coco say that stuff to you.' Raff passed a hand over his eyes. 'That's terrible, even for her.'

'It doesn't matter. I shouldn't have listened.'

Raff lifted his head. 'It was a child, telling you I knew about her. It wouldn't be your first thought not to believe her, or to believe she'd been coached to say something like that. It's horrendous.' He sat up. 'I honestly don't blame you, Soph. I really don't. Why wouldn't you believe a child? Estelle turning up like this, whenever she pleases, makes things hard for everyone. She causes havoc every single time.'

'She has rights,' Sophie said tiredly. 'But I get why it stresses you out.'

'Stresses me out? It's worse than that. And I can't stand how she's made you feel.'

Sophie pulled him back against the sofa. 'No more, Raff. I'm too tired.' She curled up against his warm, now-familiar body. He tucked his arm around her and his chin on top of her head and within minutes, the pair of them were asleep.

Fifi came down after settling Coco and watched them for a few seconds. Making sure they were both covered with a fleece, she turned the lights down low and left them to sleep.

Chapter Twenty-Three

The following morning, Raff stirred. Sophie was in his arms and it had been a long time since they'd slept like that. He was going to savour each minute until she woke up. He had around half an hour before she opened her eyes and it was bliss.

'Wow.' Sophie lifted her head. 'I was in such a deep sleep then.' She leant over and kissed him sleepily. 'This will sound crazy, but I've missed sleeping with you. Next to you. Oh, you know what I mean.'

'I do.' Raff grinned. 'And I feel the same. I've missed sleeping with you too. In every way you can imagine.'

Sophie grinned back. Their limbs were entwined and they squeezed them closer. They kissed again, more deeply, hands in each other's hair.

'God, I've missed you so badly,' Raff breathed.

'Stop talking,' Sophie said, pulling him back.

'Who would like coffee?' Fifi called down the stairs loudly.

Sophie and Raff sprang apart like teenagers.

'Er… I'd love one,' Raff called back, sitting up.

'Me too,' Sophie added sheepishly.

Fifi appeared on the stairs. 'Ah, good, you're both up.' Her eyes twinkled at them as she strode past in a smart navy skirt with a cream pussycat-bow blouse. 'I'll get us some breakfast.'

'She doesn't eat breakfast,' Sophie yawned.

Raff checked his phone. 'Estelle has messaged and asked to see me.'

'I think you should go,' Sophie said, getting up properly. Suddenly, she felt clear about Estelle. She wasn't a threat, not in the sense Sophie had thought. She had caused immense trouble, but there was also much for Sophie to reprimand herself over. And that made her feel back in control of the situation.

Coco appeared on the stairs. 'Can I come?'

'To see your mum?' Raff was surprised. 'Yes, if you want to.'

'I need to say a few things,' Coco said.

'I'll stay here and help *Grand-mère* with the shop relaunch,' Sophie said, giving Coco a hug.

'Let's go,' Raff said. 'I'll ask her to come to ours.' They left in a taxi, and as soon as they got home, Coco jumped in the shower and got changed.

'Everything alright?' Henri said, handing Raff a coffee.

Raff stared at it. His dad hadn't made him a coffee in over a year.

'Don't make a big thing of it,' Henri said gruffly. 'I've been feeling far too sorry for myself for the past year. I can only apologise.'

'What, for grieving? You don't need to apologise for that. I'm just so pleased you seem so much better.'

'I feel different,' Henri said, putting his outdoor shoes on. 'Not necessarily better yet, just... different.'

Raff rubbed his eyes tiredly. 'What are you doing?'

'Gardening. Fifi's friend Ruben is coming over shortly.'

Raff checked his watch. 'So is Estelle.'

Henri pulled a face. 'All the more reason to get out of the house then,' he joked. 'Be careful there, son.'

'Oh, don't worry about that,' Raff told him steadfastly. 'I am very clear about what I need to say. I'm pleased you're sorting out the garden, Dad.'

Henri rolled his sleeves up. 'Just clearing it for now. When it comes to planting flowers and all that, Fifi is sending her friend Margaux over.' He tapped his nose knowingly. 'I think she might have some silly notion about setting me up with her, but I know what she's up to and it won't be happening, so don't worry about that.'

'I'm not,' Raff said honestly. 'I just want you to be happy. I know you'd never try and replace mum.'

'Never,' Henri said, his eyes looking misty. 'I loved her so much.'

Raff refrained from comment. He was sure it was too soon for his father to be thinking about being with someone else, but he hoped that one day, his dad might be ready for it. He had thought he might find it weird, but he now realised that it would simply make him happy to see his dad happy.

The doorbell rang.

'If it's Ruben, send him out into the garden please,' Henri said. 'But I'll make myself scarce in case it's the other one.'

Raff hid a laugh. He knew his dad had never liked Estelle.

'Don't let Sophie go,' Henri said over his shoulder, 'but that other one is a horrible woman and I'd be happy if I never saw her again.'

Raff couldn't agree more. He got up and answered the door. It was both Ruben and Estelle. He stood aside. 'Dad is outside,' he told Ruben. 'Let's go through to the lounge,' he told Estelle. He knew he sounded cold, but he didn't care.

Estelle followed Raff. She was uncharacteristically quiet. She wore blue jeans with a khaki-coloured t-shirt – a subdued outfit by her usual standards. Coco came downstairs in a similar outfit, which she didn't seem to notice.

'Estelle. We have to talk about your visits.'

'You don't need to,' she snapped.

'Why not?' Raff frowned.

'Because I don't see any point in coming again.'

'You're Coco's mother,' Raff said, taken aback. He hadn't expected this. 'I wasn't going to suggest that you stayed away. Just that we need to talk about the visits being more regular so Coco can cope better.'

Estelle shook her head. 'I can't commit to regular visits.'

'Why not?' Coco asked calmly.

'Because of work,' Estelle shrugged.

'You're so selfish,' Raff started. 'I cannot believe you would—'

'Dad.' Coco cut in. 'Can I say something?'

Raff sat back. 'Go ahead.'

'The reason I get upset when you visit is because you made me lie to Sophie all those years ago,' Coco stated. 'And when you came back this time with Sophie here, I remembered it again properly and I felt sad and guilty and like it's all my fault that Sophie left and that dad has been unhappy for so long, when actually it was more your fault because you're an adult and you shouldn't have made me do that.'

'Made you lie to Sophie?' Estelle looked shocked at being confronted, but she did her best to bluff it out. 'I don't know what you're talking about, and it's terrible that you would make something up like—'

'Estelle.' Raff cut her off. 'Please stop. We've all had enough. You're Coco's mother, but really, only biologically speaking. Otherwise, other people have brought her up. You haven't done anything constructive. What mother leaves their child behind?'

'I'm a model. And I'm trying to start a singing career…'

Raff stared at her. 'Good for you. But you are Coco's mother first and foremost. That should be the most important thing in the world to you.'

'It's ok, Dad,' Coco assured him, putting her arm around him. 'I don't need a mum, that's the thing. I have you, dad. And you're the one who has been there for me. After *Grand-mère*, anyway and she's dead now. So dad and *Grand-père*… they are all I need.' She turned to Estelle, a calm expression on her face.

'So you don't want me to come anymore?' Estelle asked. She got up. 'Well, good. That suits me. It's a pain having to come back here when I do.'

Raff couldn't believe what he was hearing. Had it been anyone else, he would have imagined they were saying such things to cover up their own pain, but not Estelle.

'Goodbye, *Maman*,' Coco said, sounding relieved.

'Are you hoping for a new stepmum?' Estelle asked nastily. 'Sophie Marchant, perhaps? Because if you are, just remember that she left as well. She left Paris and she only came back because her mother is missing. She left Raff and she left you. And I expect she'll do it again.'

With that, Estelle flounced out of the house and slammed the door.

'Are you ok?' Raff was concerned for Coco. 'You were so brave.'

'I'm fine. I feel relieved. And I can relax now, knowing she won't turn up again.' She looked troubled. 'But it upset me, what she said about Sophie. Is she going again?'

'I don't know,' Raff answered honestly. 'I hope not. But I don't know.'

Coco nodded. 'Ok.'

'Let's wait and see.' Raff hugged her. 'When Mariele is back, I think everything will be decided one way or another.'

'Has she gone?' Henri asked, pulling off his gardening gloves.

'For good,' Coco said.

'Ah.' He patted her head. 'I'm sorry, Coco. But maybe it's for the best.'

'Definitely,' Coco agreed. 'Can I come and help in the garden?'

'Of course,' Henri put his gloves back on.

Coco kissed the top of Raff's head and went into the garden.

Raff sat back against the sofa. That had been intense, but he was certain that it was the right thing for everyone involved. Coco would be far happier. All that was needed now was for Mariele to come home.

And for Sophie to want to stay in Paris, Raff thought. Right now he had no idea whether she was going to or not.

Chapter Twenty-Four

'Are we ready?'

'We're ready,' Sophie nodded. She'd gone for a casual summer dress today for the opening: navy, with spaghetti straps and a short, slender skirt. But she was sure no one would be taking notice of what anyone was wearing today.

Sophie looked around. The macaron shop looked amazing. All the paintwork had been touched up. The new wall with the silver swirls on the pastel pink background looked fresh and modern. The new bags were lined up on the counter and the photograph looked glossy and eye-catching.

'I love the new sign,' Raff said, coming back into the shop. 'Have you seen it?'

'I had a peek this morning. It's great, isn't it?' Sophie felt absurdly nervous. Her mum might come back today and her stomach was jumping around like anything.

'I think Mariele will love it.' Raff made sure his macarons were perfectly lined up. 'Do you think she might turn up today?'

'I hope so. She sent a message this morning wishing us good luck and saying she's excited to see the changes.' Sophie thought for a second. 'Which now I come to think of it sounds more like she just means she'll see them whenever she turns up.'

'No, let's think positively.' Raff watched caterers walking in with prepared platters of food. Olives, corni-chons, rolls of ham, chunks of brie. Tiny canapés with various delicious-looking toppings. 'I could have prepared all of this.'

'I think *Grand-mère* enjoyed organising it all. I don't think she wanted to stress you out after all the Estelle stuff.'

Raff smiled. 'Cooking relaxes me. It would have helped me, not hindered me. But that's fine.'

'Are you and Coco ok about everything?' Sophie asked. Raff had told her everything that had happened the other night.

'Yes. I think we are both relieved.'

Raff refrained from saying anything about Coco's concerns about Sophie leaving. About *his* concerns about Sophie leaving. He didn't want to put any pressure on her. And Raff knew he needed to wait for Mariele to come back before anything else happened. The main thing was, Raff wanted Sophie to make her own decisions. He wasn't about to apply any emotional blackmail or say anything that might influence her either way.

Louis arrived with Anne-Marie whose stomach seemed to have popped out a little more, and Louis, dazzling in a short-sleeved shirt the colour of ripe carrots, couldn't stop rubbing Anne-Marie's tummy as though it might release a genie from a lamp.

'What do you think?' Fifi said, walking in, throwing her arms wide to encompass the shop.

'I think it looks amazing,' Raff said, kissing her cheek. 'Thank you so much for all your help. Mariele is going to love it.'

'I hope so,' Fifi said, frowning. 'She can be very... particular.'

Raff smiled. 'Where would she get that from?'

Fifi twinkled at him. 'I have no idea.' Her face faltered. 'Do you think she will come home today?'

'I don't know.' Raff glanced at Sophie who had been a bag of nerves all morning. 'I really hope so.'

'Fifi,' Louis came over and gallantly kissed her hand. 'Red shoes, I love it. And what a fantastic suit.'

Fifi glanced down at her cream Chanel and said nothing. Chanel spoke for itself.

People started to arrive for the pre-launch party. Coco and her friend Aimee, Eloise, Georges, and the boys, who had been allowed the morning off school. Eloise and Sophie hugged tightly and Eloise pulled back to look at her twin.

'Maybe we'll all be together again today,' she said in a hopeful voice.

Sophie tucked Eloise's hair behind her ear. 'She said she'd be back this weekend. We have to trust her.'

'I just want to know what's happened,' Eloise said, breaking down. Which made Sophie break down, because it always did. 'God, I've been so strong, Soph! But today, now that she's supposed to be here, it feels overwhelming.'

'I know. How silly is this? We've been without her for the past few months and because she's due back, we're falling apart.' Sophie wiped her eyes. 'We have to get a grip. Maybe she just needed a sabbatical from work or something. I'm sure it will all become clear.'

'Can't be work,' Eloise frowned. 'It has to be more than that.'

Sophie sighed. There were just too many ifs and buts with the situation. All they could do was guess and surmise until their mum came home.

'There's Pinter,' Eloise said, pulling herself together. '*Zut*, who is that gorgeous girl? And that man… he's so handsome. Oops.' She turned quickly to check Georges hadn't heard her.

'That's Mason – and Savannah. The wedding couple I photographed the other day.'

'They are so *ugly*,' Eloise giggled.

Sophie laughed. Pinter, Esther, Savannah and Mason, provided a touch of tanned, over-the-top glamour, designer labels and magnums of champagne. Just what the party needed.

'Ah,' Fifi looked pleased. 'Here is Ruben and Victor. Oh, Raff.' She put her hand on his arm. 'Henri is here!'

Raff gazed at his father, tears pricking at his eyelids. This was something he thought he would never see; his father out and about in Paris again, not confined to the house. It had been enough of a miracle in Raff's eyes that his father had ventured out into the garden.

'Dad.' He walked up and shook Henri's hand. 'I can't believe you've made it.'

Henri gave a half-smile. 'I can't say it wasn't difficult. Or strange. It feels so… bright out here. But Paris looks magnificent. I've missed it.'

Raff couldn't stop smiling.

Pinter in the meantime had cornered Sophie. 'So you're alright after the other night? After all the Estelle stuff?'

Sophie nodded. 'Yes, I'm ok. I think Raff and Coco had a difficult conversation with her and I understand that she has taken off now for good.'

Pinter shrugged. 'For the best, I'm sure. I don't advocate anyone being without their mum, but that wasn't a good mum and she was doing more harm than good.'

'Definitely. It wasn't nice seeing Coco like that. She was so upset.'

Pinter eyed her carefully. 'And... have you made any decisions yet?'

Sophie's mouth twisted. 'Yes, I think I have.'

'Are you going to tell me what that decision is?'

'Not yet. I need to speak to Raff first. Is that ok?'

Pinter smiled. 'Everything is ok with me as far as you're concerned. You know that.'

'I do love you, Pinter.' She hugged him. 'And I'll get Savannah's photos sorted in a few days' time. They look gorgeous so far.'

'She'll love them. I can't wait to see them properly. Big business, wedding photography in Paris.' He gave her a pointed stare.

Sophie rolled her eyes.

'Right. I'm on champers duty so I'm going to make sure everyone has a glass in their hands for the speeches.'

'I'll help,' Sophie offered.

Together, they opened bottles of champagne and filled up the plastic champagne flutes that Fifi had grudgingly agreed were rather more practical for the party than crystal. They made sure everyone had a glass of bubbles, apart from the kids who had plastic tumblers of orange juice, and then they lined up in front of Raff who stood in front of the macaron counter.

'Ahem.' Raff cleared his throat and everyone turned to look at him.

'I just wanted to say a few words before we crack open some more bottles and let customers in.' He looked nervous, but soon got into his stride. 'I'd worked here for a while before as you probably know, and jumped at the chance when Mariele invited me back. Why? Because I love this local business and really wanted to bring something new to it. I've worked in large pâtisseries before and other macaron shops, but I think we can all agree, that this one is special.'

There were nods and murmurs of agreement.

Raff continued. 'Mariele has worked hard over the years, mostly single-handedly, to provide a business that is both traditional in its values and commercial in its thinking. In her absence, Sophie and I have worked hard to keep everything running as Mariele wanted it, but as soon as she mentioned revamping it, we couldn't help jumping at the chance.'

Sophie felt a bit emotional at the mention; she couldn't stop herself checking the door just in case her mum was about to arrive.

'When can we eat some macarons?' Pinter called out jokingly.

'Soon, soon,' Raff laughed. 'Ok, I'll wrap this up. With Fifi's help, we have managed to revamp the inside of the shop as well as the outside. We have new bags and boxes thanks to Sophie, and I created a couple of new macarons.' He shrugged modestly. 'So. All that remains for me to say is, thank you so much for coming today. Thank you for being here to celebrate with us and enjoy this launch.' He met Sophie's eyes. 'And here is to Mariele's safe return, whenever that may be. Mariele!' he finished.

'Mariele!' everyone chorused soberly.

'And the macarons!' cried Pinter, popping open another bottle of champagne to whoops of joy.

Everyone starting tucking into Raff's colourful macarons, exclaiming in delight at how delicious they were. Raff opened up the front door and pulled down the canvas covering the new sign. There were gasps at how shiny and beautiful the new sign looked and then customers started flocking in.

Sophie stood by the door expectantly, saying hello to regulars and new faces, but struggled to hide her disappointment that none of them was her mum.

'She might still turn up,' Raff said, squeezing her waist.

Sophie leant into him. 'I know. It would just be so perfect if she walked in right now and saw all of this.' She met his eyes. 'Actually, it's not about any of this; it's just her. I really want to see her. She used to come over to England every couple of months or so... this is probably the longest amount of time I've been without her.'

Raff nodded. 'It's tough when you're so close. It's like me and Coco; we're together so much and there's only me – especially now – so I feel it more when she's not there. That's why I really felt for you when Coco went missing the other day. I know it's different, but this is what you've been dealing with for the past few months. I think I'd have gone crazy.'

'I think without the constant texts I would have done,' Sophie admitted. 'They have been an absolute lifeline. It has been like... having mum here, but not having her here. But at the same time... those texts...' She faltered.

'What?' Raff asked. 'You think there is something strange about the texts. But she did call that time, remember? You've spoken to her.'

Sophie took her phone out. 'I know and the phone call was reassuring, although very brief. But the texts... I can't explain it, Raff. They sound like her, but not like her at the same time. It's as though... I don't know. They are her words, but the texts don't read the way her texts normally do. But I know it's her because she knows things that no one else could possibly know. The things from our childhood... only Eloise and I were there. And I can't imagine she would have told anyone else such silly, insignificant details, nor would anyone be able to remember them all, I shouldn't imagine.'

'It's definitely weird,' Raff agreed. 'But I guess we're not going to be able to figure it out. We'll have to just wait until she gets here so she can explain everything.'

Sophie nudged Raff. 'Ooh look. Fifi is introducing Henri to someone. Do you think it's her friend Margaux?'

Raff turned and watch his father go into gallant mode over Fifi's friend. She was a kindly looking woman in her sixties at a guess, with blond, shoulder-length hair and a caring face. She was well turned-out and dressed in a smart pair of jeans and a thin pink sweater that matched the walls of Mariele's Macarons, and she was laughing softly as Henri held on to her hand rather longer than he was meant to.

'Well, that's something I thought I wouldn't see for a while,' Raff murmured.

'Do you mind?' Sophie probed. 'Does it feel as though it's too soon, perhaps? It's only been a year or so.'

'No.' Raff smiled as he watched his father. 'It would be odd to see him with someone else, of course… no one can replace *maman*… but I just want to see him happy. He's been so grief-stricken, so depressed. I honestly thought his agoraphobia was a permanent thing. I can't tell you how happy it makes me to see him smiling again. Out in the city he loves.' Raff grinned. 'Flirting.'

Sophie felt her phone ringing in her pocket. 'It's Jo,' she said, surprised. 'Probably phoning to wish us good luck. Hey. Are you ok?'

'I'm fine,' Jo said, sounding excited.

'What's up? I'm at the macaron shop for the re-opening. Hello, Madame Bouchon.' Sophie smiled at a regular customer.

'Oh yes, of course! I totally forgot that it was today. No, I'm phoning about something else.' Jo paused. 'You know that photo of that guy, Theo?'

'Yes. I can't find it though.'

'I took it,' Jo confessed. 'Don't be cross with me; I just thought I might be able to do a bit of digging once I was back in England.'

Sophie was taken aback. 'Ok… well, did you find anything out?'

'Yes!' Jo sounded exultant. 'You remember that it said Surrey on the back? Well, it wasn't just that; he was standing in front of this huge house with a tea shop next to it.'

'Was he?' Sophie couldn't remember. She had only looked at the man's face.

'I got on the phone and spoke to a friend of mine… another estate agent, to see if she recognised the tea shop.

She did and she said it had been sold some years ago and turned into a bakery…'

'Right…' Sophie really couldn't see where this was going. She glanced to the door to see who was coming through it. Her heart sank again when it wasn't her mum.

'I should say, a cake shop, not really a bakery.' Jo's tone was triumphant. 'A pâtisserie, if you like.'

Sophie frowned. 'A pâtisserie. Really? Ok, that's slightly weird…'

'Isn't it? Ok, so it was this guy Theo who bought it. And the house next to it. And he ran the pâtisserie himself, because he's a pastry chef.'

'Well, that must be how mum knew him. Perhaps they trained together.'

'Quite possibly, but that's not even the best bit.'

Sophie was beginning to feel impatient.

'I went to Surrey!' Jo said. 'I played detective and I went there. Guess what, Theo hasn't been around for the past few months, so someone else has been running his business for him. He was married but he left his wife two years ago.'

'Ok. I'm confused here. What's the important part: that he was married and left his wife, or that he's not been around for the past couple of months?' In spite of her confusion, Sophie felt a flash of excitement in her gut. This was significant; she could feel it.

'Both. That's all I have for now, apart from the last bit, which is his name.'

'What, Theo? We know that?' Sophie looked up. Pinter was waving his arms at her agitatedly. She started to smile, thinking it must be her mum back, then realised Pinter looked stressed out and her smile faded.

'What's wrong?' she mouthed.

Pinter stabbed a finger at the door. Sophie looked over then felt herself turn pale. Oh no. It couldn't be…

'Sophie, are you listening?' Jo was talking louder.

'Jo, I'm going to have to go…' Sophie said.

'You can't!' Jo shrieked. 'I have to tell you about his surname. It said "M" on the photo and that stands for Mar…'

Sophie hung up.

'R–Ryan…' she stammered.

Raff's head snapped round. Surely not…

But yes. Standing in the doorway, his broad shoulders filling the space, his tan deep and his smile wide but nervous, stood Ryan.

'Hey,' he said. 'You didn't tell me not to come, so here I am.' He had his fingers curled around a small box.

Sophie gaped. Oh God. She hadn't answered Ryan's text. She had got so caught up in Coco going missing and getting the shop ready for the launch and for her mum to return that she had completely forgotten to go back to her ex-boyfriend to tell him not to get a flight from Dubai to Paris.

'Oh, Ryan. I'm so sorry.' She shot a glance at Raff and shook her head.

Raff looked tight lipped, but he said nothing.

Ryan's smile faded.

Sophie went over to him and took him to one side. 'I should have come back to you. I can only apologise…'

'You didn't want me to come.' Ryan looked crestfallen. 'What an idiot I am. I shouldn't have worded the text that way. My mates told me I'd done it all wrong.'

'It's not that; there has just been a lot going on here.'

Ryan tucked the box into his pocket, looking foolish. 'I was trying to make a grand gesture. To show you how I feel. But it's too late, obviously.'

Sophie felt awful, then steeled her nerve. Ryan had broken off their engagement and their relationship and had focused on his job, leaving her high and dry. It was a lovely thing, to have flown all the way over here, but it was too late. Mostly because of Raff, but just because of… well, everything.

'It's a sweet and romantic thing to do,' Sophie told him quietly. 'But I don't feel the same any more. I didn't after you left and definitely not since I've been in Paris.'

'Anything to do with that sex god of a man over there?' Ryan commented sharply. 'The one who's been staring over since I arrived? I suspect he's important to you.'

Sophie winced. Was it that obvious? 'I'm afraid so. But that happened after I came to Paris. My feelings changed before that.'

Ryan put his head down. 'It's my fault. All I could see was job progression and pound signs. I just didn't see what was important. What was right in front of me.'

'Well, we've all been guilty of that in our lives,' Sophie said gently. 'I've done the same thing. But… yes. I'm afraid it's too late for us.'

Ryan lifted his chin. 'Ok. I'm gutted, but I guess we're just not right for each other. I shouldn't have left you and you shouldn't have been able to get over me so easily.'

Sophie nodded, feeling tearful. 'It wasn't quite as simple as that. I was gutted, I really was. But… maybe not as much as I should have been. Sorry, Ryan.'

'Don't be.' He hugged her. 'I'll leave you to it. Head back to the airport so I can just jump on the next flight back.' He nodded over in Raff's direction. 'You need to go and put that right. He's fuming.'

Sophie glanced at Raff. 'You're right. Bye, Ryan.'

He left and Sophie didn't watch him leave; she headed straight for Raff. She had important things to sort out.

Chapter Twenty-Five

'Raff.'

He was standing in the kitchen away from everyone. And he looked pissed off. Understandably.

'Right.' Sophie took stock and got herself together. 'I should have told you that Ryan messaged me saying he wanted to come over.'

'Yes,' Raff said tightly.

'But I forgot.'

'You forgot?' He looked disbelieving.

'Er… yes. I actually did. As terrible as that sounds, I forgot to mention it to you and I forgot to go back to Ryan to tell him not to come.'

Raff raised his eyebrows. 'Yes, Sophie. I gathered that.'

'I was so worried about Coco,' Sophie explained swiftly. 'Not that I'm using that as an excuse as such, but I was. And it went out of my head and I've been so concerned about the shop and about mum coming back and about you…'

'About me?' Raff looked disbelieving again.

'Yes.' Sophie bit her lip. 'But I'll get to that in a minute. Listen, I was out of order not letting you know about Ryan, especially since I gave you a hard time over you not telling me that Estelle had been in touch.'

Raff inclined his head, but didn't comment.

'And I feel awful that he flew all this way, when he didn't have a hope in hell of getting me back. But I haven't encouraged him to think that, either; I've ignored his texts pretty much from the start. And I think it speaks volumes that I forgot to go back to him on such an important text,' Sophie finished. 'I was so caught up with everything here, I wasn't even remotely focused on Ryan.'

'He looked as though he was holding a box in his hands,' Raff commented, crossing his arms. 'A small one. The kind an engagement ring comes in.'

'Yes,' Sophie admitted, cringing. 'He was. Because he thought he could let me down and come back and be with me again.' She bowed her head. 'Kind of like me. I let you down and I've come back, but I haven't assumed and actually I didn't even see it coming. But I want to be with you again.'

'Do you?' Raff unfolded his arms. 'In what capacity, Sophie? Long distance? Are you going back to England?'

'Yes.'

'Yes?' Raff looked dumbfounded. 'After everything you've just said, after everything we've been through, you're going back to England? *Mon Dieu*, Sophie! Well, ok. It's better that I know.' He shook his head, furious. 'I can't believe I actually thought you might stay in Paris. I'm an idiot, a fool. I've been so stupid... poor Coco... she will be absolutely devastated...'

'Stop.' Sophie silenced him, by kissing his mouth, hard. 'Stop talking.'

Raff held her away from him. 'No, you stop. What do you think you're doing?'

'I'm kissing the man I love and I'm trying to explain to him that I'm...'

'Sophie!'

Raff and Sophie looked up.

'Eloise…'

Sophie and Raff rushed out of the kitchen. Sophie clapped her hand to her mouth. There, in the middle of the macaron shop was her mum. She was in a wheelchair, but she was here. Here, in Paris and in her shop and she was home. She looked pale and her dark hair was longer than she normally wore it, but it was neat and tidy and she still looked like herself. Eloise was leaning over her with her arms wrapped around Mariele's shoulders. There was a dark-haired man behind her, pushing the wheelchair and he looked familiar. He was tall and handsome and his face was kindly.

Sophie was vaguely aware of Pinter in the background, looking delighted, of Fifi weeping quietly into a silk hand-kerchief and of Albert and Daniel jumping around and yelling.

'*Maman!*' Sophie walked to her and dropped to her knees so she could hug her. She fell on Mariele and held her tightly, feeling Eloise's arms on her head and her mum clutching her arms until they were all merged into one.

'Where have you been?' Sophie said tearfully.

'We've been so worried,' Eloise choked.

'I know.' Mariele stroked their hair. 'I'm so sorry, *mes filles*. I know this must have been awful for you.'

Pinter took off his jacket. 'Sophie, take your mum into the house. Me and Esther are running the shop.'

Esther looked excited. 'Are we? I've never done that before. Can I put the macarons in the boxes? How much are they?'

Coco laughed. 'I know all this stuff. I'll help.' She went behind the counter and started serving.

Sophie, Eloise and Raff headed into the house, and Mariele and the man followed. He made sure Mariele was positioned in the centre and sat down. Fifi came in and squeezed Mariele's hand.

'Shall I leave?' Raff asked.

'Don't be silly,' Mariele said. 'You're just as involved as the girls here. You helped me with the shop, and I know you've been supporting Sophie through this.'

Raff sat down and Fifi took a seat next to him. Eloise and Sophie remained standing.

'Where have you been?' Eloise cut in.

'England,' Mariele replied calmly.

'What?' Sophie was stunned. 'You've been in England? And you sent me over here?'

Mariele smiled at her weakly. 'Well, actually I didn't send you over here. I asked Eloise to get you. And you came. Which made me so happy.'

Sophie was clueless. 'Why? Why was it so important for me to be here? And for you to be there?'

'Because Raff was here. And the shop. And Paris,' Mariele replied.

Sophie was dumbfounded.

'And I had to be in England because I needed to have a heart operation,' Mariele continued. 'I was very ill and there was a specialist there. In London.'

'A heart operation?' Sophie gaped.

'Yes.'

'Oh my God.' Sophie put her hand to her face. 'I can't believe we swapped places,' she said, vexed. 'All the time,

I've assumed you've been in Paris and I've been searching and searching, and you were in England all along.'

Mariele reached out and took Sophie's hand. 'I'm so sorry, *ma chérie*.'

'What was wrong with your heart?' Eloise asked, her bottom lip trembling.

'Something very complicated and I will tell you all about it. I nearly died, but I didn't.' Mariele glossed over this huge fact quickly. 'And it took me a long time to recover. I was in a hospital in London for weeks, and then I went to Surrey to get better. I was very ill for a while... in a coma.'

'In a coma?' Eloise echoed, staring at Mariele.

'Surrey.' Sophie stared at the man who had brought Mariele in. He had taken a step backwards into the edge of the room. 'You.' She pointed at him. 'It's you, from the photos.'

Mariele looked startled. 'The photos?'

'You have photos. Of this man. You're Theo.'

He nodded and stepped forward. 'Yes, I am.'

'You have a pâtisserie in Surrey,' Sophie added, remembering what Jo had said on the phone earlier.

Theo looked impressed. 'You're quite the detective.'

Mariele was flabbergasted. 'How have you managed to get all this info, Sophie?'

'A pâtisserie?' Raff frowned. 'So that's how you know one another.'

'Not as such...' Mariele glanced at Theo. 'Well, kind of.'

Theo sat down near Mariele. 'We trained together. Here in Paris. And then... a few things happened...'

They exchanged another significant glance.

'And then I went to England,' Theo continued, 'and opened a pâtisserie there. Mariele opened the macaron shop here.'

Mariele nodded. 'But we… always stayed in touch. And then when I needed him, Theo was there for me. He is… the other piece of my heart. The one I lost all those years ago. And it was my fault.'

'It was both of our faults,' Theo corrected her.

'You wrote those texts,' Eloise said suddenly.

Theo looked up.

'You wrote those texts,' Eloise repeated. 'Not mum. You. Mum was in a coma.' She turned to Mariele. 'You were in a coma. How did you call Sophie that time?'

Mariele sighed. 'I came out of the coma and I called. But I got very sick again after that. I wasn't capable of calling or texting. So Theo took over again.'

'Right.' Sophie nodded rapidly. 'I knew there was something strange about the texts, but I forgot about it after the phone call. The texts… they were you, Mum, but not you.' She frowned at Theo. 'But how could you know all of those things? About our childhood? About mum? About us?'

'Because…' Theo started then hesitated.

'Say it,' Mariele said, clutching his hand.

'Because I'm your father,' Theo said, his voice thick with emotion. 'That's how I know all of those things. I was there, for some of it, but you don't remember me. And then I wasn't there, but Mariele told me everything. We have talked almost every day for several years. As friends.'

Sophie and Eloise found themselves holding on to one another.

'But... but you said he was a waste of space,' Eloise stammered. 'No good...'

'No, I didn't,' Mariele said. 'You assumed that and I let you think it.'

'But why?' Sophie whispered.

'Because I made a huge mistake,' Mariele confessed. 'I thought I was too young to settle down. I didn't know I was pregnant with you two. I sent Theo away because I was too proud and too pig-headed and stubborn.' She gave Sophie a pointed glance. 'And then when I had you, Theo wanted to be in your lives and I wanted him to be, but I still didn't feel ready for a relationship. How stupid is that? I sent him away and didn't speak to him for years.'

'It was a bad time,' Theo admitted. 'Eventually I met someone and we married.' He shook his head. 'But it didn't work out because I was never truly happy.'

'Theo got worried about me when he didn't hear from me for a few days and when we finally spoke and he realised I was ill, he was there for me, immediately,' Mariele said, starting to cry quietly. 'He nursed me back to health and he kept in touch with you. It's my fault we've been apart for so long.'

'It doesn't matter.' Theo stood up. 'Girls, I know this must be really strange for you, because you don't know me, but I feel as though I know you both so well. Mariele has told me everything over the years.' He sounded as though he could barely speak. 'I've missed you so much.'

Eloise tentatively went into his arms. 'We missed you too. Even though we didn't know.'

Sophie held back. Could she just accept this man as her father? He hadn't been there for them... but maybe it wasn't his fault.

Mariele met her eyes. 'It wasn't his fault, Sophie. It was mine.'

Sophie went to him and he held her in his strong arms and she sank into them. There was so much talking they needed to do.

'Don't make the same mistake I made,' Mariele said to Sophie in a low voice. 'Do not let him get away. Not this time.' She nodded at Raff.

Sophie felt shocked, but she knew what she had to do. 'Raff, can we talk?'

They went to one side.

'Are you ok?' Raff said. 'That must have been such a shock.'

Sophie nodded. 'I'm fine. I'll get my head around it later. I have to say something to you. That thing I said about going back to England... I just mean that I have to go and pack my life up there.'

'Oh.' Raff looked relieved.

'And then I'll be back. To Paris. For good... with you.'

Raff kissed her. 'I couldn't bear it if you left again.'

'Neither could I. And I won't. Because... you're the other piece of my heart,' Sophie said with a sheepish grin.

'And you are definitely mine,' Raff told her, sinking his hands into her hair. 'I lost you and now I've found you again. And I'm not letting you go.'

'You'd better not,' Sophie said. 'We've lost too much time as it is. Me, you, Paris...'

Raff grinned. 'Shall we sneak off for a while? Leave everyone to it?'

Sophie thought for a minute. 'I'm not sure I'm ready to leave mum just yet, not now I've got her back.'

'You're right. And we have the rest of our lives to be together. *Oui?*'

'*Oui*,' Sophie agreed. 'But I don't see anything wrong with you kissing the life out of me for the time being…'

Wrapping his arms around her, Raff willingly obliged.